FORWARD IN TIME

FORWARD

IN TIME

A SCIENCE FICTION STORY COLLECTION
BY
BEN BOVA

WALKER AND COMPANY • NEW YORK

First published in the United States of America in 1973 by the Walker Publishing Company, Inc.

Published simultaneously in Canada by Fitzhenry & Whiteside, Limited, Toronto.

Printed in the United States of America.

TO THE EDITORS, WHOM I NOW APPRECIATE

CONTENTS

INTRODUCTION

Since I've become editor of *Analog* Science Fiction magazine, I've been asked by many readers, scholars and interviewers to define just what science fiction is. I've often countered by asking them to define what they think science fiction is. Usually, they're laboring under a vast misconception. They believe that science fiction writers are attempting to predict the future. Nothing could be further from the truth.

For science fiction writers aren't trying to predict THE future, as if there's only one. The writers are literally creating a myriad of futures—as many different futures as there are stories. Each science fiction story is a tiny microcosm of its own, with its own reality, its own particular point of view. Each represents the writer's feelings about one possible aspect of a future that might come to be.

Science fiction is very much like the "simulation laboratories" that scientists use to test their theoretical predictions. Instead of scientific apparatus and computers, the science fiction writers use their imaginations and the arts of storytelling. They test various ideas and try to show all the many facets of all the possible tomorrows. If the history of the human race can be thought of as a vast migration through time, with billions upon billions of people wandering across the eons, then the science fiction writers are the scouts who maneuver ahead and come back with wondrous tales of the unknown territory up ahead, warnings of the deserts and badlands, glowing descriptions of the green forests and beautiful pastures that lie beyond the horizon.

The ten stories in this collection represent several different futures, reports from the territory ahead, as I've seen it. The stories were written over a span of nearly ten years, and were never intended to form a cohesive pattern when placed together (except for the three Kinsman stories). They are arranged, as the title of this book suggests, in a way that moves forward in time. The first story could happen today—maybe it has already happened. Each subsequent story could take place a little further in the future than the one previous to it. The time scale is logarithmic: the jumps in time get bigger between each story (again, with the exception of the Kinsman pieces). You might argue with the details of some of the placements, feeling that a certain story might, conceivably, take place earlier than a story I put before it. So be it; if we all agreed about the future there'd be no science fiction.

So, welcome to several different tomorrows. As you go forward in time on this brief but accelerated journey, you will visit the moon, the heart of a hurricane, the ultimate end of the universe. Fasten your seat belt and have a pleasant trip.

Ben Bova
New York City
October 1972

FORWARD IN TIME

When I first started working in the aerospace industry, I was impressed by the huge security apparatus that was designed to protect classified documents, hardware and ideas. While much of the secrecy seemed excessive and even counterproductive (like showing a pass to a guard to get to the men's room) I soon found that there were important reasons for all the elaborate security precautions. Many important reasons.

THE NEXT LOGICAL STEP

"I don't really see where this problem has anything to do with me," the CIA man said. "And, frankly, there are a lot of more important things I could be doing."

Ford, the physicist, glanced at General LeRoy. The general had that quizzical expression on his face, the look that meant he was about to do something decisive.

"Would you like to see the problem firsthand?" the general asked, innocently.

The CIA man took a quick look at his wrist watch, "Okay, if it doesn't take too long. It's late enough already."

"It won't take very long, will it, Ford?" the general said, getting out of his chair.

"Not very long," Ford agreed. "Only a lifetime."

The CIA man grunted as they went to the doorway and left the general's office. Going down the dark, deserted hallway, their footsteps echoed hollowly.

"I can't overemphasize the seriousness of the problem," General LeRoy said to the CIA man. "Eight ranking members of the General Staff have either resigned their commissions or gone straight to the violent ward after just one session with the computer."

The CIA man scowled. "Is this area Secure?"

General LeRoy's face turned red. "This entire building is as Secure as any edifice in the Free World, mister. And it's empty. We're the only living people inside here at this hour. I'm not taking any chances."

"Just want to be sure."

"Perhaps if I explain the computer a little more," Ford said, changing the subject, "you'll know what to expect."

"Good idea," said the man from CIA.

"We told you that this is the most modern, most complex and delicate computer in the world . . . nothing like it has ever been attempted before—anywhere."

"I know that They don't have anything like it," the CIA man agreed.

"And you also know, I suppose, that it was built to simulate actual war situations. We fight wars in this computer . . . wars with missiles and bombs and gas. Real wars, complete down to the tiniest detail. The computer tells us what will actually happen to every missile, every city, every man . . . who dies, how many planes are lost, how many trucks will fail to start on a cold morning, whether a battle is won or lost . . ."

General LeRoy interrupted. "The computer runs these analyses for both sides, so we can see what's happening to Them, too."

The CIA man gestured impatiently. "War-games simulations aren't new. You've been doing them for years."

"Yes, but this machine is different," Ford pointed out. "It not only gives a much more detailed war game. It's the next logical step in the development of machine-simulated war games." He hesitated dramatically.

"Well, what is it?"

"We've added a variation of the electroencephalograph . . ."

The CIA man stopped walking. "The electro-what?"

"Electroencephalograph. You know, a recording device that

reads the electrical patterns of your brain. Like the electrocardiograph."

"Oh."

"But you see, we've given the EEG a reverse twist. Instead of using a machine that makes a recording of the brain's electrical wave output, we've developed a device that will take the computer's readout tapes and turn them into electrical patterns that are put *into* your brain!"

"I don't get it."

General LeRoy took over. "You sit at the machine's control console. A helmet is placed over your head. You set the machine in operation. You *see* the results."

"Yes," Ford went on. "Instead of reading rows of figures from the computer's printer . . . you actually see the war being fought. Complete visual and auditory hallucinations. You can watch the progress of the battles, and as you change strategy and tactics you can see the results before your eyes."

"The idea, originally, was to make it easier for the General Staff to visualize strategic situations," General LeRoy said.

"But every one who's used the machine has either resigned his commission or gone insane," Ford added.

The CIA man cocked an eye at LeRoy. "You've used the computer."

"Correct."

"And you have neither resigned nor cracked up."

General LeRoy nodded. "I called you in."

Before the CIA man could comment, Ford said, "The computer's right inside this doorway. Let's get this over with while the building is still empty."

They stepped in. The physicist and the general showed the CIA man through the room-filling rows of massive consoles.

"It's all transistorized and subminiaturized, of course," Ford explained. "That's the only way we could build so much detail into the machine and still have it small enough to fit inside a single building."

"A single building?"

"Oh yes; this is only the control section. Most of this building is taken up by the circuits, the memory banks and the rest of it."

"Hm-m-m."

They showed him finally to a small desk, studded with control buttons and dials. The single spotlight above the desk lit it brilliantly, in harsh contrast to the semidarkness of the rest of the room.

"Since you've never run the computer before," Ford said, "General LeRoy will do the controlling. You just sit and watch what happens."

The general sat in one of the well-padded chairs and donned a grotesque headgear that was connected to the desk by a half-dozen wires. The CIA man took his chair, slowly.

When they put one of the bulky helmets on him, he looked up at them, squinting a little in the bright light. "This . . . this isn't going to . . . well, do me any damage, is it?"

"My goodness no," Ford said. "You mean mentally? No, of course not. You're not on the General Staff, so it shouldn't . . . it won't . . . affect you the way it did the others. Their reaction had nothing to do with the computer *per se* . . ."

"Several civilians have used the computer with no ill effects," General LeRoy said. "Ford has used it many times."

The CIA man nodded, and they closed the transparent visor over his face. He sat there and watched General LeRoy press a series of buttons, then turn a dial.

"Can you hear me?" The general's voice came muffled through the helmet.

"Yes," he said.

"All right. Here we go. You're familiar with Situation One-Two-One? That's what we're going to be seeing."

Situation One-Two-One was a standard war game. The CIA man was well acquainted with it. He watched the general flip a switch, then sit back and fold his arms over his chest. A row of lights on the desk console began blinking on and off, one, two, three . . . down to the end of the row, then back to the beginning again, on and off, on and off . . .

And then, somehow, he could see it!

He was poised, incredibly, somewhere in space, and he could see it all in a funny, blurry-double-sighted, dreamlike way. He seemed to be seeing several pictures and hearing many voices, all at once. It was all mixed up, and yet it made a weird kind of sense.

For a panicked instant he wanted to rip the helmet off his head. *It's only an illusion,* he told himself, forcing calm on his unwilling nerves. *Only an illusion.*

But it seemed strangely real.

He was watching the Gulf of Mexico. He could see Florida off to his right, and the arching coast of the southeastern United States. He could even make out the Rio Grande River.

Situation One-Two-One started, he remembered, with the discovery of missile-bearing Enemy submarines in the Gulf. Even as he watched the whole area—as though perched on a satellite—he could see, underwater and close-up, the menacing shadowy figure of a submarine gliding through the crystal-blue sea.

He saw, too, a patrol plane as it spotted the submarine and sent an urgent radio warning.

The underwater picture dissolved in a bewildering burst of bubbles. A missile had been launched. Within seconds, another burst —this time a nuclear depth charge—utterly destroyed the submarine.

It was confusing. He was everyplace at once. The details were overpowering, but the total picture was agonizingly clear.

Six submarines fired missiles from the Gulf of Mexico. Four were immediately sunk, but too late. New Orleans, St. Louis and three Air Force bases were obliterated by hydrogen-fusion warheads.

The CIA man was familiar with the opening stages of the war. The first missile fired at the United States was the signal for whole fleets of missiles and bombers to launch themselves at the Enemy. It was confusing to see the world at once; at times he could not tell if the fireball and mushroom cloud was over Chicago or Shanghai, New York or Novosibersk, Baltimore or Budapest.

It did not make much difference, really. They all got it in the first few hours of the war; as did London and Moscow, Washington and Peking, Detroit and Delhi, and many, many more.

The defensive systems on all sides seemed to operate well, except that there were never enough antimissiles. Defensive systems were expensive compared to attack rockets. It was cheaper to build a deterrent than to defend against it.

The missiles flashed up from submarines and railway cars, from underground silos and stratospheric jets; secret ones fired off automatically when a certain airbase command-post ceased beaming out a restraining radio signal. The defensive systems were simply overloaded. And when the bombs ran out, the missiles carried dust and germs and gas. On and on. For six days and six firelit nights. Launch, boost, coast, reenter, death.

And now it was over, the CIA man thought. The missiles were all gone. The airplanes were exhausted. The nations that had built the weapons no longer existed. By all the rules he knew of, the war should have been ended.

Yet the fighting did not end. The machine knew better. There were still many ways to kill an enemy. Time-tested ways. There were armies fighting in four continents, armies that had marched overland, or splashed ashore from the sea, or dropped out of the skies.

Incredibly, the war went on. When the tanks ran out of gas, and the flame throwers became useless, and even the prosaic artillery pieces had no more rounds to fire, there were still simple guns and even simpler bayonets and swords.

The proud armies, the descendants of the Alexanders and Caesars and Timujins and Wellingrons and Grants and Rommels, relived their evolution in reverse.

The war went on. Slowly, inevitably, the armies split apart into smaller and smaller units, until the tortured countryside that so recently had felt the impact of nuclear war once again knew the tread of bands of armed marauders. The tiny savage groups, stranded in alien lands, far from the homes and families that they knew to be destroyed, carried on a mockery of war, lived off the land, fought their own countrymen if the occasion suited, and revived the ancient terror of hand-wielded, personal, one-head-at-a-time killing.

The CIA man watched the world disintegrate. Death was an individual business now, and none the better for no longer being mass-produced. In agonized fascination he saw the myriad ways in which a man might die. Murder was only one of them. Radiation, disease, toxic gases that lingered and drifted on the once-innocent winds, and—finally—the most efficient destroyer of them all: starvation.

Three billion people (give or take a meaningless hundred-million) lived on the planet Earth when the war began. Now, with the tenuous thread of civilization burned away, most of those who were not killed by the fighting itself succumbed, inexorably, to starvation.

Not everyone died, of course. Life went on. Some were lucky.

A long darkness settled on the world. Life went on for a few, a pitiful few, a bitter, hateful, suspicious, savage few. Cities became pestholes. Books became fuel. Knowledge died. Civilization was completely gone from the planet Earth.

The helmet was lifted slowly off his head. The CIA man found that he was too weak to raise his arms and help. He was shivering and damp with perspiration.

"Now you see," Ford said quietly, "why the military men cracked up when they used the computer."

General LeRoy, even, was pale. "How can a man with any conscience at all direct a military operation when he knows that *that* will be the consequence?"

The CIA man struck up a cigarette and pulled hard on it. He exhaled sharply. "Are all the war games . . . like that? Every plan?"

"Some are worse," Ford said. "We picked an average one for you. Even some of the 'brushfire' games get out of hand and end up like that."

"So . . . what do you intend to do? Why did you call me in? What can I do?"

"You're with CIA," the general said. "Don't you handle espionage?"

"Yes, but what's that got to do with it?"

The general looked at him. "It seems to me that the next logical step is to make damned certain that *They* get the plans to this computer . . . and fast!"

The ability to predict earthquakes could be
an unqualified boon, especially to residents of
such jittery places as the California coast. But
science doesn't always produce foolproof results
. . . especially new science.

A SLIGHT MISCALCULATION

Nathan French was a pure mathematician. He worked for a research laboratory perched on a California hill that overlooked
the Pacific surf, but his office had no windows. When his laboratory earned its income by doing research on nuclear bombs, Nathan doodled out equations for placing men on the moon with a
minimum expenditure of rocket fuel. When his lab landed a fat
contract for developing a lunar-flight profile, Nathan began worry-
ing about air pollution.

   Nathan didn't look much like a mathematician. He was tall
and gangly, liked to play handball, spoke with a slight lisp when
he got excited and had a face that definitely reminded you of a
horse. Which helped him to remain pure in things other than
mathematics. The only possible clue to his work was that,
lately, he had started to squint a lot. But he didn't look the slightest bit nervous or highstrung, and he still often smiled his great
big toothy, horsey smile.

When the lab landed its first contract (from the State of California), to study air pollution, Nathan's pure thoughts turned—naturally—elsewhere.

"I think it might be possible to work out a method of predicting earthquakes," Nathan told the laboratory chief, kindly old Dr. Moneygrinder.

Moneygrinder peered at Nathan over his half-lensed bifocals. "Okay, Nathan my boy," he said heartily. "Go ahead and try it. You know I'm always interested in furthering man's understanding of his universe."

When Nathan left the chief's sumptuous office, Moneygrinder hauled his paunchy little body out of its plush desk chair and went to the window. *His* office had windows on two walls: one set overlooked the beautiful Pacific; the other looked down on the parking lot, so the chief could check on who got to work at what time.

And behind that parking lot, which was half-filled with aging cars (business had been deteriorating for several years), back among the eucalyptus trees and paint-freshened grass, was a remarkably straight little ridge of ground, no more than four feet high. It ran like an elongated step behind the whole length of the laboratory and out past the abandoned pink stucco church on the crest of the hill. A little ridge of grass-covered earth that was called the San Andreas Fault.

Moneygrinder often stared at the Fault from his window, rehearsing in his mind exactly what to do when the ground started to tremble. He wasn't afraid, merely careful. Once a tremor had hit in the middle of a staff meeting. Moneygrinder was out the window, across the parking lot, and on the far side of the Fault (the eastern, or "safe" side), before men half his age had gotten out of their chairs. The staff talked for months about the astonishing agility of the fat little waddler.

A year, almost to the day, later the parking lot was slightly fuller and a few of the cars were new. The pollution business was starting to pick up, since the disastrous smog in San Clemente. And the laboratory had also managed to land a few quiet little Air Force contracts—for six times the amount of money it got from the pollution work.

Moneygrinder was leaning back in the plush desk chair, trying to look both interested and noncommittal at the same time, which was difficult to do, because he never could follow Nathan when the mathematician was trying to explain his work.

"Then it's a thimple matter of transposing the progression," Nathan was lisping, talking too fast because he was excited as he scribbled equations on the fuchsia-colored chalkboard with nerve-ripping squeaks of the yellow chalk.

"You thee?" Nathan said at last, standing beside the chalkboard. It was totally covered with his barely legible numbers and symbols. A pall of yellow chalk dust hovered about him.

"Um . . ." said Moneygrinder. "Your conclusion, then . . ."

"It's perfectly clear," Nathan said. "If you have any reasonable data base at all, you can not only predict when an earthquake will hit and where, but you can altho predict its intensity."

Moneygrinder's eyes narrowed. "You're sure?"

"I've gone over it with the CalTech geophysicists. They agree with the theory."

"H'mm." Moneygrinder tapped his desktop with his pudgy fingers. "I know this is a little outside your area of interest, Nathan, but . . . ah, can you really predict actual earthquakes? Or is this all theoretical?"

"Sure you can predict earthquakes," Nathan said, grinning like Francis, the movie star. "Like next Thursday's."

"Next Thursday's?"

"Yeth. There's going to be a major earthquake next Thursday."

"Where?"

"Right here. Along the Fault."

"Ulp."

Nathan tossed his stubby piece of chalk into the air nonchalantly, but missed the catch and it fell to the carpeted floor.

Moneygrinder, slightly paler than the chalk, asked, "A major quake, you say?"

"Uh-huh."

"Did . . . did the CalTech people make this prediction?"

"No, I did. They don't agree. They claim I've got an inverted gamma factor in the fourteenth set of equations. I've got the computer checking it right now."

Some of the color returned to Moneygrinder's flabby cheeks.

"Oh . . . oh, I see. Well, let me know what the computer says."

"Sure."

The next morning, as Moneygrinder stood behind the gauzy drapes of his office window, watching the cars pull in, his phone rang. His secretary had put in a long night, he knew, and she wasn't in yet. Pouting, Moneygrinder went over to the desk and answered the phone himself.

It was Nathan. "The computer still agrees with the CalTech boys. But I think the programming's slightly off. Can't really trust computers, they're only as good as the people who feed them, you know."

"I see," Moneygrinder answered. "Well, keep checking on it."

He chuckled as he hung up. "Good old Nathan. Great at theory, but hopeless in the real world."

Still, when his secretary finally showed up and brought him his morning coffee and pill and nibble on the ear, he said thoughtfully:

"Maybe I ought to talk with those bankers in New York, after all."

"But you said that you wouldn't need their money now that business is picking up," she purred.

He nodded, bulbously. "Yes, but still . . . arrange a meeting with them for next Thursday. I'll leave Wednesday afternoon. Stay the weekend in New York."

She stared at him. "But you said we'd . . ."

"Now, now . . . business comes first. You take the Friday night jet and meet me at the hotel."

Smiling, she answered, "Yes, Cuddles."

Matt Climber had just come back from a Pentagon lunch when Nathan's phone call reached him.

Climber had worked for Nathan several years ago. He had started as a computer programmer, assistant to Nathan. In two years he had become a section head, and Nathan's direct supervisor. (On paper only. Nobody bossed Nathan, he worked independently.) When it became obvious to Moneygrinder that Climber was heading his way, the lab chief helped his young assistant to a government job in Washington. Good experience for an up-and-coming executive.

"Hiya Nathan, how's the pencil-pushing game?" Climber shouted into the phone as he glanced at his calendar-appointment pad. There were three interagency conferences and two staff meetings going this afternoon.

"Hold it now, slow down," Climber said, sound'ng friendly but looking grim. "You know people can't understand you when you talk too fast."

Thirty minutes later, Climber was leaning back in his chair, feet on the desk, tie loosened, shirt collar open, and the first two meetings on his afternoon's list crossed off.

"Now let me get this straight, Nathan," he said into the phone. "You're predicting a major quake along the San Andreas Fault next Thursday afternoon at two-thirty Pacific Standard Time. But the CalTech people and your own computer don't agree with you."

Another ten minutes later, Climber said, "Okay, okay . . . sure, I remember how we'd screw up the programming once in a while. But you made mistakes, too. Okay, look—tell you what, Nathan. Keep checking. If you find out definitely that the computer's wrong and you're right, call me right away. I'll get the President himself, if we have to. Okay? Fine. Keep in touch."

He slammed the phone back onto its cradle and his feet on the floor, all in one weary motion.

Old Nathan's really gone 'round the bend, Climber told himself. *Next Thursday. Hah! Next Thursday. H'mmm . . .*

He leafed through the calendar pages. Sure enough, he had a meeting with the Boeing people in Seattle next Thursday.

If there is a major 'quake, the whole damned West Coast might slide into the Pacific. Naw . . . don't be silly. Nathan's cracking up, that's all. Still . . . how far north does the Fault go?

He leaned across the desk and tapped the intercom button.

"Yes, Mr. Climber?" came his secretary's voice.

"That conference with Boeing on the hypersonic ramjet transport next Thursday," Climber began, then hesitated a moment. But, with absolute finality, he snapped, "Cancel it."

Nathan French was not a drinking man, but by Tuesday of the following week he went straight from the laboratory to a friendly little bar that hung from a rocky ledge over the surging ocean.

It was a strangely quiet Tuesday afternoon, so Nathan had the undivided attention of both the worried-looking bartender and the freshly-painted whore, who worked the early shift in a low-cut, black cocktail dress and overpowering perfume.

"Cheez, I never seen business so lousy as yesterday and today," the bartender mumbled. He was sort of fidgeting around behind the bar, with nothing to do. The only dirty glass in the place was Nathan's, and he was holding on to it because he liked to chew the ice cubes.

"Yeah," said the girl. "At this rate, I'll be a virgin again by the end of the week."

Nathan didn't reply. His mouth was full of ice cubes, which he crunched in absent-minded cacophony. He was still trying to figure out why he and the computer didn't agree about the fourteenth set of equations. Everything else checked out perfectly: time, place, force level on the Richter scale. But the vector, the directional value—somebody was still misreading his programming instructions. That was the only possible answer.

"The stock market's dropped through the floor," the bartender said darkly. "My broker says Boeing's gonna lay off half their people. That ramjet transport they was gonna build is getting scratched. And the lab up the hill is getting bought out by some East Coast banks." He shook his head.

The girl, sitting beside Nathan with her elbows on the bar and her styrofoam bra sharply profiled, smiled at him and said, "Hey, how about it, big guy? Just so I don't forget how to, huh?"

With a final crunch on the last ice cube, Nathan said, "Uh, excuse me. I've got to check that computer program."

By Thursday morning, Nathan was truly upset. Not only was the computer still insisting that he was wrong about equation fourteen, but none of the programmers had shown up for work. Obviously, one of them—maybe all of them—had sabotaged his program. But why?

He stalked up and down the hallways of the lab searching for a programmer, somebody, anybody—but the lab was virtually empty. Only a handful of people had come in, and after an hour or so of wide-eyed whispering among themselves in the cafeteria over coffee, they started to sidle out to the parking lot and get into their cars and drive away.

Nathan happened to be walking down a corridor when one of the research physicists—a new man, from a department Nathan never dealt with—bumped into him.

"Oh, excuse me," the physicist said hastily, and started to head for the door down at the end of the hall.

"Wait a minute," Nathan said, grabbing him by the arm. "Can you program the computer?"

"Uh, no, I can't."

"Where is everybody today?" Nathan wondered aloud, still holding the man's arm. "Is it a national holiday?"

"Man, haven't you heard?" the physicist asked, goggle-eyed. "There's going to be an earthquake this afternoon. The whole damned state of California is going to slide into the sea!"

"Oh, that."

Pulling his arm free, the physicist scuttled down the hall. As he got to the door he shouted over his shoulder, "Get out while you can! East of the Fault! The roads are jamming up fast!"

Nathan frowned. "There's still an hour or so," he said to himself. "And I still think the computer's wrong. I wonder what the tidal effects on the Pacific Ocean would be if the whole state collapsed into the ocean?"

Nathan didn't really notice that he was talking to himself. There was no one else to talk to.

Except the computer.

He was sitting in the computer room, still poring over the stubborn equations, when the rumbling started. At first it was barely audible, like very distant thunder. Then the room began to shake and the rumbling grew louder.

Nathan glanced at his wristwatch: two-thirty-two.

"I knew it!" he said gleefully to the computer. "You see? And I'll bet all the rest of it is right, too. Including equation fourteen."

Going down the hallway was like walking through the passage-way of a storm-tossed ship. The floor and walls were swaying violently. Nathan kept his feet, despite some awkward lurches here and there.

It didn't occur to him that he might die until he got outside. The sky was dark, the ground heaving, the roaring deafened him.

A violent gale was blowing dust everywhere, adding its shrieking fury to the earth's tortured groaning.

Nathan couldn't see five feet ahead of him. With the wind tearing at him and the dust stinging his eyes, he couldn't tell which way to go. He knew the other side of the Fault meant safety, but where was it?

Then there was a biblical crack of lightning and the ultimate grinding, screaming, ear-shattering roar. A tremendous shock wave knocked Nathan to the ground and he blacked out. His last thought was, "I was right and the computer was wrong."

When he woke up, the sun was shining feebly through a gray overcast. The wind had died away. Everything was strangely quiet.

Nathan climbed stiffly to his feet and looked around. The lab building was still there. He was standing in the middle of the parking lot; the only car in sight was his own, caked with dust.

Beyond the parking lot, where the eucalyptus trees used to be, was the edge of a cliff, where still-steaming rocks and raw earth tumbled down to a foaming sea.

Nathan staggered to the cliff's edge and looked out across the water, eastward. Somehow he knew that the nearest land was Europe.

"Son of a bitch," he said with unaccustomed vehemence. "The computer was right after all."

All right, it was a joke. The story was literally cooked up over a bowl of Mulligatawny soup in an Indian restaurant one afternoon when Judy-Lynn del Rey and I lunched together. The final joke was that her chief editor at Galaxy magazine rejected the story; it was ultimately published by The Magazine of Fantasy and Science Fiction.

Many people—experts and laymen alike—fail to understand that teenage gangs represent a response to chaos, the same kind of response that primitive human beings make when they start to form clan and tribal groupings. Faced with a social environment that either ignores them or tries to herd them into institutions that they can't or won't accept, the teenagers in most cities end up by forming their own society. Called gangs, or associations, or clubs, they're all startlingly similar to the tribal society as a threat to Law and Order. If modern technology can be applied, however, and "reform" the gangs and make them useful to the adult society—what's the harm?

Indeed!

BLOOD OF TYRANTS

Still photo . . .

Danny Romano, switchblade in hand, doubling over as the bullet hits slightly above his groin. His face going from rage to shock. In the background other gang members battling: tire chains, pipes, knives. Behind them a grimy wall bearing a tattered political poster of some WASP promising "EQUAL OPPORTUNITY FOR ALL."

Fast montage of scenes, quick cutting from one to the next. Background music: Gene Kelly singing, "You Are My Lucky Star" . . .

Long shot of the street. Kids still fighting. Danny crawling painfully on all fours. CUT TO tight shot of Danny, eyes fixed on the skinny kid who shot him, switchblade still in hand. The kid, goggleeyed, tries to shoot again, gun jams, he runs. CUT TO long shot again, police cruisers wailing into view, lights flashing. CUT TO Danny being picked up off the street by a pair of angry-faced cops. He struggles, feebly. Nightstick fractures skull, ends his struggling. CUT TO Danny being slid out of an ambulance at hospital emergency entrance. CUT TO green-gowned surgeons (backs visible only), working with cool indifference under the glaring overhead lights. CUT TO Danny lying unconscious in hospital bed. Head bandaged. IV stuck in arm. Private room. Uniformed cop opens door from hallway, admits two men. One is obviously a plainclothes policeman: stocky, hard-faced, tired-eyed. The other looks softer, unembittered, even smiles. He peers at Danny through rimless glasses, turns to the plainclothesman and nods.

Establishing shots . . .

Washington, D.C.: Washington monument, Capitol build'ng (seen from foreground of Northeast district slums), pickets milling around White House fence.

An office interior . . .

Two men are present. Brockhurst, sitting behind the desk, is paunchy, bald, hooked on cigarettes, frowning with professional skepticism. The other man, Hansen, is the rimless-glasses man from the hospital scene.

"I still don't like it; it's risky," says Brockhurst from behind his desk.

"What's the risk?" Hansen has a high, thin voice. "If we can rehabilitate these gang leaders, and then use them to rehabilitate their fellow delinquents, what's the risk?"

"It might not work."

"Then all we've lost is time and money." Brockhurst glowers, but says nothing.

Another montage of fast-cut scenes. Background music: Mahalia Jackson stomping, "He's Got the Whole World in His Hands" . . .

Danny, between two cops, walks out of the hospital side door and into a police van. Bandages gone now. CUT TO Danny being unloaded from van, still escorted, at airport. He is walked to a twin-engine plane. CUT TO interior of plane. Five youths are already aboard: two Negroes, two Puerto Ricans, one white. Each is sitting, flanked by a white guard. A sixth guard takes Danny's arm at the entry-hatch and sits him in the only remaining pair of seats. Danny tries to look cool, but he's really delighted to be next to the window.

Interior of a "classroom" . . .

A large room. No windows, cream-colored walls, perfectly blank. About fifty boys are fidgeting in metal folding-chairs. Danny is sitting toward the rear. All the boys are now dressed in identical gray coveralls. Two uniformed guards stand by the room's only exit, a pair of large double doors.

The boys are mostly quiet; they don't know each other, they're trying to size up the situation. Hansen comes through the double doors (which a guard quickly closes behind him) and strides to the two-steps-up platform in the front of the room. He has a small microphone in his hand. He smiles and tries to look confident as he speaks.

"I'm not going to say much. I'd like to introduce myself. I'm Dr. Hansen. I'm not a medical doctor, I'm a specialist in education . . ."

A loud collective groan.

"No, no . . ." Hansen chuckles slightly. "No, it's not what you think. I work with teaching machines. You know, computers? Have you heard of them? Well, never mind . . ."

One of the kids stands up and starts for the door. A guard points a cattle prod toward the kid's chair. He gets the idea, goes back sullenly and sits down.

"You're here whether you like it or not," Hansen continues, minus the smile. "I'm confident that you'll soon like it. We're going to change you. We're going to make your lives worth living. And it doesn't matter in the slightest whether you like it or not. You'll learn to like it soon enough. No one's going to hurt you, unless you try to get rough. But we *are* going to change you."

Interior of the "reading room" . . .

A much smaller room. Danny and Hansen are alone in it. Same featureless plastic walls. No furniture except an odd-looking chair in the middle of the floor. It somewhat resembles an electric chair. Danny is trying to look contemptuous to cover up his fear.

"You ain't gettin' me in that!"

"It's perfectly all right; there's nothing here to hurt you. I'm merely going to determine how well you can read."

"I can read."

"Yes, of course." Doubtfully. "But how well? That's what I need to know."

"I don't see no books around."

"When you sit in the chair and the electrodes are attached to your scalp . . ."

"You gonna put those things on my head?"

"It's completely painless."

"No you ain't!"

Hansen speaks with great patience. "There's no use arguing about it. If I have to, I'll get the guards to strap you in. But it will be better if you cooperate. Mr. Carter—the one you call, uh, 'Spade,' I believe—he took the test without hesitating a moment. You wouldn't want him to know that we had to hold you down, would you?"

Danny glowers, but edges toward the chair. "Mother-humpin' sonofabitch . . ."

Series of fadeins and fadeouts . . .

Danny in the "reading room," sitting in the chair, cranium covered by electrode network. The wall before him has become a projection screen, and he is reading the words on it. MUSIC UNDER is Marine Corps Band playing Cornell University *Alma Mater* ("Far Above Cayuga's Waters . . .")

DANNY (hesitantly): The car . . . hummed . . . cut . . . quiet-ly to it-self . . .

FADEOUT
FADEIN

DANNY (tense with concentration): So my fellow Americans . . . ask not what your country can do for you . . .

FADEOUT
FADEIN

DANNY: "Surrender?" he shouted. "I have not yet begun to fight!"

FADEOUT
FADEIN

DANNY (enjoying himself): Robin pulled his bowstring back

carefully, knowing that the Sheriff and all the townspeople were watching him . . .

FADEOUT

Interior of Brockhurst's office . . .

Hansen is pacing impatiently before the desk, an intense smile on his face.

"I tell you, it's succeeding beyond my fondest hopes! Those boys are soaking it up like sponges. That Romano boy alone has absorbed more knowledge . . ."

Brockhurst is less than optimistic. "They're really learning?"

"Not only learning. They're beginning to change. The process is working. We're changing their attitudes, their value systems, everything. We're going to make useful citizens out of them!"

"All of them?"

"No, of course not. Only the best of them: half a dozen, I'd say, out of the fifty here—Romano, 'Spade' Carter, three or four others. At least six out of fifty, better than one out of ten. And this is just the first batch! When we start processing larger numbers of them . . ."

Brockhurst cuts Hansen short with a gesture. "Do you actually think these—students—of yours will go back to their old neighborhoods and start to rehabilitate their fellow gang members?"

"Yes, of course they will. They'll have to! They're being programmed for it!"

Interior of library . . .

Danny is sitting at a reading table, absorbed in a book. Bookshelves line the walls. A lumpy-faced redhead sits one table away, also reading. Hansen enters quietly, walks to Danny. "Hello Danny. How's it going today?"

Danny looks up and smiles pleasantly. "Fine, Mr. Hansen."

"I just got the computer's scoring of your economics exam. You got the highest mark in the class."

"Did I? Great. I was worried about it. Economics is kind of hard to grasp. Those booster pills you gave me must have helped."

"You did extremely well. . . . What are you reading?"

"Biography, by Harold Lamb. It's about Genghis Khan."

Hansen nods. "I see, look, it's about time we started thinking about what you're going to do when you go back home. Why don't you drop over to my office tonight, after supper?"

"Okay."

"See you then."

"Right."

Hansen moves away, toward the other boy. Danny closes his book, stands up. He turns to the bookshelf directly behind him and reaches unhesitatingly for another volume. He puts the two books under his arm and starts for the door. The title of the second book is *Mein Kampf*.

Brockhurst's office . . .

Six boys are standing in front of Brockhurst's desk, the six Hansen spoke of. They are now dressed in casual slacks, shirts, sport coats. Hansen is sitting beside the desk, beaming at them. Brockhurst, despite himself, looks impressed.

"You boys understand how important your mission is." Brockhurst is lapsing into a military tone. "You can save your friends a lot of grief . . . perhaps save their lives."

Danny nods gravely. "It's not just our friends that we'll be saving. It'll be our cities, all the people in them, our whole country."

"Exactly."

Hansen turns to Brockhurst. "They've been well-trained. They're ready to begin their work."

"Very well. Good luck, boys. We're counting on you."

Exterior shot, a city street . . .

Mid-afternoon, a hot summer day. A taxi pulls to the curb of the dingy, sun-baked street. Danny steps out, ducks down to pay the cabbie. He drives away quickly. Danny stands alone, in front of a magazine/tobacco store. He is dressed as he was in Brockhurst's office. Taking off the jacket, he looks slowly up and down the street. Deserted, except for a few youngsters sitting, listlessly, in the shade. With a shrug, he steps to the store.

Interior, the store . . .

Magazine racks on one side of the narrow entrance; store counter featuring cigarettes and candy on the other. No one at the counter. Overhead, a battered fan drones ineffectually. Farther back, a grimy table surrounded by rickety chairs. Three boys, two girls, all Danny's age, sit there. The boys in jeans and tee shirts, girls in shorts and sleeveless tops. They turn as he shuts the door, gape at him.

"Nobody going to say hello?" He grins at them.

"Danny!"

They bounce out of the chairs, knocking one over.

"We thought you was dead!"

"Or in jail . . . nobody knew what happened to you . . ."

"It's been almost a year!"

They cluster around him as he walks slowly back toward the table. But no one touches him.

"What happened to ya?"

"You look . . . different, sort of." The girl gestures vaguely.

"What'd they do to you? Where were you?"

Danny sits down. "It's a long story. Somebody get me a coke, huh? Who's been running things, Marco? Find him for me, I want to see him. And, Speed . . . get word to the Bloodhounds. I want to see their Prez . . . is it still Waslewski? And the one who shot me . . ."

"A war council?"

Danny smiles. "Sort of. Tell them that, if that's what it'll take to bring them here."

Interior, the back of the store . . .

It is night. Danny sits at the table, his shirt-sleeves rolled up, watching the front door. Two boys flank him: Marco, slim and dark, his thin face very serious; and Speed, bigger, lighter, obviously excited but managing to keep it contained. Both boys are trying to hide their nervousness with cigarettes. The door opens, and a trio of youths enter. Their leader, Waslewski, is stocky, blond, intense. His eyes cover the whole store with a flick. Behind him is the skinny kid who shot Danny, and a burlier boy who's trying to look cool and menacing.

"Come on in," Danny calls from his chair. "Nobody's going to hurt you."

Waslewski fixes his eyes on Danny and marches to the table. He takes a chair. His cohorts remain standing behind him. "So you ain't dead after all."

"Not yet."

"Guess you're pretty lucky."

Danny grins. "Luckier than you'll ever know." Nodding toward the boy who shot him, "What's his name?"

"O'Banion."

"All right, O'Banion. You put a bullet in me; I lived through it. You were doing your job for the Bloodhounds; I'm doing my job for the Champions. Nothing personal and no hard feelings on my part."

Waslewski's eyes narrow. "What're you pullin'? I thought this was gonna be a war council . . ."

"It is, but not the regular kind." Danny leans forward, spreads his hands on the table. "Know where I've been the past ten months? In Washington, in a special school the government set up, just to handle jay-dees. They pump knowledge into you with a computer . . . just like opening your head and sticking a hose in it."

The other boys, Bloodhounds and Champions alike, squirm a bit.

"You know what they taught me? They taught me we're nuts to fight each other. That's right . . . gangs fighting each other is strictly crazy. What's it get us? Lumps, is all. And dead."

Waslewski is obviously disgusted. "You gonna preach a sermon?"

"Damned right I am. You know why the gangs fight each other? Because *they* keep us up tight. They've got the money, they've got the power that runs this city, and they make sure we gangs stay down in the garbage. By fighting each other, we keep them sitting high and running the big show."

"They? Who the hell's they?"

"The people who run this city. The fat cats. The rich cats. The ones who've got limosines and broads with diamonds hanging from each tit. They *own* this city. They own the buildings and the people in the buildings. They own the cops. They own us."

"Nobody owns me!" says the burly kid behind Waslewski.

"Shuddup." Waslewski is frowning with thought now, trying to digest Danny's words.

"Look," Danny says. "This city is filled with money. It's filled with broads and good food and everything a guy could want for the rest of his life. What do we get out of it? Shit, that's what! And why? Because we let them run us, that's why. We fight each other over a crummy piece of turf, a couple of blocks of lousy street, while *they* sit back in plush restaurants and penthouses with forty-two-inch broads bending over them."

"So . . . what d'you expect us to do?"

"Stop fighting each other. Make the gangs work together to take over this city. We can do it! We can crack this city wide open, like a peanut. Instead of fighting each other, we can conquer this whole fucking city and run it for ourselves!"

Waslewski sags back in his seat. The other boys look at each other, amazed, unbelieving, yet obviously attracted by the idea.

"Great . . . real cool." Waslewski's voice and face exude sarcasm. "And what do the cops do? Sit back and let us take over? And what about the rest of the people? There's millions of 'em."

"Listen! We know how to fight. What we've got to do is get all the gangs together and fight together, like an army. It's just a matter of using the right strategy, the right tactics. We can do it. But we've got to work together. Not just the Bloodhounds and the Champions, but *all* the gangs! All of us, together, striking all at once. We can rack up the fuzz and take this town in a single night. They'll never know what hit them."

Marco objects, "But Danny, we can't . . ."

"Look, I know it'll take a lot of work. I figure we'll need two years, at least. We've got to get our guys spotted at key places all over the city: the power plants, all the radio and TV stations. We'll need guys inside the National Guard armories, inside the precinct stations, if we can do it. It'll mean a lot of guys will have to take jobs, learn to work hard for a couple years. But in the end, we'll have this city for ourselves!"

"You got it all figured out?"

"To the last inch."

Waslewski unconsciously pushes his chair slightly back from the table. He glances at his two lieutenants; they are wide-eyed.

"I gotta think about this. . . . I can't say yes or no just like that."

"Okay, you think about it. But don't spill it to anybody except your top boys. And remember, I'm going to be talking to all the gangs around here . . . and then to the gangs in the rest of the city. They'll go for it, I know. Don't get yourself left out."

Waslewski gets up slowly. "Okay, I'll get back to you right away. I think you can count us in." His aides nod agreement.

"Good. Now we're rolling." Danny gets up and sticks out his hand. Waslewski hesitates a beat, and then—acting rather stunned —shakes hands with Danny.

Montage of scenes. Background music: "The Army Caisson Song" . . .

Danny escorting Waslewski and two other boys into a Job Corps training-center office. CUT TO half-a-dozen boys sitting in a personnel-office waiting room. CUT TO a boy signing up in a National Guard armory.

Interior, Brockhurst's office . . .

Hansen is sitting on the front inch of the chair beside the desk, tense with excitement.

"It's a brilliant idea. Romano is working out better than any of his classmates, and this idea simply proves it!"

Brockhurst looks wary, probing for the weak point. "Why's he doing it? What's the sense of having gang members formed into a police auxiliary?"

"Sense? It's perfect sense. The boys can work hand-in-hand with the police, clue them in on trouble before it erupts into violence. The police can get to know the boys and the boys will get to know the police. Mutual exposure will breed mutual trust and confidence. Instead of working against each other, they'll be working together. With violence between the gangs and the police dwindling, a major source of trouble will be eliminated . . ."

"It just doesn't sound right to me. I can't picture those young punks turning into volunteer cops."

"But it's worth a try, isn't it? What do we have to lose?"

Brockhurst makes a sour face. "I suppose you're right. It's worth a try."

Interior, a one-room apartment . . .

The room is small but neat. The bed in the corner is made up in military style. The walls are covered with street maps of the city, over which are colored markings showing the territory of each gang. Danny sits at the only table, together with five other boys. One is a Negro, two others are Puerto Rican. The table is heaped high with papers.

"Okay," Danny says, "the Hellcats will handle the power station in their turf and the precinct house. And they've offered to put eight of their guys on our task force for the downtown area. What else?" He looks around at his aides.

The Negro boy says, "The Hawks have a beef. They claim the Jaguars have been cuttin' into their turf pretty regular for the past month. They've tried talkin' it out with 'em, but no dice. I tried talkin' to both sides, but they're up pretty tight about it."

Danny frowns. "Those damned Hawks have been screwing up for months."

"They're gonna rumble 'less you can stop 'em."

Thoughtfully, "There hasn't been a rumble all winter. Even the newspapers are starting to notice it. Maybe it'd be a good idea to let them fight it out . . . so long as nobody winds up spilling his guts about us to the squares."

"Somebody's gonna get hurt bad if they rumble. Lotta bad blood between them two gangs."

"I know." Danny thinks it over for a moment. "Look, tell them if they've got to rumble, do it without artillery. No guns, nothing that'll tip the squares to what we've got stashed away."

"Okay."

Interior, a Congressman's office . . .

The room is high-ceilinged, ornately decorated. The Congressman's broad desk is covered with mementos, framed photographs, neat piles of papers. The Congressman, himself, is in his mid-forties, just starting to turn fleshy. Sitting before him are Brockhurst, Hansen and—in a neat business suit—Danny.

"And so, with the annual appropriation coming up," Brockhurst is saying, "I thought you should have a personal report on the program."

The Congressman nods. "From all I've heard, it seems to be highly successful."

"It is." Brockhurst allows himself to smile. "Of course, this is only the beginning; only a half-dozen cities have been touched so far, although we have a hundred more boys in training at the moment. But I think you can judge the results for yourself."

Hansen interrupts. "And I hope you can realize the necessity for keeping the program secret, for the time being. Premature publicity . . ."

"Could ruin everything. I understand." Turning his gaze to Danny, "And this is your star pupil, eh?"

Danny smiles. "I . . . uh, Sir, I'd merely like to add my thanks for what this program has done for me and my friends. It's just like Dr. Hansen has been saying: all we boys need is some training and opportunity."

Interior, a fire house . . .

A boy sits at a tiny desk in the deserted garage. Behind him are the powerful fire trucks. No one else is in sight. Through the window alongside the desk, snow is falling on a city street. The window has a holiday wreath on it.

The boy is thumbing through the big calendar on the desk. He flips past December and into the coming year. He stops on July, notes that the Fourth falls on a Sunday. Smiling, he puts a red circle around the date.

Interior, a Congressional hearing room . . .

The committee members, half of them chatting with each other, sit at a long table in the front of the room. Brockhurst is sitting at the witness's desk, reading from a prepared text. Hansen sits beside him. The visitors' pews are completely empty, and a uniformed guard stands impassively at the door.

"Mr. Chairman, since the inception of this program, juvenile gang violence has decreased dramatically in five of the six cities where we have placed rehabilitated subjects. In one city, gang violence has dwindled to truly miniscule proportions. The boys are being rehabilitated, using Job Corps and other OEO facilities to train themselves for useful work, and then taking on—and keeping —full-time jobs." Brockhurst looks up from his text. "Mr. Chairman, if I may be allowed a new twist on an old saying, we're beating their switchblades into plowshares."

Interior, Danny's apartment . . .

Danny is pacing angrily across the room, back and forth. Three abject youths sit on the bed in the corner. At the table sit Marco and Speed.

"He nearly blew it!" Danny's voice is not loud, but clearly close to violence. "You stupid ass-holes can't keep your own people happy. He gets sore over a bitch and goes to the cops! If we didn't have a man in the precinct station last night, the whole plan would've been blown sky-high!"

One of the boys on the bed says, miserably, "But we didn't know . . ."

"That's even worse! You're supposed to know. You're the Prez of the Belters, you're supposed to know every breath your people take."

"Well . . . whaddawe do now?"

"You do nothing! You go back to your hole and sit tight. Don't even go to the can unless you get the word from me. Understand? If the cops tumble to us because you've got one half-wit who can't keep his mouth shut, every gang in the city is going to be after your blood. And they'll get it!"

Danny motions them to the door. They leave quickly. He turns to his lieutenants.

"Speed, you know anybody in the Belters who can do a good job as Prez?"

Speed hesitates only a beat before answering, "Yeah . . . kid named Molie. Sharp. He'd keep 'em in line okay."

"All right. Good. Get him here. Tonight. If I like him, we get that ass-hole who just left and his half-wit fink to kill each other. Then Molie becomes their President."

"Kill each other?"

"Right. Can't let the fink hang around. And we can't make the cops worry that he was killed because he knew something. And that ass-hole is no good for us. So we make it look like they had a fight over the bitch. And fast, before something else happens. We've only got a month to go."

Speed nods. "Okay, Danny. I'm movin' . . ." He is already halfway to the door.

Exterior, night . . .

A park in the city. Holiday crowd is milling around. City skyline is visible over the trees. A band finishes the final few bars of "Stars and Stripes Forever." A hush. Then the small thud of a skyrocket being launched, and overhead, a red-white-and-blue firework blossoms against the night sky. The crowd gives its customary gasp of delight.

Danny stands at the edge of the crowd. In the flickering light of the fireworks, he looks at his wrist watch, then turns to Speed and Marco and nods solemnly. They hurry off into the darkness.

Exterior, tollbooth across a major bridge . . .

A car full of youths pulls up at one of the three open tollgates. The boys spill out, guns in hands, club down the nearest tollbooth collector. The next closest one quickly raises his hands. The third collector starts to run, but he's shot down.

Interior, National Guard armory . . .

One hugely grinning boy in Army fatigues is handing out automatic weapons to a line-up of other boys, from a rack that has an unlocked padlock hanging from its open door.

Interior, subway train . . .

Four adults—two old ladies, a middle-aged man and a younger man—ride along sleepily. The train stops, the doors open. A combat team of twenty boys steps in through the three open doors. Their dress is ragged, but each boy carries a newly-oiled automatic weapon. The adults gasp. One boy yanks open the motorman's cubicle door and drags out the portly motorman. Another boy steps into the cubicle and shuts the doors. The train starts up again with the boys wordlessly standing, guns ready, while the adults huddle in a corner of the car.

Interior, police precinct station . . .

The desk sergeant is yawning. The radio operator, in the back of the room, is thumbing through a magazine. A boy—one of the police auxiliary—sits quietly on a bench by the door. He gets up, stretches, opens the front door. In pour a dozen armed boys. The desk sergeant freezes in mid-yawn. Two boys sprint toward the radio operator. He starts to grab for his microphone, but a blast of fire cuts him down.

Interior, a city power station . . .

Over the rumbling, whining noise of the generators, a boy walks calmly up to his supervisor, who's sitting in front of a board full of dials and switches, and pokes a pistol in his face. The man, startled, gets slowly out of his chair. Two other boys appear and take the man away. The first boy sits in the chair and reaches for the phone hanging on the instrument board.

Interior, newspaper office . . .

There is no sign of the usual news staff. All the desks are manned by boys, with Danny sitting at one of the desks in the center of the complex. Boys are answering phones, general hubbub of many simultaneous conversations. The mood is excited, almost jubilant. A few boys stand at the windows behind Danny, with carbines and automatic rifles in their hands. But they look relaxed.

Speed comes over to Danny from another desk, carrying a bundle of papers. "Here's the latest reports: every damned precinct station in town. We got 'em all! And the armories, the power stations, the TV studios. All the bridges and tunnels are closed down. Everything!"

Danny doesn't smile. "What about City Hall?"

"Took some fighting, but Shockie says we've got it nailed down. A few diehards in the cellblock, that's all. Our guys are usin' their own tear gas on 'em."

"The Mayor and the Councilmen?"

"The Mayor's outta town for the holidays, but we got most of the Councilmen, and the Police Chief, and the local FBI guys, too!"

Danny glances at his watch. "Okay, time for Phase Two. Round up every cop in town. On duty or off. Knock their doors down if you have to, pull them out of bed. But get them all into cells before dawn."

"Right!" Speed's grin is enormous.

Exterior, sun rising over city skyline . . .

From the air, the city appears normal. Nothing out of the ordinary. No fires, no milling crowds, not even much motor traffic on the streets. ZOOM TO the toll plaza at one of the city's main bridges. A lone sedan is stopped at an impromptu roadblock, made up of old cars and trucks strung lengthwise across the traffic lanes. A boy with an automatic rifle in the crook of one arm is standing atop a truck cab, waving the amazed automobile driver back into the city. On the other side of the tollbooth, an oil truck and moving van are similarly stopped before another roadblock.

Interior, a TV studio . . .

Danny is sitting at a desk, the hot lights on him. He is now wearing an Army shirt, open at the collar. A Colt automatic rests on the desk before him. Adults are manning the cameras, mike boom, lights, control booth; but armed boys stand behind each one.

"Good morning," Danny allows himself to smile pleasantly. "Don't bother trying to change channels. I'm on every station in town. Your city has been taken over. It's now our city. My name is Danny Romano; I'm your new Mayor. Also your Police Chief, Fire Chief, District Attorney, Judge, and whatever other jobs I want to take on. The kids you've been calling punks, jay-dees . . . the kids from the street gangs . . . we've taken over your city. You'll do what we tell you from now on. If you cooperate, nobody's going to hurt you. If you don't, you'll be shot. Life is going to be a lot simpler for all of us from now on. Do as you're told and you'll be okay."

Interior, Brockhurst's office . . .

General uproar. Brockhurst is screaming into a telephone. A couple dozen people are shouting at each other, waving their arms. Hansen is prostrate on the couch.

"No, I don't know anything more about it than you do!" Brockhurst's voice is near frenzy. His shirt is open at the neck, tie ripped off, jacket rumpled, face sweaty. "How the hell do I know? The FBI . . . the Army . . . somebody's got to do *something!*"

His secretary fights her way through the crowd. "Mr. Brockhurst . . . on line three . . . it's the *President!*"

Every voice hushes. Brockhurst slams the phone down, takes his hand off it, looks at it for a long moment. Then, shakily, he punches a button at the phone's base and lifts the receiver.

"Yessir. Yes, this is Brockhurst. . . . No, sir, I have no idea of how this came about . . . it . . . it seems to be genuine, sir. Yes, we've tried to communicate with them. . . . Yessir, Romano is one of our, eh, graduates. No, sir. No, I don't . . . but . . . I agree, we can't let them get away with it. The Army? Isn't there any other way? I'm afraid he's got several million people bottled up in that city, and he'll use them as hostages. If the Army attacks, he might start executing them wholesale."

Hansen props himself up on one elbow and speaks weakly, "Let me go to them. Let me talk to Danny. Something's gone wrong . . . something . . ."

Brockhurst waves him silent with a furious gesture. "Yes, Mr. President, I agree. If they won't surrender peacefully, then there's apparently no alternative. But if they fight the Army, a lot of innocent people are going to be hurt. . . . Yes, I know you can't just . . . but . . . no other way, yes, I see. Very well, sir, you are the Commander-in-Chief. Yessir. Of course, sir. Before the day is out. Yessir . . ."

Exterior, city streets . . .

Tanks rumbling down the streets. Kids firing from windows, throwing Molotov cocktails. One tank bursts into flames. The one behind it fires its cannon pointblank into a building: the entire structure explodes and collapses. Soldiers crouching in doorways, behind burned-out automobiles, firing at kids running crouched-down a half-block away. Two boys go sprawling. A soldier kicks a door in and tosses in a grenade. A few feet up the street, a teenage girl lies dead. A tank rolls past a children's playground, while a dazed old man sits bloody-faced on the curbstone, watching. Flames and smoke and the constant pock-pock-pock sound of automatic rifles, punctuated by explosions.

No picture, sound only . . .

The sounds of a phone being dialed, the click of circuits, the buzz of a phone ringing, another click as it is picked up.

"Yeah?"

"Hey, Spade, that you?"

"It's me."

"This is Midget."

"I know the voice, Midge."

"You see what Danny did?"

"I see what happened to him. How many dead, how many thousands? Or is it millions?"

"They ain't tellin'. Gotta be millions, though. Whole damned city's flattened. Army must've lost fifty thousand men all by itself."

"They killed Danny."

"They claim they killed him, but I ain't seen pictures of his body yet."

"It's a mess, all right."

"Yeah. Listen . . . they got Federal men lookin' for us now, you know?"

"I know. All Danny's 'classmates' are in for it."

"You gonna be okay?"

"They won't find me, don't worry. There's plenty of places to hide and plenty of people to hide me."

"Good. Now listen, this mess of Danny's oughtta teach us a lesson."

"Damned right."

"Yeah. We gotta work together now. When we make our move, it's gotta be in all the cities. Not just one. Every big city in the god damn country."

"Gonna take a long time to do it."

"I know, but we can make it. And when we do, they can't send the Army against every big city all at once."

"Specially if we take Washington and get *their* Prez."

"Right. Okay, gotta run now. Stay loose and keep in touch."

"Check. See you in Washington one of these days."

"You bet your sweet ass."

These three stories tell a connected tale about
the early life of an Air Force astronaut named
Chester A. Kinsman. Essentially, these stories
deal with his loss of innocence and his first
step toward real maturity. Or, to thoroughly
mix metaphors and sources, the stories taken
together form a miniature Paradise Lost and
Purgatorio. Kinsman has been with me since
the late 1940s. I knew him from birth to
death. There will be more stories about
him, including a novel.

Someday.

ZERO GEE

Joe Tenny looked like a middle linebacker for the Pittsburgh
Steelers. Sitting in the cool shadows of the Astro Motel's bar,
swarthy, barrel-built, scowling face clamped on a smoldering cigar,
he would never be taken for that rarest of all birds: a good engineer
who is also a good military officer.

"Afternoon, Major."

Tenny turned on his stool to see old Cy Calder, the dean of the
press-service reporters covering the base.

"Hi. Whatcha drinking?"

"I'm working," Calder answered with dignity. But he settled
his once-lanky frame onto the next stool.

"Double scotch," Tenny called to the bartender. "And refill
mine."

"An officer and a gentleman," murmured Calder. His voice was
gravelly, matching his face.

As the bartender slid the drinks to them, Tenny said, "You
wanna know who got the assignment."

"I told you I'm working."

Tenny grinned. "Keep your mouth shut 'til tomorrow? Murdock'll make the official announcement then, at his press conference."

"If you can save me the tedium of listening to the good colonel for two hours to get a single name out of him, I'll buy the next round, shine your shoes for a month, and arrange to lose an occasional poker pot to you."

"The hell you will!"

Calder shrugged. Tenny took a long pull on his drink. Calder did likewise.

"Okay. You'll find out anyway. But keep it quiet until Murdock's announcement. It's going to be Kinsman."

Calder put his glass down on the bar carefully. "Chester A. Kinsman, the pride of the Air Force? That's hard to believe."

"Murdock picked him."

"I know this mission is strictly for publicity," Calder said, "but Kinsman? In orbit for three days with *Photo Day* magazine's prettiest female? Does Murdock want publicity or a paternity suit?"

"Come on, Chet's not that bad. . . ."

"Oh no? From the stories I hear about your few weeks up at the NASA Ames center, Kinsman cut a swath from Berkeley to North Beach."

Tenny countered, "He's young and good-looking. And the girls haven't had many single astronauts to play with. NASA's gang is a bunch of old farts compared to my kids. But Chet's the best of the bunch, no fooling."

Calder looked unconvinced.

"Listen. When we were training at Edwards, know what Kinsman did? Built a biplane, an honest-to-God replica of a Spad fighter. From the ground up. He's a solid citizen."

"Yes, and then he played Red Baron for six weeks. Didn't he get into trouble for buzzing an airliner?"

Tenny's reply was cut off by a burst of talk and laughter. Half a dozen lean, lithe young men in Air Force blues—captains, all of them—trotted down the carpeted stairs that led into the bar.

"There they are," said Tenny. "You can ask Chet about it yourself."

Kinsman looked no different from the other Air Force astronauts. Slightly under six feet tall, thin with the leanness of youth, dark hair cut in the short, flat military style, blue-gray eyes, long bony face. He was grinning broadly at the moment, as he and the other five astronauts grabbed chairs in one corner of the bar and called their orders to the lone bartender.

Calder took his drink and headed for their table, followed by Major Tenny.

"Hold it," one of the captains called out. "Here comes the press."

"Tight security."

"Why, boys," Calder tried to make his rasping voice sound hurt, "don't you trust me?"

Tenny pushed a chair toward the newsman and took another one for himself. Straddling it, he told the captains, "It's okay. I spilled it to him."

"How much he pay you, boss?"

"That's between him and me."

As the bartender brought a tray of drinks, Calder said, "Let the Fourth Estate pay for this round, gentlemen. I want to pump some information out of you."

"That might take a lot of rounds."

To Kinsman, Calder said, "Congratulations, my boy. Colonel Murdock must think very highly of you."

Kinsman burst out laughing. "Murdock? You should've seen his face when he told me it was going to be me."

"Looked like he was sucking on lemons."

Tenny explained. "The choice for this flight was made mostly by computer. Murdock wanted to be absolutely fair, so he put everybody's performance ratings into the computer and out came Kinsman's name. If he hadn't made so much noise about being impartial, he could've reshuffled the cards and tried again. But I was right there when the machine finished its run, so he couldn't back out of it."

Calder grinned. "All right then, the computer thinks highly of you, Chet. I suppose that's still something of an honor."

"More like a privilege. I've been watching that *Photo Day* chick all through her training. She's ripe."

"She'll look even better up in orbit."

"Once she takes off the pressure suit . . . etcetera."

"Hey, y'know, nobody's ever done it in orbit."

"Yeah . . . free fall, zero gravity."

Kinsman looked thoughtful. "Adds a new dimension to the problem, doesn't it?"

"Three-dimensional." Tenny took the cigar butt from his mouth and laughed.

Calder got up slowly from his chair and silenced the others. Looking down fondly on Kinsman, he said:

"My boy—back in 1915, in London, I became a charter member of the Mile High Club. At an altitude of exactly 5,280 feet, while circling St. Paul's, I successfully penetrated an Army nurse in an open cockpit . . . despite fogged goggles, cramped working quarters, and a severe case of windburn.

"Since then, there's been damned little to look forward to. The skin-divers claimed a new frontier, but in fact they are retrogressing. Any silly-ass dolphin can do it in the water."

"But you've got something new going for you: weightlessness. Floating around in free fall, chasing tail in three dimensions. It beggars the imagination!

"Kinsman, I pass the torch to you. To the founder of the Zero Gee Club!"

As one man, they rose and solemnly toasted Captain Kinsman.

As they sat down again, Major Tenny burst the balloon. "You guys haven't given Murdock credit for much brains. You don't think he's gonna let Chet go up with that broad all alone, do you?"

Kinsman's face fell, but the others lit up.

"It'll be a three-man mission!"

"Two men and the chick."

Tenny warned, "Now don't start drooling. Murdock wants a chaperon, not an assistant rapist."

It was Kinsman who got it first. Slouching back in his chair, chin sinking to his chest, he muttered, "Sonofabitch . . . he's sending Jill along."

A collective groan.

"Murdock made up his mind an hour ago," Tenny said. "He was stuck with you, Chet, so he hit on the chaperon idea. He's also giving you some real chores to do, to keep you busy. Like mating the power pod."

"Jill Meyers," said one of the captains disgustedly.

"She's qualified, and she's been taking the *Photo Day* girl through her training. I'll bet she knows more about the mission than any of you guys do."

"She would."

"In fact," Tenny added maliciously, "I think she's the senior captain among you satellite-jockeys."

Kinsman had only one comment: "Shit."

The bone-rattling roar and vibration of liftoff suddenly died away. Sitting in his contour seat, scanning the banks of dials and gauges a few centimeters before his eyes, Kinsman could feel the pressure and tension slacken. Not back to normal. To zero. He was no longer plastered up against his seat, but touching it only lightly, almost floating in it, restrained only by his harness.

It was the fourth time he had felt weightlessness. It still made him smile inside the cumbersome helmet.

Without thinking about it, he touched a control stud on the chair's armrest. A maneuvering jet fired briefly and the ponderous, lovely bulk of planet Earth slid into view through the port in front of Kinsman. It curved huge and serene, blue, mostly, but tightly wrapped in the purest, dazzling white of clouds, beautiful, peaceful, shining.

Kinsman could have watched it forever, but he heard sounds of motion in his earphones. The two girls were sitting behind him, side by side. The spacecraft cabin made a submarine look roomy: the three seats were shoe-horned in among racks of instruments and equipment.

Jill Meyers, who came to the astronaut program from the Aerospace Medical Division, was officially second pilot and biomedical officer. *And chaperon,* Kinsman knew. The photographer, Linda Symmes, was simply a passenger.

Kinsman's earphones crackled with a disembodied link from Earth. "AF-9, this is ground control. We have you confirmed in orbit. Trajectory nominal. All systems go."

"Check," Kinsman said into his helmet mike.

The voice, already starting to fade, switched to ordinary conversational speech. "Looks like you're right on the money, Chet. We'll get the orbital parameters out of the computer and have 'em for you by the time you pass Ascension. You probably won't need much maneuvering to make rendezvous with the lab."

"Good. Everything here on the board looks green."

"Okay. Ground control out." Faintly. "And hey . . . good luck, Founding Father."

Kinsman grinned at that. He slid his faceplate up, loosened his harness and turned in his seat. "Okay, girls, you can take off your helmets if you want to."

Jill Meyers snapped her faceplate open and started unlocking the helmet's neck seal.

"I'll go first," she said, "and then I can help Linda with hers."

"Sure you won't need any help?" Kinsman offered.

Jill pulled her helmet off. "I've had more time in orbit than you. And shouldn't you be paying attention to the instruments?"

So this is how it's going to be, Kinsman thought.

Jill's face was round and plain and bright as a new penny. Snub nose, wide mouth, short hair of undistinguished brown. Kinsman knew that under the pressure suit was a figure that could most charitably be described as ordinary.

Linda Symmes was entirely another matter. She had lifted her faceplate and was staring out at him with wide, blue eyes that combined feminine curiosity with a hint of helplessness. She was tall, nearly Kinsman's own height, with thick honey-colored hair and a body that he had already memorized down to the last curve.

In her sweet, high voice she said, "I think I'm going to be sick."

"Oh for . . ."

Jill reached into the compartment between their two seats. "I'll take care of this. You stick to the controls." And she whipped a white plastic bag open and stuck it over Linda's face.

Shuddering at the thought of what could happen in zero gravity, Kinsman turned back to the control panel. He pulled his faceplate shut and turned up the air blower in his suit, trying to cut off the obscene sound of Linda's struggles.

"For Chrissake," he yelled, "unplug her radio! You want me chucking all over, too?"

"AF-9, this is Ascension."

Trying to blank his mind to what was going on behind him, Kinsman thumbed the switch on his communications panel. "Go ahead, Ascension."

For the next hour Kinsman thanked the gods that he had plenty of work to do. He matched the orbit of their three-man spacecraft to that of the Air Force orbiting laboratory, which had been up for more than a year now, and intermittently occupied by two- or three-man crews.

The lab was a fat, cylindrical shape, silhouetted against the brilliant white of the cloud-decked Earth. As he pulled the spacecraft close, Kinsman could see the antennas and airlock and other odd pieces of gear that had accumulated on it. *Looking more like a junkheap every trip.* Riding behind it, unconnected in any way, was the massive cone of the new power pod.

Kinsman circled the lab once, using judicious squeezes of his maneuvering jets. He touched a command-signal switch, and the lab's rendezvous-radar-beacon came to life, announced by a light on his control panel.

"All systems green," he said to ground control. "Everything looks okay."

"Roger, Niner. You are cleared for docking."

This was a bit more delicate. *Be helpful if Jill could read off the computer . . .*

"Distance, eighty-eight meters," Jill's voice pronounced firmly in his earphones. "Approach angle . . ."

Kinsman instinctively turned, but his helmet cut off any possible sight of her. "Hey, how's your patient?"

"Empty. I gave her a sedative. She's out."

"Okay," Kinsman said. "Let's get docked."

He inched the spacecraft into the docking-collar on one end of the lab, locked on and saw the panel lights confirm that the docking was secure.

"Better get Sleeping Beauty zipped up," he told Jill as he touched the buttons that extended the flexible access-tunnel from the hatch over their heads to the main hatch of the lab. The lights on the panel turned from amber to green when the tunnel locked its fittings around the lab's hatch.

Jill said, "I'm supposed to check the tunnel."

"Stay put. I'll do it." Sealing his faceplate shut, Kinsman unbuckled and rose effortlessly out of the seat to bump his helmet lightly against the overhead hatch.

"You two both buttoned tight?"

"Yes."

"Keep an eye on the air gauge." He cracked the hatch open a few millimeters.

"Pressure's okay. No red lights."

Nodding, Kinsman pushed the hatch open all the way. He pulled himself easily up and into the shoulder-wide tunnel, propelling himself down its curving length by a few flicks of his fingers against the ribbed walls.

Light and easy, he reminded himself. *No big motions, no sudden moves.*

When he reached the laboratory hatch he slowly rotated, like a swimmer doing a lazy rollover, and inspected every inch of the tunnel seal in the light of his helmet lamp. Satisfied that it was locked in place, he opened the lab hatch and pushed himself inside. Carefully, he touched his slightly adhesive boots to the plastic flooring and stood upright. His arms tended to float out, but they touched the equipment racks on either side of the narrow central passageway. Kinsman turned on the lab's interior lights, checked the air supply, pressure and temperature gauges, then shuffled back to the hatch and pushed himself through the tunnel again.

He reentered the spacecraft upside-down and had to contort himself in slow motion around the pilot's seat to regain a "normal" attitude.

"Lab's okay," he said finally. "Now how the hell do we get her through the tunnel?"

Jill had already unbuckled the harness over Linda's shoulders. "You pull, I'll push. She ought to bend around the corners all right."

And she did.

The laboratory was about the size and shape of the interior of a small transport plane. On one side, nearly its entire length was taken up by instrument racks, control equipment and the computer, humming almost inaudibly behind light plastic panels. Across the narrow separating aisle were the crew stations: control desk, two observation ports, biology and astrophysics benches. At the far end, behind a discreet curtain, was the head and a single hammock.

Kinsman sat at the control desk, in his fatigues now, one leg hooked around the webbed chair's single supporting column to keep him from floating off. He was running through a formal check of all the lab's life systems: air, water, heat, electrical power. All green lights on the main panel. Communications gear. Green. The radar screen to his left showed a single large blip close by—the power pod.

He looked up as Jill came through the curtain from the bunk-room. She was still in her pressure suit, with only the helmet removed.

"How is she?"

Looking tired, Jill answered, "Okay. Still sleeping. I think she'll be all right when she wakes up."

"She'd better be. I'm not going to have a wilting flower around here. I'll abort the mission."

"Give her a chance, Chet. She just lost her cookies when free-fall hit her. All the training in the world can't prepare you for those first few minutes."

Kinsman recalled his first orbital flight. *It doesn't shut off. You're falling. Like skiing, or skydiving. Only better.*

Jill shuffled toward him, keeping a firm grip on the chairs in front of the work benches and the handholes set into the equipment racks.

Kinsman got up and pushed toward her. "Here, let me help you out of the suit."

"I can do it myself."

"Shut up."

After several minutes, Jill was free of the bulky suit and sitting in one of the webbed chairs in her coverall-fatigues. Ducking slightly because of the curving overhead, Kinsman glided into the galley. It was about half the width of a phone booth, and not as deep nor as tall.

"Coffee, tea or milk?"

Jill grinned at him. "Orange juice."

He reached for a concentrate bag. "You're a hard girl to satisfy."

"No I'm not. I'm easy to get along with. Just one of the fellas."

Feeling slightly puzzled, Kinsman handed her the orange juice container.

For the next couple of hours they checked out the lab's equipment in detail. Kinsman was reassembling a high resolution camera after cleaning it, parts hanging in midair all around him as he sat intently working, while Jill was nursing a straggly-looking philo-dendron that had been smuggled aboard and was inching from the biology bench toward the ceiling light panels. Linda pushed back the curtain from the sleeping area and stepped, uncertainly, into the main compartment.

Jill noticed her first. "Hi, how're you feeling?"

Kinsman looked up. She was in tight-fitting coveralls. He bounced out of his web-chair toward her, scattering camera parts in every direction.

"Are you all right?" he asked.

Smiling sheepishly. "I think so. I'm rather embarrassed . . ." Her voice was high and soft.

"Oh, that's all right," Kinsman said eagerly. "It happens to practically everybody. I got sick myself my first time in orbit."

"That," said Jill as she dodged a slowly-tumbling lens that rico-cheted gently off the ceiling, "is a little white lie, meant to make you feel at home."

Kinsman forced himself not to frown. *Why'd Jill want to cross me?*

Jill said, "Chet, you'd better pick up those camera pieces before they get so scattered you won't be able to find them all."

He wanted to snap an answer, thought better of it, and replied simply, "Right."

As he finished the job on the camera, he took a good look at Linda. The color was back in her face. She looked steady, clear-eyed, not frightened or upset. *Maybe she'll be okay after all.* Jill made her a cup of tea, which she sipped from the lid's plastic spout.

Kinsman went to the control desk and scanned the mission schedule sheet.

"Hey, Jill, it's past your bedtime."

"I'm not really very sleepy," she said.

"Maybe. But you've had a busy day, little girl. And tomorrow will be busier. Now you get your four hours, and then I'll get mine. Got to be fresh for the mating."

"Mating?" Linda asked from her seat at the far end of the aisle, a good five strides from Kinsman. Then she remembered, "Oh . . . you mean linking the pod to the laboratory."

Suppressing a half-dozen possible jokes, Kinsman nodded. "Extra-vehicular activity."

Jill reluctantly drifted off her web-chair. "Okay, I'll sack in. I am tired, but I never seem to get really sleepy up here."

Wonder how much Murdock's told her? She's sure acting like a chaperon.

Jill shuffled into the sleeping area and pulled the curtain firmly shut. After a few moments of silence, Kinsman turned to Linda.

"Alone at last."

She smiled back.

"Uh, you just happen to be sitting where I've got to install this camera." He nudged the finished hardware so that if floated gently toward her.

She got up slowly, carefully, and stood behind the chair, holding its back with both hands as if she were afraid of falling. Kinsman slid into the web-chair and stopped the camera's slow-motion flight with one hand. Working on the fixture in the bulkhead that it fit into, he asked:

"You really feel okay?"

"Yes, honestly."

"Think you'll be up to EVA tomorrow?"

"I hope so . . . I want to go outside with you."

I'd rather be inside with you. Kinsman grinned as he worked.

An hour later they were sitting side by side in front of one of the observation ports, looking out at the curving bulk of Earth, the blue and white splendor of the cloud-spangled Pacific. Kinsman had just reported to the Hawaii ground station. The mission flight plan was floating on a clipboard between the two of them. He was trying to study it, comparing the time when Jill would be sleeping with the long stretches between ground stations, when there would be no possibility of being interrupted.

"Is that land?" Linda asked, pointing to a thick band of clouds wrapping the horizon.

Looking up from the clipboard, Kinsman said, "South American coast. Chile."

"There's another tracking station there."

"NASA station. Not part of our network. We only use Air Force stations."

"Why is that?"

He felt his face frowning. "Murdock's playing soldier. This is supposed to be a strictly military operation. Not that we do anything warlike. But we run as though there weren't any civilian stations around to help us. The usual hup-two-three crap."

She laughed. "You don't agree with the Colonel?"

"There's only one thing he's done lately that I'm in complete agreement with."

"What's that?"

"Bringing you up here."

The smile stayed on her face but her eyes moved away from him. "Now you sound like a soldier."

"Not an officer and a gentleman?"

She looked straight at him again. "Let's change the subject."

Kinsman shrugged. "Sure. Okay. You're here to get a story. Murdock wants to get the Air Force as much publicity as NASA gets. And the Pentagon wants to show the world that we don't have any weapons on board. We're military, all right, but *nice* military."

"And you?" Linda asked, serious now. "What do you want? How does an Air Force captain get into the space cadets?"

"The same way everything happens—you're in a certain place at a certain time. They told me I was going to be an astronaut. It was all part of the job . . . until my first orbital flight. Now it's a way of life."

"Really? Why is that?"

Grinning, he answered, "Wait'll we go outside. You'll find out."

Jill came back into the main cabin precisely on schedule, and it was Kinsman's turn to sleep. He seldom had difficulty sleeping on Earth, never in orbit. But he wondered about Linda's reaction to being outside while he strapped on the pressure-cuffs to his arms and legs. The medics insisted on them, claimed they exercised the cardiovascular system while you slept.

Damned stupid nuisance, Kinsman grumbled to himself. *Some ground-based MD's idea of how to make a name for himself.*

Finally he zippered himself into the gossamer cocoon-like hammock and shut his eyes. He could feel the cuffs pumping gently. His last conscious thought was a nagging worry that Linda would be terrified of EVA.

When he awoke, and Linda took her turn in the hammock, he talked it over with Jill.

"I think she'll be all right, Chet. Don't hold that first few minutes against her."

"I don't know. There's only two kinds of people up here: you either love it or you're scared sh . . . witless. And you can't fake it. If she goes ape outside . . ."

"She won't," Jill said firmly. "And anyway, you'll be there to help her. I've told her that she won't be going outside until you're finished with the mating job. She wanted to get pictures of you actually at work, but she'll settle for a few posed shots."

Kinsman nodded. But the worry persisted. *I wonder if Calder's Army nurse was scared of flying?*

He was pulling on his boots, wedging his free foot against an equipment rack to keep from floating off, when Linda returned from her sleep.

"Ready for a walk around the block?" he asked her.

She smiled and nodded without the slightest hesitation. "I'm looking forward to it. Can I get a few shots of you while you zipper up your suit?"

Maybe she'll be okay.

At last he was sealed into the pressure suit. Linda and Jill stood back as Kinsman shuffled to the airlock-hatch. It was set into the floor at the end of the cabin where the spacecraft was docked. With Jill helping him, he eased down into the airlock and shut the hatch. The airlock chamber itself was coffin-sized. Kinsman had to half-bend to move around in it. He checked out his suit, then pumped the air out of the chamber. Then he was ready to open the outer hatch.

It was beneath his feet, but as it slid open to reveal the stars, Kinsman's weightless orientation flip-flopped, like an optical illusion, and he suddenly felt that he was standing on his head and looking up.

"Going out now," he said into the helmet-mike.

"Okay," Jill's voice responded.

Carefully, he eased himself through the open hatch, holding onto its edge with one gloved hand once he was fully outside, the way a swimmer holds the rail for a moment when he first slides into the deep water. Outside. Swinging his body around slowly, he took in the immense beauty of Earth, dazzlingly bright even through his tinted visor. Beyond its curving limb was the darkness of infinity, with the beckoning stars watching him in unblinking solemnity.

Alone now. His own tight, self-contained universe, independent of everything and everybody. He could cut the life-giving umbilical line that linked him with the laboratory and float off by himself, forever. And be dead in two minutes. *Ay, there's the rub.*

Instead, he unhooked the tiny gas gun from his waist and, trailing the umbilical, squirted himself over toward the power pod. It was riding smoothly behind the lab, a squat truncated cone, shorter, but fatter, than the lab itself, one edge brilliantly lit by the sun; the rest of it bathed in the softer light reflected from the dayside of Earth below.

Kinsman's job was to inspect the power pod, check its equipment, and then mate it to the electrical system of the laboratory. There was no need to physically connect the two bodies, except to link a pair of power lines between them. Everything necessary for the task—tools, power lines, checkout instruments—had been built into the pod, waiting for a man to use them.

It would have been simple work on Earth. In zero gee, it was complicated. The slightest motion of any part of your body started you drifting. You had to fight against all the built-in mannerisms of a lifetime; had to work constantly to keep in place. It was easy to get exhausted in zero gee.

Kinsman accepted all this with hardly a conscious thought. He worked slowly, methodically, using as little motion as possible, letting himself drift slightly until a more-or-less natural body motion counteracted and pulled him back in the opposite direction. *Ride the waves, slow and easy.* There was a rhythm to his work, the natural dreamlike rhythm of weightlessness.

His earphones were silent, he said nothing. All he heard was the purring of the suit's air-blowers and his own steady breathing. All he saw was his work.

Finally he jetted back to the laboratory, towing the pair of thick cables. He found the connectors waiting for them on the side wall of the lab and inserted the cable plugs. *I pronounce you lab and power source.* He inspected the checkout lights alongside the connectors. All green. *May you produce many kilowatts.*

Swinging from handhold-to-handhold along the length of the lab, he made his way back toward the airlock.

"Okay, it's finished. How's Linda doing?"

Jill answered, "She's all set."

"Send her out."

She came out slowly, uncertain wavering feet sliding out first from the bulbous airlock. It reminded Kinsman of a film he had seen of a whale giving birth.

"Welcome to the real world," he said when her head cleared the airlock-hatch.

She turned to answer him and he heard her gasp and he knew that now he liked her.

"It's . . . it's . . ."

"Staggering," Kinsman suggested. "And look at you—no hands."

She was floating freely, pressure-suit laden with camera gear, umbilical flexing easily behind her. Kinsman couldn't see her face through the tinted visor, but he could hear the awe in her voice, even in her breathing.

"I've never seen anything so absolutely overwhelming. . . ."

And then, suddenly, she was all business, reaching for a camera, snapping away at the Earth and stars and distant moon, rapidfire. She moved too fast and started to tumble. Kinsman jetted over and steadied her, holding her by the shoulders.

"Hey, take it easy. They're not going away. You've got lots of time."

"I want to get some shots of you, and the lab. Can you get over by the pod and go through some of the motions of your work on it?"

Kinsman posed for her, answered her questions, rescued a camera when she fumbled it out of her hands and couldn't reach it as it drifted away from her.

"Judging distances gets a little whacky out here," he said, handing the camera back to her.

Jill called them twice and ordered them back inside. "Chet, you're already fifteen minutes over the limit!"

"There's plenty slop in the schedule; we can stay out a while longer."

"You're going to get her exhausted."

"I really feel fine," Linda said, her voice lyrical.

"How much more film do you have?" Kinsman asked her.

She peered at the camera. "Six more shots."

"Okay, we'll be in when the film runs out, Jill."

"You're going to be in darkness in another five minutes!"

Turning to Linda, who was floating upside-down with the cloud-laced Earth behind her, he said, "Save your film for the sunset, then shoot like hell when it comes."

"The sunset? What'll I focus on?"

"You'll know when it happens. Just watch."

It came fast, but Linda was equal to it. As the lab swung in its orbit toward the Earth's night-shadow, the sun dropped to the horizon and shot off a spectacular few moments of the purest reds and oranges and finally a heart-catching blue. Kinsman watched in silence, hearing Linda's breath going faster and faster as she worked the camera.

Then they were in darkness. Kinsman flicked on his helmet lamp. Linda was just hanging there, camera still in hand.

"It's . . . impossible to describe." Her voice sounded empty, drained. "If I hadn't seen it . . . if I didn't get it on film, I don't think I'd be able to convince myself that I wasn't dreaming."

Jill's voice rasped in his earphones. "Chet, get inside! This is against every safety reg, being outside in the dark."

He looked over toward the lab. Lights were visible along its length and the ports were lighted from within. Otherwise, he could barely make it out, even though it was only a few meters away.

"Okay, okay. Turn on the airlock-light so we can see the hatch."

Linda was still bubbling about the view outside, long after they had pulled off their pressure-suits and eaten sandwiches and cookies.

"Have you ever been out there?" she asked Jill.

Perched on the biology bench's edge, near the mice colony, Jill nodded curtly. "Twice."

"Isn't it spectacular? I hope the pictures come out; some of the settings on the camera . . ."

"They'll be all right," Jill said. "And if they're not, we've got a backlog of photos you can use."

"Oh, but they wouldn't have the shots of Chet working on the power pod."

Jill shrugged. "Aren't you going to take more photos in here?

If you want to get some pictures of real space veterans, you ought to snap the mice here. They've been up for months now, living fine and raising families. And they don't make such a fuss about it, either."

"Well, some of us do exciting things," Kinsman said, "and some of us tend mice."

Jill glowered at him.

Glancing at his wristwatch, Kinsman said, "Girls, it's my sack time. I've had a trying day: mechanic, tourist guide, and cover boy for *Photo Day*. Work, work, work."

He glided past Linda with a smile, kept it for Jill as he went by her. She was still glaring.

When he woke up again and went back into the main cabin, Jill was talking pleasantly with Linda as the two of them stood over the microscope and specimen-rack of the biology bench.

Linda saw him first. "Oh, hi. Jill's been showing me the spores she's studying. And I photographed the mice. Maybe they'll go on the cover instead of you."

Kinsman grinned. "She been poisoning your mind against me." But to himself he wondered, *What the hell has Jill been telling her about me?*

Jill drifted over to the control desk, picked up the clipboard with the mission log on it and tossed it lightly toward Kinsman.

"Ground control says the power pod checks out all green," she said. "You did a good job."

"Thanks." He caught the clipboard. "Whose turn in the sack is it?"

"Mine," Jill answered.

"Okay. Anything special cooking?"

"No. Everything's on schedule. Next data transmission comes up in twelve minutes. Kodiak station."

Kinsman nodded. "Sleep tight."

Once Jill had shut the curtain to the bunkroom, Kinsman carried the mission log to the control desk and sat down. Linda stayed at the biology bench, about three paces away.

He checked the instrument board with a quick glance, then turned to Linda. "Well, now do you know what I meant about this being a way of life?"

"I think so. It's so different . . ."

"It's the real thing. Complete freedom. Brave new world. After ten minutes of EVA, everything else is just toothpaste."

"It was certainly exciting."

"More than that. It's living. Being on the ground is a drag, even flying a plane is dull now. This is where the fun is . . . out here in orbit and on the moon. It's as close to heaven as anybody's gotten."

"You're really serious?"

"Damned right. I've even been thinking of asking Murdock for a transfer to NASA duty. Air Force missions don't include the moon, and I'd like to walk around on the new world, see the sights."

She smiled at him. "I'm afraid I'm not that enthusiastic."

"Well, think about it for a minute. Up here, you're free. Really free, for the first time in your life. All the laws and rules and prejudices they've been dumping on you all your life . . . they're all *down there*. Up here it's a new start. You can be yourself and do your own thing . . . and nobody can tell you different."

"As long as somebody provides you with air and food and water and . . ."

"That's the physical end of it, sure. We're living in a microcosm, courtesy of the aerospace industry and AFSC. But there're no strings on us. The brass can't make us follow their rules. We're writing the rule books ourselves. . . . For the first time since 1776, we're writing new rules."

Linda looked thoughtful now. Kinsman couldn't tell if she was genuinely impressed by his line, or if she knew what he was trying to lead up to. He turned back to the control desk and studied the mission flight plan again.

He had carefully considered all the possible opportunities, and narrowed them down to two. *Both of them tomorrow, over the Indian Ocean. Forty to fifty minutes between ground stations, and Jill's asleep both times.*

"AF-9, this is Kodiak."

He reached for the radio switch. "AF-9 here, Kodiak. Go ahead."

"We are receiving your automatic data transmission loud and clear."

"Roger Kodiak. Everything normal here; mission profile unchanged."

"Okay, Niner. We have nothing new for you. Oh wait . . . Chet, Lew Regneson is here and he says he's betting on you to uphold the Air Force's honor. Keep 'em flying."

Keeping his face as straight as possible, Kinsman answered, "Roger, Kodiak. Mission profile unchanged."

"Good luck!"

Linda's thoughtful expression had deepened. "What was that all about?"

He looked straight into those cool blue eyes and answered, "Damned if I know. Regneson's one of the astronaut team; been assigned to Kodiak for the past six weeks. He must be going ice-happy. Thought it'd be best just to humor him."

"Oh. I see." But she looked unconvinced.

"Have you checked any of your pictures in the film processor?"

Shaking her head, Linda said, "No, I don't want to risk them on your automatic equipment. I'll process them myself when we get back."

"Damned good equipment," said Kinsman.

"I'm fussy."

He shrugged and let it go.

"Chet?"

"What?"

"That power pod . . . what's it for? Colonel Murdock got awfully coy when I asked him."

"Nobody's supposed to know until the announcement's made in Washington . . . probably when we get back. I can't tell you officially," he grinned, "but generally reliable sources believe that it's going to power a radar set that'll be orbited next month. The radar will be part of our ABM warning system."

"Antiballistic missile?"

With a nod, Kinsman explained, "From orbit you can spot missile launches farther away, give the States a longer warning time."

"So your brave new world is involved in war, too."

"Sort of." Kinsman frowned. "Radars won't kill anybody, of course. They might save lives."

"But this *is* a military satellite."

"Unarmed. Two things this brave new world doesn't have yet: death and love."

"Men have died . . ."

"Not in orbit. On reentry. In ground or air accidents. No one's died up here. And no one's made love, either."

Despite herself, it seemed to Kinsman, she smiled. "Have there been any chances for it?"

"Well, the Russians have had women cosmonauts. Jill's been the first American girl in orbit. You're the second."

She thought it over for a moment. "This isn't exactly the bridal suite of the Waldorf . . . in fact, I've seen better motel rooms along the Jersey Turnpike."

"Pioneers have to rough it."

"I'm a photographer, Chet, not a pioneer."

Kinsman hunched his shoulders and spread his hands helplessly, a motion that made him bob slightly on the chair. "Strike three, I'm out."

"Better luck next time."

"Thanks." He returned his attention to the mission flight plan. *Next time will be in exactly sixteen hours, chickie.*

When Jill came out of the sack it was Linda's turn to sleep. Kinsman stayed at the control desk, sucking on a container of lukewarm coffee. All the panel lights were green. Jill was taking a blood specimen from one of the white mice.

"How're they doing?"

Without looking up, she answered, "Fine. They've adapted to weightlessness beautifully. Calcium level's evened off, muscle tone is good . . ."

"Then there's hope for us two-legged types?"

Jill returned the mouse to the colony entrance and snapped the lid shut. It scampered through to rejoin its clan in the transparent plastic maze of tunnels.

"I can't see any physical reason why humans can't live in orbit indefinitely," she answered.

Kinsman caught a slight but definite stress on the word *physical*. "You think there might be emotional problems over the long run?"

"Chet, I can see emotional problems on a three-day mission." Jill forced the blood specimen into a stoppered test tube.

"What do you mean?"

"Come on," she said, her face a mixture of disappointment and distaste. "It's obvious what you're trying to do. Your tail's been wagging like a puppy's whenever she's in sight."

"You haven't been sleeping much, have you?"

"I haven't been eavesdropping, if that's what you mean. I've simply been watching you watching her. And some of the messages from the ground . . . is the whole Air Force in on this? How much money's being bet?"

"I'm not involved in any betting. I'm just . . ."

"You're just taking a risk on fouling up this mission and maybe killing the three of us, just to prove you're Tarzan and she's Jane."

"Goddammit, Jill, now you sound like Murdock."

The sour look on her face deepened. "Okay. You're a big boy. If you want to play Tarzan while you're on duty, that's your business. I won't get in your way. I'll take a sleeping pill and stay in the sack."

"You will?"

"That's right. You can have your blonde Barbie doll, and good luck to you. But I'll tell you this . . . she's a phony. I've talked to her long enough to dig that. You're trying to use her, but she's using us, too. She was pumping me about the power pod while you were sleeping. She's here for her own reasons, Chet, and if she plays along with you it won't be for the romance and adventure of it all."

My God Almighty, Jill's jealous!

It was tense and quiet when Linda returned from the bunkroom. The three of them worked separately: Jill fussing over the algae colony on the shelf above the biology bench; Kinsman methodically taking film from the observation cameras for return to Earth and reloading them; Linda efficiently clicking away at both of them.

Ground control called up to ask how things were going. Both Jill and Linda threw sharp glances at Kinsman. He replied merely:

"Following mission profile. All systems green."

They shared a meal of pastes and squeeze-tubes together, still mostly in silence, and then it was Kinsman's turn in the sack. But not before he checked the mission flight plan. *Jill goes in next, and we'll have four hours alone, including a stretch over the Indian Ocean.*

Once Jill retired, Kinsman immediately called Linda over to the control desk under the pretext of showing her the radar image of a Russian satellite.

"We're coming close now." They hunched side by side at the desk to peer at the orange-glowing radar screen, close enough for Kinsman to scent a hint of very feminine perfume. "Only a thousand kilometers away."

"Why don't you blink our lights at them?"

"It's unmanned."

"Oh."

"It *is* a little like World War I up here," Kinsman realized, straightening up. "Just being here is more important than which nation you're from."

"Do the Russians feel that way, too?"

Kinsman nodded. "I think so."

She stood in front of him, so close that they were almost touching.

"You know," Kinsman said, "when I first saw you on the base, I thought you were a photographer's model . . . not the photographer."

Gliding slightly away from him, she answered, "I started out as a model. . . ." Her voice trailed off.

"Don't stop. What were you going to say?"

Something about her had changed, Kinsman realized. She was still coolly friendly, but alert now, wary, and . . . sad?

Shrugging, she said, "Modeling is a dead end. I finally figured out that there's more of a future on the other side of the camera."

"You had too much brains for modeling."

"Don't flatter me."

"Why on earth should I flatter you?"

"We're not on Earth."

"*Touché.*"

She drifted over toward the galley. Kinsman followed her.

"How long have you been on the other side of the camera?" he asked.

Turning back toward him, "I'm supposed to be getting your life story, not vice versa."

"Okay . . . ask me some questions."

"How many people know you're supposed to lay me up here?"

Kinsman felt his face smiling, an automatic delaying action. *What the hell,* he thought. Aloud, he replied, "I don't know. It started as a little joke among a few of the guys . . . apparently the word has spread."

"And how much money do you stand to win or lose?" She wasn't smiling.

"Money?" Kinsman was genuinely surprised. "Money doesn't enter into it."

"Oh no?"

"No, not with me," he insisted.

The tenseness in her body seemed to relax a little. "Then why . . . I mean . . . what's it all about?"

Kinsman brought his smile back and pulled himself down into the nearest chair. "Why not? You're damned pretty, neither one of us has any strings, nobody's tried it in zero gee before. . . . Why the hell not?"

"But why should I?"

"That's the big question. That's what makes an adventure out of it."

She looked at him thoughtfully, leaning her tall frame against the galley paneling. "Just like that. An adventure. There's nothing more to it than that?"

"Depends," Kinsman answered. "Hard to tell ahead of time."

"You live in a very simple world, Chet."

"I try to. Don't you?"

She shook her head. "No, my world's very complex."

"But it includes sex."

Now she smiled, but there was no pleasure in it. "Does it?"

"You mean never?" Kinsman's voice sounded incredulous, even to himself.

She didn't answer.

"Never at all? I can't believe that. . . ."

"No," she said, "not never at all. But never for . . . for an adventure. For job security, yes. For getting the good assignments; for teaching me how to use a camera, in the first place. But never for fun . . . at least, not for a long, long time has it been for fun."

Kinsman looked into those ice-blue eyes and saw that they were completely dry and aimed straight back at him. His insides felt odd. He put a hand out toward her, but she didn't move a muscle.

"That's . . . that's a damned lonely way to live," he said.

"Yes, it is." Her voice was a steel knifeblade, without a trace of self-pity in it.

"But . . . how'd it happen? Why . . ."

She leaned her head back against the galley paneling, her eyes looking away, into the past. "I had a baby. He didn't want it. I had to give it up for adoption—either that or have it aborted. The kid should be five years old now. . . . I don't know where she is." She straightened up, looked back at Kinsman. "But I found out that sex is either for making babies or making careers; not for fun."

Kinsman sat there, feeling like he had just taken a low blow. The only sound in the cabin was the faint hum of electrical machinery, the whisper of the air fans.

Linda broke into a grin. "I wish you could see your face . . . Tarzan, the Ape-Man, trying to figure out a nuclear reactor."

"The only trouble with zero gee," he mumbled, "is that you can't hang yourself."

Jill sensed something was wrong, it seemed to Kinsman. From the moment she came out of the sack, she sniffed around, giving quizzical looks. Finally, when Linda retired for her final rest period before their return, Jill asked him:

"How're you two getting along?"

"Okay."

"Really?"

"Really. We're going to open a Playboy Club in here. Want to be a bunny?"

Her nose wrinkled. "You've got enough of those."

For more than an hour they worked their separate tasks in silence. Kinsman was concentrating on recalibrating the radar mapper when Jill handed him a container of hot coffee.

He turned in the chair. She was standing beside him, not much taller than his own seated height.

"Thanks."

Her face was very serious. "Something's bothering you, Chet. What did she do to you?"

"Nothing."

"Really?"

"For Chrissake, don't start that again! Nothing, absolutely nothing happened. Maybe that's what's bothering me."

Shaking her head, "No, you're worried about something, and it's not about yourself."

"Don't be so damned dramatic, Jill."

She put a hand on his shoulder. "Chet . . . I know this is all a game to you, but people can get hurt at this kind of game, and . . . well . . . nothing in life is ever as good as you expect it will be."

Looking up at her intent brown eyes, Kinsman felt his irritation vanish. "Okay, kid. Thanks for the philosophy. I'm a big boy, though, and I know what it's all about. . . ."

"You just think you do."

Shrugging, "Okay, I think I do. Maybe nothing is as good as it ought to be, but a man's innocent until proven guilty, and everything new is as good as gold until you find some tarnish on it. That's *my* philosophy for the day!"

"All right, slugger," Jill smiled, ruefully. "Be the ape-man. Fight it out for yourself. I just don't want to see her hurt you."

"I won't get hurt."

Jill said, "You hope. Okay, if there's anything I can do . . ."

"Yeah, there is something."

"What?"

"When you sack in again, make sure Linda sees you take a sleeping pill. Will you do that?"

Jill's face went expressionless. "Sure," she answered flatly. "Anything for a fellow officer."

She made a great show, several hours later, of taking a sleeping pill so that she could rest well on her final nap before reentry. It seemed to Kinsman that Jill deliberately layed it on too thickly.

"Do you always take sleeping pills on the final time around?" Linda asked, after Jill had gone into the bunkroom.

"Got to be fully alert and rested," Kinsman replied, "for the return flight. Reentry's the trickiest part of the operation."

"Oh. I see."

"Nothing to worry about, though," Kinsman added.

He went to the control desk and busied himself with the tasks that the mission profile called for. Linda sat lightly in the next chair, within arm's reach. Kinsman chatted briefly with Kodiak station, on schedule, and made an entry in the log.

Three more ground stations and then we're over the Indian Ocean, with world enough and time.

But he didn't look up from the control panel; he tested each system aboard the lab, fingers flicking over control buttons, eyes focused on the red, amber and green lights that told him how the laboratory's mechanical and electrical machinery was functioning.

"Chet?"

"Yes."

"Are you . . . sore at me?"

Still not looking at her, "No, I'm busy. Why should I be sore at you?"

"Well, not sore maybe, but . . ."

"Puzzled?"

"Puzzled, hurt, something like that."

He punched an entry on the computer's keyboard at his side, then turned to face her. "Linda, I haven't really had time to figure out what I feel. You're a complicated girl; maybe too complicated for me. Life's got enough twists in it."

Her mouth drooped a little.

"On the other hand," he added, "we WASPS ought to stick together. Not many of us left."

That brought a faint smile. "I'm not a WASP. My real name's Szymanski. . . . I changed it when I started modeling."

"Oh. Another complication."

She was about to reply when the radio speaker crackled, "AF-9, this is Cheyenne. Cheyenne to AF-9."

Kinsman leaned over and thumbed the transmitter switch. "AF-9 to Cheyenne. You're coming through faint but clear."

"Roger, Nine. We're receiving your telemetry. All systems look green from here."

"Manual check of systems also green," Kinsman said. "Mission profile okay, no deviations. Tasks about ninety percent complete."

"Roger. Ground control suggests you begin checking out your spacecraft on the next orbit. You are scheduled for reentry in ten hours."

"Right. Will do."

"Okay, Chet. Everything looks good from here. Anything else to report, ol' Founding Father?"

"Mind your own business." He turned the transmitter off.

Linda was smiling at him.

"What's so funny?"

"You are. You're getting very touchy about this whole business."

"It's going to stay touchy for a long time to come. Those guys'll hound me for years about this."

"You could always tell lies."

"About you? No, I don't think I could do that. If the girl was anonymous, that's one thing. But they all know you, know where you work . . ."

"You're a gallant officer. I suppose that kind of rumor would get back to New York."

Kinsman grinned. "You could even make the front page of the *National Enquirer.*"

She laughed at that. "I'll bet they'd pull out some of my old bikini pictures."

"Careful now," Kinsman put up a warning hand. "Don't stir up my imagination any more than it already is. I'm having a hard enough time being gallant right now."

They remained apart, silent, Kinsman sitting at the control desk, Linda drifting back toward the galley, nearly touching the curtain that screened off the sleeping area.

The ground control center called in and Kinsman gave a terse report. When he looked up at Linda again, she was sitting in front of the observation port across the aisle from the galley. Looking back at Kinsman, her face was troubled now, her eyes . . . he wasn't sure what was in her eyes. They looked different: no longer ice-cool, no longer calculating; they looked aware, concerned, almost frightened.

Still Kinsman stayed silent. He checked and double-checked the control board, making absolutely certain that every valve and transistor aboard the lab was working perfectly. Glancing at his watch: *Five more minutes before Ascension calls.* He checked the lighted board again.

Ascension called in exactly on schedule. Feeling his innards tightening, Kinsman gave his standard report in a deliberately calm and mechanical way. Ascension signed off.

With a long last look at the controls, Kinsman pushed himself out of the seat and drifted, hands faintly touching the grips along the aisle, toward Linda.

"You've been awfully quiet," he said, standing over her.

"I've been thinking about what you said a while ago." What was it in her eyes? Anticipation? Fear? "It . . . it has been a damned lonely life, Chet."

He took her arm and lifted her gently from the chair and kissed her.

"But . . ."

"It's all right," he whispered. "No one will bother us. No one will know."

She shook her head. "It's not that easy, Chet. It's not that simple."

"Why not? We're here together . . . what's so complicated?"

"But—doesn't anything bother you? You're floating around in a dream. You're surrounded by war machines, you're living every minute with danger. If a pump fails or a meteor hits . . ."

"You think it's any safer down there?"

"But life *is* complex, Chet. And love . . . well, there's more to it than just having fun."

"Sure there is. But it's meant to be enjoyed, too. What's wrong with taking an opportunity when you have it? What's so damned complicated or important? We're above the cares and worries of Earth. Maybe it's only for a few hours, but it's here and now, it's us. They can't touch us, they can't force us to do anything or stop us from doing what we want to. We're on our own. Understand? Completely on our own."

She nodded, her eyes still wide with the look of a frightened animal. But her hands slid around him, and together they drifted back toward the control desk. Wordlessly, Kinsman turned off all the overhead lights, so that all they saw was the glow of the control board and the flickering of the computer as it murmured to itself.

They were in their own world now, their private cosmos, floating freely and softly in the darkness. Touching, drifting, coupling, searching the new seas and continents, they explored their world.

Jill stayed in the hammock until Linda entered the bunkroom, quietly, to see if she had awakened yet. Kinsman sat at the control desk feeling, not tired, but strangely numb.

The rest of the flight was strictly routine. Jill and Kinsman did their jobs, spoke to each other when they had to. Linda took a brief nap, then returned to snap a few last pictures. Finally, they crawled back into the spacecraft, disengaged from the laboratory, and started the long curving flight back to Earth.

Kinsman took a last look at the majestic beauty of the planet, serene and incompatible among the stars, before touching the button that slid the heat-shield over his viewport. Then they felt the surge of rocket thrust, dipped into the atmosphere, knew that air heated beyond endurance surrounded them in a fiery grip and made their tiny craft into a flaming, falling star. Pressed into his seat by the acceleration, Kinsman let the automatic controls bring them through reentry, through the heat and buffeting turbulence, down to an altitude where their finned craft could fly like a rocket-plane.

He took control and steered the craft back toward Patrick Air Force Base, back to the world of men, of weather, of cities, of hierarchies and official regulations. He did this alone, silently; he didn't need Jill's help or anyone else's. He flew the craft from inside his buttoned-tight pressure suit, frowning at the panel-displays through his helmet's faceplate.

Automatically, he checked with ground control and received permission to slide the heat-shield back. The viewpoint showed him a stretch of darkening clouds spreading from the sea across the beach and well inland. His earphones were alive with other men's voices now: wind conditions, altitude checks, speed esti-mates. He knew, but could not see, that two jet planes were trail-ing along behind him, cameras focused on the returning spacecraft. *To provide evidence if I crash.*

They dipped into the clouds and a wave of gray mist hurtled up and covered the viewport. Kinsman's eyes flicked to the radar screen slightly off to his right. The craft shuddered briefly, then they broke below the clouds and he could see the long, black gouge of the runway looming before him. He pulled back slightly on the controls, hands and feet working instinctively, flashed over some scrubby vegetation, and flared the craft onto the runway. The landing skids touched once, bounced them up momentarily, then touched again with a grinding shriek. They skidded for more than a mile before stopping.

He leaned back in the seat and felt his body oozing sweat.

"Good landing," Jill said.

"Thanks." He turned off all the craft's systems, hands moving automatically in response to long training. Then he slid his faceplate up, reached overhead and popped the hatch open.

"End of the line," he said tiredly. "Everybody out."

He clambered up through the hatch, feeling his own weight with a sullen resentment, then helped Linda and finally Jill out of the spacecraft. They hopped down onto the blacktop runway. Two vans, an ambulance, and two fire trucks were rolling toward them from their parking stations at the end of the runway, a half-mile ahead.

Kinsman slowly took off his helmet. The Florida heat and humidity annoyed him now. Jill walked a few paces away from him, toward the approaching trucks.

He stepped toward Linda. Her helmet was off, and she was carrying a bag full of film.

"I've been thinking," he said to her. "That business about having a lonely life. . . . You know, you're not the only one. And it doesn't have to be that way. I can get to New York whenever . . ."

"Now who's taking things seriously?" Her face looked calm again, cool, despite the glaring heat.

"But I mean . . ."

"Listen, Chet. We had our kicks. Now you can tell your friends about it, and I can tell mine. We'll both get a lot of mileage out of it. It'll help our careers."

"I never intended to . . . I didn't . . ."

But she was already turning away from him, walking toward the men who were running up to meet them from the trucks. One of them, a civilian, had a camera in his hands. He dropped to one knee and took a picture of Linda holding the film out and smiling broadly.

Kinsman stood there with his mouth open.

Jill came back to him. "Well? Did you get what you were after?"

"No," he said slowly. "I guess I didn't."

She started to put her hand out to him. "We never do, do we?"

TEST IN ORBIT

Kinsman snapped awake when the phone went off. Before it could complete its first ring he had the receiver off its cradle.

"Captain Kinsman?" The motel's night clerk.

"Yes," he whispered back, squinting at the luminous dial of his wristwatch: *three twenty-three.*

"I'm awfully sorry to disturb you, Captain, but Colonel Murdock called . . ."

"How the hell did he know I was here?"

"He said he's calling all the motels around the base. I didn't tell him you were here. He said when he found you he wanted you to report to him at once. Those were his words. Captain: at once."

Kinsman frowned in the darkness. "Okay. Thanks for playing dumb."

"Not at all, sir. Hope it isn't trouble."

"Yeah." Kinsman hung up. He sat for a half-minute on the edge of the bed. *Murdock making the rounds of the motels at three in the morning and the clerk hopes it's not trouble.* Very *funny.*

He stood up, stretched his wiry frame and glanced at the girl still sleeping quietly on the other side of the bed. With a wistful shake of his head, he padded out to the bathroom.

He flipped the light switch and turned on the coffee machine on the wall next to the doorway. *It's lousy but it's coffee.* As the machine started gurgling, he softly closed the door and rummaged through his travel kit for the electric razor. The face that met him in the mirror was lean and long-jawed, with jet black hair cut down to military length and soft gray eyes that were, at the moment, just the slightest bit bloodshot.

Within a few minutes he was shaved, showered, and back in Air Force blues. He left a scribbled note on motel stationery leaning against the dresser mirror, took a final long look at the girl, and went out to find his car.

He put down the top of his old convertible and gunned her out onto the coast road. As he raced through the pre-dawn darkness, wind whistling all around him, Kinsman could feel the excitement building up. A pair of cars zoomed past him, doing eighty, heading for the base. Kinsman held to the legal limit and caught them again at the main gate, lined up while the guard sergeant checked ID badges with extra care. Kinsman's turn came.

"What's the stew, Sergeant?"

The guard flashed his hand-light on the badge Kinsman held in his outstretched hand.

"Dunno, sir. We got the word to look sharp."

The light flashed full in Kinsman's face. *Painfully sharp,* he thought to himself.

The guard waved him on.

There was that special crackle in the air as Kinsman drove toward the Administration Building. The kind that comes only when a launch is imminent. As if in answer to his unspoken hunch, the floodlights on Complex 17 bloomed into life, etching the tall, silver rocket standing there, embraced by the dark spiderwork of the gantry tower.

Pad 17. Manned shot.

People were scurrying in and out of the Administration Building: sleepy-eyed, disheveled, but their feet were moving double time. Colonel Murdock's secretary was coming down the hallway as Kinsman signed in at the reception desk.

"What's up, Annie?"

"I just got here myself," she said. There were hair-clips still in her blonde curls. "The boss told me to flag you down the instant you arrived."

Even from completely across the colonel's spacious office, Kinsman could see that Murdock was a round little kettle of nerves. He was standing by the window behind his desk, watching the activity on Pad 17, clenching and unclenching his hands behind his back. His bald head was glistening with perspiration, despite the frigid air conditioning. Kinsman stood at the door with the secretary.

"Colonel?" she said softly.

Murdock spun around. "Kinsman. So here you are."

"What's going on? I thought the next manned shot wasn't until . . ."

The colonel waved a pudgy hand. "The next manned shot is as fast as we can damned well make it." He walked around the desk and eyed Kinsman. "You look a mess."

"Hell, it's four in the morning!"

"No excuses. Get over to the medical section for pre-flight checkout. They've been waiting for you."

"I'd still like to know . . ."

"Probably ought to test your blood for alcohol content," Murdock grumbled.

"I've been celebrating my transfer," Kinsman said. "I'm not supposed to be on active duty. Six more days and I'm a civilian spaceman. Get my picture in *Photo Day* and off to the moon. Remember?"

"Cut the clowning. General Hatch is flying in from Norton Field and he wants you."

"Hatch?"

"That's right. He wants the most experienced man available."

"Twenty guys on base and you have to make me available."

Murdock fumed. "Listen. This is a military operation. I may not insist on much discipline, but don't think you're a civilian glamor boy yet. You're still in the Air Force and there's a hell of a bind on. Hatch wants you. Understand?"

Kinsman shrugged. "If you saw what I had to leave behind me to report for duty here, you'd put me up for the Medal of Honor."

Murdock frowned in exasperation. The secretary tried unsuccessfully to suppress a smile.

"All right, joker. Get down to the medical section. On the double. Anne, you stick with him and bring him to the briefing room the instant he's finished. General Hatch will be here in twenty minutes; I don't want to keep him waiting any longer than I have to."

Kinsman stood at the doorway, not moving. "Will you please tell me just what this scramble is all about?"

"Ask the general," Murdock said, walking back toward his desk. He glanced out the window again, then turned back to Kinsman. "All I know is that Hatch wants the man with the most hours in orbit ready for a shot, immediately . . ."

"Manned shots are all volunteer missions," Kinsman pointed out.

"So?"

"I'm practically a civilian. There are nineteen other guys who . . ."

"Dammit Kinsman, if you . . ."

"Relax, Colonel. Relax. I won't let you down. Not when there's a chance to get a few hundred miles away from all the brass on Earth."

Murdock stood there glowering as Kinsman took the girl out to his car. As they sped off toward the medical section, she looked at him.

"You shouldn't bait him like that," she said. "He feels the pressure a lot more than you do."

"He's insecure," Kinsman said, grinning. "There're only twenty men in the Air Force qualified for orbital missions, and he's not one of them."

"And you are."

"Damned right, honey. It's the only thing in the world worth doing. You ought to try it."

She put a hand up to her wind-whipped hair. "Me? Flying in orbit? No gravity?"

"It's a clean world, Annie. Brand new every time. Just you and your own little cosmos. Your life is completely your own. Once you've done it, there's nothing left on Earth but to wait for the next shot."

"My God, you sound as though you really mean it."

"I'm serious," he insisted. "The Reds have female cosmonauts. We're going to be putting women in orbit, eventually. Get your name on the top of the list."

"And get locked in a capsule with you?"

His grin returned. "It's an intriguing possibility."

"Some other time, captain," she said. "Right now we have to get you through your pre-flight and off to meet the general."

General Lesmore D. ("Hatchet") Hatch sat in dour silence in the small briefing room. The oblong conference table was packed with colonels and a single civilian. *They all look so damned serious,* Kinsman thought as he took the only empty chair, directly across from the general.

"Captain Kinsman." It was a flat statement of fact.

"Good, em, morning, General."

Hatch turned to a moon-faced aide. "Borgeson, let's not waste time."

Kinsman only half-listened as the hurried introductions went around the table. He felt uncomfortable already, and it was only partly due to the stickiness of the crowded little room. Through the only window he could see the first glow of dawn.

"Now then," Borgeson said, introductions finished, "very briefly, your mission will involve orbiting and making rendezvous with an unidentified satellite."

"Unidentified?"

Borgeson nodded. "Whoever launched it has made no announcement whatsoever. Therefore, we must consider the satellite as potentially hostile. To begin at the beginning, we'll have Colonel McKeever of SPADATS give you the tracking data first."

As they went around the table, each colonel adding his bit of information, Kinsman began to build up the picture in his mind.

The satellite had been launched from the mid-Pacific, nine hours ago. Probably from a specially rigged submarine. It was now in a polar orbit, so that it covered every square mile on Earth in twelve hours. Since it went up, not a single radio transmission had been detected going to it or from it. And it was big, even heavier than the ten-ton V*oshkods* the Russians had been using for manned flights.

"A satellite of that size," said the colonel from the Special Weapons Center, "could easily contain a nuclear warhead of 100 megatons or more."

If the bomb were large enough, he explained, it could heat the atmosphere to the point where every combustible thing on the ground would ignite. Kinsman pictured trees, plants, grass, buildings, people, the sky itself, all bursting into flame.

"Half the United States could be destroyed at once with such a bomb," the colonel said.

"And in a little more than two hours," Borgeson added, "the satellite will pass over Chicago and travel right across the heartland of America."

Murdock paled. "You don't think they'd . . . set it off?"

"We don't know," General Hatch answered. "And we don't intend to sit here waiting until we find out."

"Why not just knock it down?" Kinsman asked. "We can hit it, can't we?"

Hatch frowned. "We could reach it with a missile, yes. But we've been ordered by the Pentagon to inspect the satellite and determine whether or not it's actually hostile."

"In two hours?"

"Perhaps I can explain," said the civilian. He had been introduced as a State Department man; Kinsman had already forgotten his name. He had a soft, sheltered look about him.

"You may know that the disarmament meeting in Geneva is discussing nuclear weapons in space. It seemed last week we were on the verge of an agreement to ban weapons in space, just as testing weapons in the atmosphere has already been banned. But three days ago the conference suddenly became deadlocked on some very minor issues. It's been very difficult to determine who is responsible for the deadlock and why. The Russians, the Chinese, the French, even some of the smaller nations, are apparently stalling for time . . . waiting for something to happen."

"And this satellite might be it," Kinsman said.

"The Department of State believes that this satellite is a test, to see if we can detect and counteract weapons placed in orbit."

"But they know we can shoot them down!" the general snapped.

"Yes, of course," the civilian answered softly. "But they also know we would not fire on a satellite that might be a peaceful research station. Not unless we were certain that it was actually a bomb in orbit. We must inspect this satellite to prove to the world that we can board any satellite and satisfy ourselves that it is not a threat to us. Otherwise we will be wide open to nuclear blackmail, in orbit."

The general shook his head. "If they've gone to the trouble of launching a multi-ton vehicle, then military logic dictates that they placed a bomb in it. By damn, that's what I'd do, in their place."

"Suppose it is a bomb," Kinsman asked, "and they explode it over Chicago?"

Borgeson smiled uneasily. "It could take out everything between New England and the Rockies."

Kinsman heard himself whistle in astonishment.

"No matter whether it's a bomb or not, the satellite is probably rigged with booby traps to prevent us from inspecting it," one of the other colonels pointed out.

Thanks a lot, Kinsman said to himself.

Hatch focused his gunmetal eyes on Kinsman. "Captain, I want to impress a few thoughts on you. First, the Air Force has been working for nearly twenty years to achieve the capability of placing a military man in orbit on an instant's notice. Your flight will be the first practical demonstration of all that we've battled to achieve over those years. You can see, then, the importance of this mission."

"Yessir."

"Second, this is strictly a voluntary mission. Because it is so important to us, I don't want you to try it unless you're absolutely certain . . ."

"I realize that, sir. I'm your man."

"I understand you're transferring out of the Air Force next week."

Kinsman nodded. "That's next week. This is now."

Hatch's well-seamed face unfolded into a smile. "Well said, captain. And good luck."

The general rose and everyone snapped to attention. As the

others filed out of the briefing room, Murdock drew Kinsman aside.

"You had your chance to beg off."

"And miss this? A chance to play cops and robbers in orbit?"

The colonel flushed angrily. "We're not in this for laughs. This is damned important. If it really is a bomb . . ."

"I'll be the first to know," Kinsman snapped. To himself he added, *I've listened to you long enough for one morning.*

Countdowns took minutes instead of days, with solid-fueled rockets. But there were just as many chances of a man or machine failing at a critical point and turning the intricate, delicately poised booster into a flaming pyre of twisted metal.

Kinsman sat tautly in the contoured couch, listening to them tick off the seconds. He hated countdowns. He hated being helpless, completely dependent on a hundred faceless voices that flickered through his earphones, waiting childlike in a mechanical womb, not alive, waiting, doubled up and crowded by the unfeeling, impersonal machinery that automatically gave him warmth and breath and life. He could feel the tiny vibrations along his spine that told him the ship was awakening. Green lights started to blossom across the control panel, a few inches in front of his faceplate, telling him that everything was ready. Still the voices droned through his earphones in carefully measured cadence: *three . . . two . . . one . . .*

And she bellowed into life. Acceleration pressure flattened Kinsman into the couch. Vibration rattled his eyes in their sockets. Time became meaningless. The surging, engulfing, overpowering noise of the mighty rocket engines made his head ring, even after they burned out into silence.

Within minutes he was in orbit, the long slender rocket stages falling away behind, together with all sensations of weight. Kinsman was alone now in the squat, delta-shaped capsule: weightless, free of Earth.

Still he was the helpless, unstirring one. Computers sent guidance instructions from the ground to the capsule's controls. Tiny vectoring rockets placed around the capsule's black hull squirted on and off, microscopic puffs of thrust that maneuvered the capsule into the precise orbit needed for catching the unidentified satellite.

Completely around the world Kinsman spun, southward over the Pacific, past the gleaming whiteness of Antarctica, and then north again over the wrinkled, cloud-spattered land mass of Asia. As he crossed the night-shrouded Arctic, nearly two hours after being launched, the voices from his base began crackling in his earphones again. He answered them as automatically as the machines did, reading off the numbers on the control panel, proving to them that he was alive and functioning properly.

Then Murdock's voice cut in: "There's been another launch, fifteen minutes ago. From somewhere near Mongolia as near as we can determine it. It's a high-energy boost; looks as though you're going to have company."

Kinsman acknowledged the information, but still sat unmoving.

Then he saw it looming ahead of him, seemingly hurtling toward him.

He came to life. To meet and board the satellite he had to match its orbit and speed, exactly. He was approaching it too fast. No computer on Earth could handle this part of the job. Radar and stabilizing gyros helped, but it was his own eyes and the fingers that manipulated the retrorocket controls that finally eased the capsule into a rendezvous orbit.

Finally, the big satellite seemed to be stopped in space, dead ahead of his capsule, a huge inert hulk of metal, dazzlingly brilliant where the sun lit its curving side, totally invisible where it was in shadow. It looked ridiculously like a crescent moon made of flush-welded aluminum. A smaller crescent puzzled Kinsman until he realized it was a dead rocket-nozzle hanging from the satellite's tailcan.

"I'm parked alongside her, about fifty feet off," he reported into his helmet microphone. "She looks like the complete upper stage of a *Saturn*-class booster. Can't see any markings from this angle. I'll have to go outside."

"You'd better make it fast," Murdock's voice answered. "That second ship is closing in fast."

"What's the E.T.A.?"

A pause while voices mumbled in the background. "About fifteen minutes . . . maybe less."

"Great."

"You can abort if you want to."

Same to you, pal, Kinsman said to himself. Aloud, he replied, "I'm going to take a close look at her. Maybe get inside, if I can. Call you back in fifteen minutes."

Murdock didn't argue. Kinsman smiled grimly at the realization that the colonel had not reminded him that the satellite might be booby-trapped. Old Mother Murdock hardly forgot such items. He simply had decided not to make the choice of aborting the mission too attractive.

Gimmicked or not, the satellite was too near and too enticing to turn back now. Kinsman quickly checked out his pressure suit, pumped the air out of his cabin and into storage tanks, and then opened the airlock hatch over his head.

Out of the womb and into the world.

He climbed out and teetered on the lip of the airlock, balancing weightlessly. *The real world.* No matter how many times he saw it, it always caught his breath. The vast sweep of the multi-hued Earth, hanging at an impossible angle, decked with dazzling clouds, immense and beautiful beyond imagining. The unending black of space, sprinkled with countless, gleaming jewels of stars that shone steadily, solemnly, the unblinking eyes of infinity.

I'll bet this is all there is to heaven, he said to himself. *You don't need anything more than this.*

Then he turned, with the careful deliberate motions of a deep-sea diver, and looked at the fat crescent of the nearby satellite. Only ten minutes now. Even less.

He pushed off from his capsule and sailed effortlessly, arms outstretched. Behind him trailed the umbilical cord that carried his air and electrical power for heating/cooling. As he approached the satellite, the sun rose over the humped curve of its hull and nearly blinded him, despite the automatic darkening of the photo-chromic plastic in his faceplate visor. He kicked downward and ducked behind the satellite's protective shadow again.

Still half-blind from the sudden glare, he bumped into the satellite's massive body and rebounded gently. With an effort, he twisted about, pushed back to the satellite, and planted his magnetized boots on the metal hull.

I claim this island for Isabella of Spain, he muttered foolishly. *Now where the hell's the hatch?*

The hatch was over on the sunlit side, he found, at last. It wasn't too hard to figure out how to operate it, even though there were absolutely no printed words in any language anywhere on the hull. Kinsman knelt down and turned the locking mechanism. He felt it click open.

For a moment he hesitated. *It might be booby-trapped,* he heard the colonel warn.

The hell with it.

Kinsman yanked the hatch open. No explosion, no sound at all. A dim light came from within the satellite. Carefully he slid down inside. A trio of faint emergency lights were on; there were other lights in place, he saw, but not operating.

"Saving the juice," he muttered to himself.

It took a moment for his eyes to accustom themselves to the dimness. Then he began to appreciate what he saw. The satellite was packed with equipment. He couldn't understand what most of it was, but it was clearly not a bomb. Surveillance equipment, he guessed. Cameras, recording instruments, small telescopes. Three contoured couches lay side by side beneath the hatch. He was standing on one of them. Up forward of the couches was a gallery of compact cabinets.

"All very cozy."

He stepped off the couch and onto the main deck, crouching to avoid bumping his head on the instrument rack, above. He opened a few of the cabinets. *Murdock'll probably want a few samples to play with.* He found a set of small hand-wrenches, unfastened them from their setting.

With the wrenches in one hand, Kinsman tried the center couch. By lying all the way back on it, he could see through the satellite's only observation port. He scanned the instrument panel: Cyrillic letters and Arabic numerals on all the gauges.

Made in CCR. Kinsman put the wrenches down on the armrest of the couch. They stuck, magnetically. Then he reached for the miniature camera at his belt. He took four snaps of the instrument panel.

Something flashed in the corner of his eye.

He tucked the camera back in its belt holster and looked at the observation port. Nothing but the stars: beautiful, impersonal. Then another flash, and this time his eye caught and held the slim crescent of another ship gliding toward him. Most of the ship was in impenetrable shadow; he would have never found it without the telltale burst of the retrorockets.

She's damned close! Kinsman grabbed his tiny horde of stolen wrenches and got up from the couch. In his haste, he stumbled over his trailing umbilical cord and nearly went sprawling. A weightless fall might not hurt you, but it could keep you bouncing around for precious minutes before you regained your equilibrium.

Kinsman hoisted himself out of the satellite's hatch just as the second ship make its final rendezvous maneuver. A final flare of its retrorockets, and the ship seemed to come to a stop alongside the satellite.

Kinsman ducked across the satellite's hull and crouched in the shadows of the dark side. Squatting in utter blackness, safely invisible, he watched the second ship.

She was considerably smaller than the satellite, but built along the same general lines. Abruptly, a hatch popped open. A strange-looking figure emerged and hovered, dreamlike, for a long moment.

The figure looked like a tapered cannister, with flexible arms and legs and a plastic bubble over the head. Kinsman could see no umbilical cord. There were bulging packs of equipment attached all around the cannister.

Selfcontained capsule, Kinsman said to himself. *Very neat.*

A wispy plume of gas jetted from the cannister, and the cosmonaut sailed purposefully over to the satellite's hatch.

Got his own reaction motor, too. Kinsman was impressed.

Unconsciously, he hunched down deeper in the shadows as the figure approached. Only one of them; no one else appeared from the second ship. The newcomer touched down easily beside the still-open hatch of the satellite. For several minutes he did not move. Then he edged away from the satellite slightly and, hovering, turned toward Kinsman's capsule, still hanging only a few hundred feet away.

Kinsman felt himself start to sweat, even in the cold darkness.

The cosmonaut jetted away from the satellite, straight toward the American capsule.

Damn! Kinsman snapped at himself. *First rule of warfare, you stupid slob: keep your line of retreat open!*

He leaped off the satellite and started floating back toward his own capsule. It was nightmarish, drifting through space with agonizing slowness while the weird-looking cosmonaut sped on ahead. The cosmonaut spotted Kinsman as soon as he cleared the shadow of the satellite and emerged into the sunlight.

For a moment they simply stared at each other, separated by a hundred feet of nothingness.

"Get away from that capsule!" Kinsman shouted, even though he knew that the intruder could not possibly hear him.

As if to prove the point, the cosmonaut put a hand on the lip of the capsule's hatch and peered inside. Kinsman flailed his arms and legs, trying to raise some speed, but still he moved with hellish slowness. Then he remembered the wrenches he was carrying.

Almost without thinking, he tossed the whole handful at the cosmonaut. The effort spun him wildly off-balance. The Earth slid across his field of vision, then the stars swam by dizzingly. He caught a glimpse of the cosmonaut as the wrenches reached the capsule—most of them missed and bounced noiselessly off the capsule. But one banged into the intruder's helmet hard enough to jar him, then rebounded crazily out of sight.

Kinsman lost sight of the entire capsule as he spun around. Grimly, he fought to straighten himself, using his arms and legs as counterweights. Finally, the stars stopped whirling. He turned and found the capsule again, but it was upside-down. Very carefully, Kinsman turned himself to the same orientation as the cosmonaut.

The intruder still had his hand on the capsule hatch, and his free hand was rubbing along the spot where the wrench had hit. He looked ludicrously like a little boy rubbing a bump on his head.

"That means get off, stranger," Kinsman muttered. "No trespassing. U.S. property. Beware of the eagle. Next time I'll crack your helmet in half."

The newcomer turned slightly and reached for one of the equipment packs on the cannister-suit. A weird-looking tool appeared in his hand. Kinsman drifted helplessly and watched the cosmonaut take up a section of the umbilical line. Then he applied the hand tool to it. Sparks flared.

Electrical torch! He's trying to cut the line! He'll kill me!

Frantically, Kinsman began clambering along the umbilical line, hand-over-hand. All he could see, all he could think of, was that flashing torch eating into his lifeline.

Almost without thinking, he grabbed the line in both hands and snapped it, viciously. Again he tumbled wildly, but he saw the wave created by his snap race down the line. The intruder found the section of line he was holding suddenly bounce violently out of his hand. The torch spun away from him and winked off.

Both men moved at once.

The cosmonaut jetted away from the capsule, looking for the torch. Kinsman hurled himself directly toward the hatch. He planted his magnetized boots on the capsule's hull and grasped the open hatch in both hands.

Duck inside, slam shut, and get the hell out of here.

But he did not move. Instead, he watched the cosmonaut, a weird sun-etched outline figure now, mostly in shadow, drifting quietly some fifty feet away, sizing up the situation.

That glorified tin can tried to kill me.

Kinsman coiled like a cat on the edge of the hatch and then sprang at his enemy. The cosmonaut reached for the jet controls at his belt but Kinsman slammed into him and they both went hurtling through space, tumbling and clawing at each other. It was an unearthly struggle, human fury in the infinite calm of star-studded blackness. No sound, except your own harsh breath and the bone-carried shock of colliding arms and legs.

They wheeled out of the capsule's shadow and into the painful glare of the sun. In a cold rage, Kinsman grabbed the air hose that connected the cosmonaut's oxygen tank and helmet. He hesitated a moment and glanced into the bulbous plastic helmet. All he could see was the back of the cosmonaut's head, covered with a dark, skin-tight flying hood. With a vicious yank, he ripped out the airhose. The cosmonaut jerked twice, spasmodically, then went inert.

With a conscious effort, Kinsman unclenched his teeth. His jaws ached. He was trembling, and covered with a cold sweat. He released his death-grip on the enemy. The two human forms drifted slightly apart. The dead cosmonaut turned, gently, as Kinsman floated beside him. The sun glinted brightly on the metal cannister and shone full onto the enemy's lifeless, terror-stricken face.

Kinsman looked into that face for an eternally long moment, and felt the life drain out of him. He dragged himself back to the capsule, sealed the hatch and cracked open the air tanks with automatic, unthinking motions. He flicked on the radio and ignored the flood of interrogating voices that streamed in from the ground.

"Bring me in. Program the autopilot to bring me in. Just bring me in."

It was six days before Kinsman saw Colonel Murdock again. He sat tensely before the wide mahogany desk while Murdock beamed at him, almost as brightly as the sun outside.

"You look thinner in civvies," the colonel said.

"I've lost a little weight."

Murdock made a meaningless gesture. "I'm sorry I haven't had a chance to see you sooner. What with the Security and State Department people holding you for debriefings, and now your mustering-out . . . I haven't had a chance to, eh, congratulate you on your mission. It was a fine piece of work."

Kinsman said nothing.

"General Hatch was very pleased. You'd be up for a decoration, but . . . well, you know, this has to be quiet."

"I know."

"But you're a hero, son. A real honest-to-God hero."

"Stow it."

Murdock suppressed a frown. "And the State Department man tells me the Reds haven't even made a peep about it. They're keeping the whole thing hushed up. The disarmament meeting is going ahead again, and we might get a complete agreement on banning bombs in orbit. Guess we showed them they can't put anything over on us. We called their bluff, all right!"

"I committed a murder."

"Now listen, son . . . I know how you feel. But it had to be done."

"No, it didn't," Kinsman insisted quietly. "I could've gotten back inside the capsule and de-orbited."

"You killed an enemy soldier. You protected your nation's frontier. Sure, you feel like hell now, but you'll get over it."

"You didn't see the face I saw inside that helmet."

Murdock shuffled some papers on his desk. "Well . . . okay, it was rough. But it's over. Now you're going to Florida and be a civilian astronaut and get to the moon. That's what you've wanted all along."

"I don't know . . . I've got to take some time and think everything over."

"What?" Murdock stared at him. "What're you talking about?"

"Read the debriefing report," Kinsman said tiredly.

"It hasn't come down to my level and it probably won't. Too sensitive. But I don't understand what's got you spoofed. You killed an enemy soldier. You ought to be proud . . ."

"Enemy," Kinsman echoed bleakly. "She couldn't have been more than twenty years old."

Murdock's face went slack. "She?"

Kinsman nodded. "Your honest-to-God hero murdered a terrified girl. That's something to be proud of, isn't it?"

FIFTEEN MILES

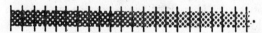

SEN. ANDERSON: Does that mean that man's mobility on the moon will be severely limited?

MR. WEBB: Yes, sir; it is going to be severely limited, Mr. Chairman. The moon is a rather hostile place . . .

U.S. Senate Hearings on National
Space Goals, 23 August 1965

"Any word from him yet?"

"Huh? No, nothing."

Kinsman swore to himself as he stood on the open platform of the little lunar rocket-jumper.

"Say, where are you now?" The astronomer's voice sounded gritty with static in Kinsman's helmet earphones.

"Up on the rim. He must've gone inside the damned crater."

"The rim? How'd you get . . ."

"Found a flat spot for the jumper. Don't think I walked this far, do you? I'm not as nutty as the priest."

"But you're supposed to stay down here on the plain! The crater's off limits."

"Tell it to our holy friar. He's the one who marched up here. I'm just following the seismic rigs he's been planting every three-four miles."

He could sense Bok shaking his head. "Kinsman, if there're twenty officially approved ways to do a job, I swear you'll pick the twenty-second."

"If the first twenty-one are lousy."

"You're not going inside the crater, are you? It's too risky."

Kinsman almost laughed. "You think sitting in that aluminum casket of ours is *safe?*"

The earphones went silent. With a scowl, Kinsman wished for the tenth time in an hour that he could scratch his twelve-day beard. *Get zipped into the suit and the itches start.* He didn't need a mirror to know that his face was haggard, sleepless, and his black beard was mean-looking.

He stepped down from the jumper—a rocket motor with a railed platform and some equipment on it, nothing more—and planted his boots on the solid rock of the ringwall's crest. With a twist of his shoulders to settle the weight of the pressure-suit's bulky back-pack, he shambled over to the packet of seismic instruments and fluorescent marker that the priest had left there.

"He came right up to the top, and now he's off on the yellow brick road, playing moon explorer. Stupid bastard."

Reluctantly, he looked into the crater Alphonsus. The brutally short horizon cut across its middle, but the central peak stuck its worn head up among the solemn stars. Beyond it was nothing but dizzying blackness, an abrupt end to the solid world and the beginning of infinity.

Damn the priest! God's gift to geology . . . and I've got to play guardian angel for him.

"Any sign of him?"

Kinsman turned back and looked outward from the crater. He could see the lighted radio mast and squat return rocket, far below on the plain. He even convinced himself that he saw the mound of rubble marking their buried base shelter, where Bok lay curled safely in his bunk. It was two days before sunrise, but the Earth-light lit the plain well enough.

"Sure," Kinsman answered. "He left me a big map with an X to mark the treasure."

"Don't get sore at me!"

"Why not? You're sitting inside. I've got to find our fearless geologist."

"Regulations say one man's got to be in the base at all times."

But not the same one man, Kinsman flashed silently.

"Anyway," Bok went on, "he's got a few hours' oxygen left. Let him putter around inside the crater for a while. He'll come back."

"Not before his air runs out. Besides, he's officially missing. Missed two check-in calls. I'm supposed to scout his last known position. Another of those sweet regs."

Silence again. Bok didn't like being alone in the base, Kinsman knew.

"Why don't you come on back," the astronomer's voice returned, "until he calls in. Then you can get him with the jumper. You'll be running out of air yourself before you can find him inside the crater."

"I'm supposed to try."

"But why? You sure don't think much of him. You've been tripping all over yourself trying to stay clear of him when he's inside the base."

Kinsman suddenly shuddered. *So it shows! If you're not careful you'll tip them both off.*

Aloud he said, "I'm going to look around. Give me an hour. Better call Earthside and tell them what's going on. Stay in the shelter until I come back." *Or until the relief crew shows up.*

"You're wasting your time. And taking an unnecessary chance."

"Wish me luck," Kinsman answered.

"Good luck. I'll sit tight here."

Despite himself, Kinsman grinned. Shutting off the radio, he said to himself, "I know damned well you'll sit tight. Two scientific adventurers. One goes over the hill and the other stays in his bunk two weeks straight."

He gazed out at the bleak landscape, surrounded by starry emptiness. Something caught at his memory:

"They can't scare me with their empty spaces," he muttered. There was more to the verse but he couldn't recall it.

"Can't scare me," he repeated softly, shuffling to the inner rim. He walked very carefully and tried, from inside the cumbersome helmet, to see exactly where he was placing his feet.

The barren slopes fell away in gently terraced steps until, more than half a mile below, they melted into the crater floor. *Looks easy . . . too easy*. With a shrug that was weighted down by the pressure-suit, Kinsman started to descend into the crater.

He picked his way across the gravelly terraces and crawled feet first down the breaks between them. The bare rocks were slippery and sometimes sharp. Kinsman went slowly, step by step, trying to make certain he didn't puncture the aluminized fabric of his suit.

His world was cut off now and circled by the dark rocks. The only sounds he knew were the creakings of the suit's joints, the electrical hum of its motor, the faint whir of the helmet's air blower, and his own heavy breathing. Alone, all alone. A solitary microcosm. One living creature in the one universe.

They cannot scare me with their empty spaces
Between stars—on stars where no human race is.

There was still more to it: the tag line that he couldn't remember.

Finally he had to stop. The suit was heating up too much from his exertion. He took a marker-beacon from the back-pack and planted it on the broken ground. The moon's soil, churned by meteors and whipped into a frozen froth, had an unfinished look about it, as though somebody had been black-topping the place but stopped before he could apply the final smoothing touches.

From a pouch on his belt Kinsman took a small spool of wire. Plugging one end into the radio outlet on his helmet, he held the spool at arm's length and released the catch. He couldn't see it in the dim light, but he felt the spring fire the wire antenna a hundred yards or so upward and out into the crater.

"Father Lemoyne," he called as the antenna drifted in the moon's easy gravity. "Father Lemoyne, can you hear me? This is Kinsman."

No answer.

Okay. Down another flight.

After two more stops and nearly an hour of sweaty descent, Kinsman got his answer.

"Here . . . I'm here . . ."

"Where?" Kinsman snapped. "Do something. Make a light."

". . . can't . . ." The voice faded out.

Kinsman reeled in the antenna and fired it out again. "Where the hell are you?"

A cough, with pain behind it. "Shouldn't have done it. Disobeyed. And no water, nothing . . ."

Great! Kinsman frowned. *He's either hysterical or delirious. Or both.*

After firing the spool antenna again, Kinsman flicked on the lamp atop his helmet and looked at the radio direction-finder dial on his forearm. The priest had his suit radio open and the carrier beam was coming through even though he was not talking. The gauges alongside the radio-finder reminded Kinsman that he was about halfway down on his oxygen, and more than an hour had elapsed since he had spoken to Bok.

"I'm trying to zero in on you," Kinsman said. "Are you hurt? Can you . . ."

"Don't, don't, don't. I disobeyed and now I've got to pay for it. Don't trap yourself too . . ." The heavy, reproachful voice lapsed into a mumble that Kinsman couldn't understand.

Trapped. Kinsman could picture it. The priest was using a canister-suit: a one-man walking cabin, a big, plexidomed rigid can with flexible arms and legs sticking out of it. You could live in it for days at a time—but it was too clumsy for climbing. Which is why the crater was off limits.

He must've fallen and now he's stuck.

"The sin of pride," he heard the priest babbling. "God forgive us our pride. I wanted to find water; the greatest discovery a man can make on the moon. . . . Pride, nothing but pride. . . ."

Kinsman walked slowly, shifting his eyes from the direction-finder to the roiled, pocked ground underfoot. He jumped across an eight-foot drop between terraces. The finder's needle snapped to zero.

"Your radio still on?"

"No use . . . go back . . ."

The needle stayed fixed. *Either I busted it or I'm right on top of him.*

He turned full circle, scanning the rough ground as far as his light could reach. No sign of the canister. Kinsman stepped to the terrace-edge. Kneeling with deliberate care, so that his back-pack wouldn't unbalance and send him sprawling down the tumbled rocks, he peered over.

In a zigzag fissure a few yards below him was the priest, a giant, armored insect gleaming white in the glare of the lamp, feebly waving its one free arm.

"Can you get up?" Kinsman saw that all the weight of the cumbersome suit was on the pinned arm. *Banged up his back-pack, too.*

The priest was mumbling again. It sounded like Latin.

"Can you get up?" Kinsman repeated.

"Trying to find the secrets of natural creation . . . storming heaven with rockets. . . . We say we're seeking knowledge, but we're really after our own glory. . . ."

Kinsman frowned. He couldn't see the older man's face, behind the canister's heavily tinted window.

"I'll have to get the jumper down here."

The priest rambled on, coughing spasmodically. Kinsman started back across the terrace.

"Pride leads to death," he heard in his earphones. "You know that, Kinsman. It's pride that makes us murderers."

The shock boggled Kinsman's knees. He turned, trembling. "What . . . did you say?"

"It's hidden. The water is here, hidden . . . frozen in fissures. Strike the rock and bring forth water . . . like Moses. Not even God himself was going to hide this secret from me. . . ."

"What did you say," Kinsman whispered, completely cold inside, "about murder?"

"I know you, Kinsman . . . anger and pride. . . . Destroy not my soul with men of blood . . . whose right hands are . . . are . . ."

Kinsman ran away. He fought back toward the crater-rim, storming the terraces blindly, scrabbling up the inclines with four-yard-high jumps. Twice he had to turn up the air blower in his helmet to clear the sweaty fog from his faceplate. He didn't dare stop. He raced on, breath racking his lungs, heart pounding until he could hear nothing else.

But in his mind he still saw those savage few minutes in orbit, when he had been with the Air Force, when he became a killer. He had won a medal for that secret mission; a medal and a conscience that never slept.

Finally he reached the crest. Collapsing on the deck of the jumper, he forced himself to breathe normally again, forced himself to sound normal as he called Bok.

The astronomer said guardedly, "It sounds as though he's dying."

"I think his regenerator's shot. His air must be pretty foul by now."

"No sense going back for him, I guess."

Kinsman hesitated. "Maybe I can get the jumper down close to him." *He found out about me.*

"You'll never get him back in time. And you're not supposed to take the jumper near the crater, let alone inside of it. It's too dangerous."

"You want to just let him die?" *He's hysterical. If he babbles about me where Bok can hear it . . .*

"Listen," the astronomer said, his voice rising, "you can't leave me stuck here with both of you gone! I know the regulations, Kinsman. You're not allowed to risk yourself or the third man on the team in an effort to help a man in trouble."

"I know. I know." *But it wouldn't look right for me to start minding regulations now. Even Bok doesn't expect me to.*

"You don't have enough oxygen in your suit to get down there and back again," Bok insisted.

"I can tap some from the jumper's propellant tank."

"But that's crazy! You'll get yourself stranded!"

"Maybe." *It's an Air Force secret. No discharge: just transferred to the space agency. If they find out about it now, I'll be finished. Everybody'll know. No place to hide . . . newspapers, TV, everybody!*

"You're going to kill yourself over that priest. And you'll be killing me, too!"

"He's probably dead by now," Kinsman said. "I'll just put a

marker beacon there, so another crew can get him when the time comes. I won't be long."

"But the regulations . . ."

"They were written Earthside. The brass never planned on something like this. I've got to go back, just to make sure."

He flew the jumper back down the crater's inner slope, leaning over the platform railing to see his marker-beacons as well as listening to their tinny radio beeping. In a few minutes, he was easing the spraddle-legged platform down on the last terrace before the helpless priest.

"Father Lemoyne."

Kinsman stepped off the jumper and made it to the edge of the fissure in four lunar strides. The white shell was inert, the lone arm unmoving.

"Father Lemoyne!"

Kinsman held his breath and listened. Nothing . . . wait . . . the faintest, faintest breathing. More like gasping. Quick, shallow, desperate.

"You're dead," Kinsman heard himself mutter. "Give it up, you're finished. Even if I got you out of here, you'd be dead before I could get you back to the base."

The priest's faceplate was opaque to him; he only saw the reflected spot of his own helmet lamp. But his mind filled with the shocked face he once saw in another visor, a face that had just realized it was dead.

He looked away, out to the too-close horizon and the uncompromising stars beyond. Then he remembered the rest of it:

They cannot scare me with their empty spaces
Between stars—on stars where no human race is.
I have it in me so much nearer home
To scare myself with my own desert places.

Like an automaton, Kinsman turned back to the jumper. His mind was blank now. Without thought, without even feeling, he rigged a line from the jumper's tiny winch to the metal lugs in the canister-suit's chest. Then he took apart the platform railing and wedged three rejoined sections into the fissure above the fallen man, to form a hoisting angle. Looping the line over the projecting arm, he started the winch.

He climbed down into the fissure and set himself as solidly as he could on the bare, scoured-smooth rock. He grabbed the priest's armored shoulders, and guided the oversized canister up from the crevice, while the winch strained silently.

The railing arm gave way when the priest was only partway up, and Kinsman felt the full weight of the monstrous suit crush down on him. He sank to his knees, gritting his teeth to keep from crying out.

Then the winch took up the slack. Grunting, fumbling, pushing, he scrabbled up the rocky slope with his arms wrapped halfway round the big canister's middle. He let the winch drag them to the jumper's edge, then reached out and shut the motor.

With only a hard breath's pause, Kinsman snapped down the suit's supporting legs, so the priest could stay upright even though unconscious. Then he clambered onto the platform and took the oxygen line from the rocket tankage. Kneeling at the bulbous suit's shoulders, he plugged the line into its emergency air tank.

The older man coughed once. That was all.

Kinsman leaned back on his heels. His faceplate was fogging over again, or was it fatigue blurring his sight?

The regenerator was hopelessly smashed, he saw. *The old bird must've been breathing his own juices.* When the emergency tank registered full, he disconnected the oxygen line and plugged it into a special fitting below the regenerator.

"If you're dead, this is probably going to kill me, too," Kinsman said. He purged the entire suit, forcing the contaminating fumes out and replacing them with the oxygen that the jumper's rocket needed to get them back to the base.

He was close enough now to see through the canister's tinted visor. The priest's face was grizzled, eyes closed. Its usual smile was gone; the mouth hung open limply.

Kinsman hauled him up onto the railless platform and strapped him down on the deck. Then he went to the controls and inched the throttle forward just enough to give them the barest minimum of lift.

The jumper almost made it to the crest before its rocket died and bumped them gently on one of the terraces. There was a small emergency tank of oxygen that could have carried them a little farther, Kinsman knew. But he and the priest would need it for breathing.

"Wonder how many Jesuits have been carried home on their shields?" he asked himself as he unbolted the section of decking that the priest was lying on. By threading the winch line through the bolt holes, he made a sort of sled, which he carefully lowered to the ground. Then he took down the emergency oxygen tank and strapped it to the deck-section, too.

Kinsman wrapped the line around his fists and leaned against the burden. Even in the moon's light gravity, it was like trying to haul a truck.

"Down to less than one horsepower," he grunted, straining forward.

For once he was glad that the scoured rocks had been smooth clean by micrometeors. He would climb a few steps, wedge himself as firmly as he could, and drag the sled up to him. It took a painful half-hour to reach the ringwall crest.

He could see the base again, tiny and remote as a dream. "All downhill from here," he mumbled.

He thought he heard a groan.

"That's it," he said, pushing the sled over the crest, down the gentle outward slope. "That's it. Stay with it. Don't you die on me. Don't put me through this for nothing!"

"Kinsman!" Bok's voice. "Are you all right?"

The sled skidded against a yard-high rock. Scrambling after it, Kinsman answered, "I'm bringing him in. Just shut up and leave us alone. I think he's alive. Now stop wasting my breath."

Pull it free. Push to get it started downhill again. Strain to hold it back . . . don't let it get away from you. Haul it out of craterlets. Watch your step, don't fall.

"Too damned much uphill in this downhill."

Once he sprawled flat and knocked his helmet against the edge of the improvised sled. He must have blacked out for a moment. Weakly, he dragged himself up to the oxygen tank and refilled his suit's supply. Then he checked the priest's suit and topped off his tank.

"Can't do that again," he said to the silent priest. "Don't know if we'll make it. Maybe we can. If neither one of us has sprung a leak. Maybe . . ."

Time slid away from him. The past and future dissolved into an endless now, a forever of pain and struggle, with the heat of his toil welling up in Kinsman drenchingly.

"Why don't you say something?" Kinsman panted at the priest. "You can't die. Understand me? You can't die! I've got to explain it to you. . . . I didn't mean to kill her. I didn't even know she was a girl. You can't tell, can't even see a face until you're too close. She must've been just as scared as I was. She tried to kill me. I was inspecting their satellite . . . how'd I know their cosmonaut was a scared kid. I could've pushed her off, didn't have to kill her. But the first thing I knew I was ripping her air lines open. I didn't know she was a girl, not until it was too late. It doesn't make any difference, but I didn't know it, I didn't know . . ."

They reached the foot of the ringwall and Kinsman dropped to his knees. "Couple more miles now . . . straightaway . . . only a couple more . . . miles." His vision was blurred, and something in his head was buzzing angrily.

Staggering to his feet, he lifted the line over his shoulder and slogged ahead. He could just make out the lighted tip of the base's radio mast.

"Leave him, Chet," Bok's voice pleaded from somewhere. "You can't make it unless you leave him!"

"Shut . . . up."

One step after another. Don't think, don't count. Blank your mind. Be a mindless plow horse. Plod along, one step at a time. Steer for the radio mast. . . . Just a few . . . more miles.

"Don't die on me. Don't you . . . die on me. You're my ticket back. Don't die on me, priest . . . don't die . . ."

It all went dark. First in spots, then totally. Kinsman caught a glimpse of the barren landscape tilting weirdly, then the grave stars slid across his view, then darkness.

"I tried," he heard himself say in a far, far distant voice. "I tried."

For a moment or two he felt himself falling, dropping effortlessly into blackness. Then even that sensation died and he felt nothing at all.

A faint vibration buzzed at him. The darkness started to shift, turn gray at the edges. Kinsman opened his eyes and saw the low, curved ceiling of the underground base. The noise was the electrical machinery that lit and warmed and brought good air to the tight little shelter.

"You okay?" Bok leaned over him. His chubby face was frowning worriedly.

Kinsman weakly nodded.

"Father Lemoyne's going to pull through," Bok said, stepping out of the cramped space between the two bunks. The priest was awake but unmoving, his eyes staring blankly upward. His canister-suit had been removed and one arm was covered with a plastic cast.

Bok explained. "I've been getting instructions from the Earth-side medics. They're sending a team up; should be here in another thirty hours. He's in shock, and his arm's broken. Otherwise he seems pretty good . . . exhausted, but no permanent damage."

Kinsman pulled himself up to a sitting position on the bunk and leaned his back against the curving metal wall. His helmet and boots were off, but he was still wearing the rest of his pressure suit.

"You went out and got us," he realized.

Bok nodded. "You were only about a mile away. I could hear you on the radio. Then you stopped talking. I had to go out."

"You saved my life."

"And you saved the priest's."

Kinsman stopped a moment, remembering. "I did a lot of raving out there, didn't I?"

"Any of it intelligible?"

Bok wormed his shoulders uncomfortably. "Sort of. It's, uh . . . it's all on the automatic recorder, you know. All conversations. Nothing I can do about that."

That's it. Now everybody knows.

"You haven't heard the best of it, though," Bok said. He went to the shelf at the end of the priest's bunk and took a little plastic container. "Look at this."

Kinsman took the container. Inside was a tiny fragment of ice, half melted into water.

"It was stuck in the cleats of his boots. It's really water! Tests out okay, and I even snuck a taste of it. It's water all right."

"He found it after all," Kinsman said. "He'll get into the history books now." *And he'll have to watch his pride even more.*

Bok sat on the shelter's only chair. "Chet, about what you were saying out there . . ."

Kinsman expected tension, but instead he felt only numb. "I know. They'll hear the tapes Earthside."

"There've been rumors about an Air Force guy killing a cosmonaut during a military mission, but I never thought . . . I mean . . ."

"The priest figured it out," Kinsman said. "Or at least he guessed it."

"It must've been rough on you," Bok said.

"Not as rough as what happened to her."

"What'll they do about you?"

Kinsman shrugged. "I don't know. It might get out to the press. Probably I'll be grounded. Unstable. It could be nasty."

"I'm . . . sorry." Bok's voice trailed off helplessly.

"It doesn't matter."

Surprised, Kinsman realized that he meant it. He sat straight upright. "It doesn't matter anymore. They can do whatever they want to. I can handle it. Even if they ground me and throw me to the newsmen . . . I think I can take it. I did it, and it's over with, and I can take what I have to take."

Father Lemoyne's free arm moved slightly. "It's all right," he whispered hoarsely. "It's all right. I thought we were in hell, but it was only purgatory."

The priest turned his face toward Kinsman. His gaze moved from the astronaut's eyes to the plastic container, still in Kinsman's hands. "It's all right," he repeated, smiling. Then he closed his eyes and his face relaxed into sleep. But the smile remained, strangely gentle in that bearded, haggard face; ready to meet the world or eternity.

The origins of this story go back to one of
the finest essays ever written on a scientific
subject, "What Makes the Weather: the
Seven American Airs," by Rudolph Langweisch.
Many years after I first read it, I found
myself deeply involved in the aerospace industry,
in the role of trying to convince skeptical
bureaucrats that certain proposed research
programs could result in great gains in
knowledge and, ultimately, new and practical
devices. Often frustrated by the stand-
patedness of most bureaucrats, I pounded out a
full-length novel on the subject of weather
control. This excerpt, published by John
Campbell in Analog, deals with the culmination
of a massive weather control project, and with
the realization that some research can—and
must—affect the entire world.

THE WEATHERMAKERS

Ted Marrett gathered us around the mammoth viewscreen-map
that loomed over his desk in the THUNDER control center. The
map showed a full-fledged hurricane—Nora—howling up the
mid-Atlantic. Four more tropical disturbances, marked by red
danger symbols, were strung out along the fifteenth parallel from
the Antilles Islands to the Cape Verde's.

"There's the story," Ted told us, prowling impatiently along the
foot of the viewscreen. He moved his tall, powerful body with
the feline grace of a professional athlete. His stubborn red hair
and rough-hewn face made him look more like a football gladiator
than "the whiz-kid boss of Project THUNDER," as the news
magazines had called him.

Gesturing toward the map, Ted said, "Nora's no problem,
she'll stay out at sea. Won't even bother Bermuda much. But
these four Lows'll bug us."

Tuli Noyon, Ted's closest buddy and chief of the Air Chemistry Section, said in his calm Oriental way, "This is the day we have all been dreading. There are more disturbances than we can handle. One of them, possibly two, will get past us and form hurricanes."

Ted looked sharply at him, then turned to me. "How about it, Jerry? What's the logistics picture?"

"Tuli's right," I admitted. "The planes and crews have been working around the clock for the past few weeks and we just don't have enough . . ."

"Skip the flute music. How many of these Lows can we hit?"

I shrugged. "Two, I'd say. Maybe three if we really push it."

Barney—Priscilla Barneveldt—said, "The computer just finished an updated statistical analysis on the four disturbances. Their storm tracks all threaten the East Coast. The two closest ones have point-eight probabilities of reaching hurricane strength. The farther pair are only point-five."

"Fifty-fifty," Ted muttered, "for the last two. But they've got the longest time to develop. Chances'll be better for 'em by tomorrow."

Barney was slim and blond as a Dutch jonquil, and had a true Hollander's stubborn spirit. "It's those two closest disturbances that are the most dangerous," she insisted. "They each have an eighty percent chance of turning into hurricanes that will hit the East Coast."

"We can't stop them all," Tuli said. "What will we do, Ted?"

Project THUNDER: Threatening Hurricane Neutralization, Destruction and Recording. Maybe we were young and daring and slightly fanatical, as the newsmen had said of us. But it took more than knowledge and skill. THUNDER was Ted Marret's creation, the result of nearly four years of his single-minded determination. None of us would have dared it, even if there were a hundred more of us, without Ted to lead the way. He had brought the Project into being, practically with his own strong hands.

Yet it wasn't enough, not for Ted Marrett. He wasn't satisfied with an experimental program to modify potential hurricanes. Ted wanted to control the weather, fully. Nothing less. To him THUNDER was only a small shadow of what could be done toward controlling the weather. He had said as much to the press, and now the world expected us to prevent all hurricanes from striking the islands of the Caribbean and the North American mainland.

It was an impossible task.

"Where's the analysis?" Ted asked Barney. "I want to go over the numbers."

She looked around absently. "I must have left it on my desk. I'll go get it."

Ted's phone buzzed. He leaned across the desk and flicked the switch. "Dr. Weis calling from Washington," the operator said.

He made a sour face. "Okay, put him on." Sliding into his desk chair, Ted waved us away as Dr. Weis's tanned, well-creased face came on the phone viewscreen.

"I've just seen this morning's weather map," the President's Science Advisor said, with no preliminaries. "It looks to me as though you're in trouble."

"Got our hands full," Ted said.

I started back for my own cubicle. I could hear Dr. Weis's nasal voice, a little edgier than usual, saying, "The opposition has turned Project THUNDER into a political issue, with only six weeks to the election. If you hadn't made the newsmen think that you cou'd stop every hurricane . . ."

The rest was lost in the chatter and bustle of the control room. THUNDER's nerve center filled the entire second floor of our Miami bayfront building. It was a frenetic conglomeration of people, desks, calculating machines, plotting boards, map printers, cabinets, teletypes, phones, viewscreens and endless piles of paper. Over it all hung Ted's giant electronic plotting screen, showing our battlefield—all of North America and the North Atlantic Ocean. I made my way across the cluttered, windowless room and stepped into my glass-walled cubicle.

It was quiet inside, with the door closed. Phone screens lined the walls, and half my desk was covered with a private switchboard that put me in direct contact with a network of THUNDER support stations ranging from New Orleans to ships off the coast of Africa to the Atlantic Satellite Station, in synchronous orbit 23,000 miles above the mouth of the Amazon River.

I looked across the control center again, and saw Ted still talk-

ing earnestly into the phone. Dr. Weis called every day. THUN-
DER was important to him, and to the President. If we failed . . .
I didn't like to think of the consequences.

There was work to be done. I began alerting the Navy and Air
Force bases that were supporting THUNDER, trying to get
ready to hit those hurricane threats as hard and fast as we could.

While I worked, I watched Barney and Ted plowing through the
thick sheaf of computer printout sheets that contained the detailed
analysis of the storm threats. They made a good-looking couple,
and everyone assumed that she was Ted's girl. Including Ted himself. But he never bothered to ask Barney about it. Or me.

As soon as I could, I went down and joined them.

"Okay," he was saying, "if we leave those two farther-out Lows
alone, they'll develop into hurricanes overnight. We can knock 'em
out now without much sweat, but by tomorrow they'll be too
much for us."

"The same applies to the second disturbance," Barney said,
"only more so. It's already better developed than the two farther
Lows."

"We'll have to skip the second one. The first one—off the Lee-
wards—is too close to ignore. So we'll hit Number One, skip the
second, and hit Three and Four."

Barney took her glasses off. "That won't work, Ted," she said
firmly. "If we don't stop the second one today it certainly will
develop into . . ."

"A walloping big hurricane. I know." He shrugged. "But if we
throw enough planes at Number Two to smother it, we'll have to
leave Three and Four alone. Then they'll both develop and we'll
have two brutes on our hands."

"But this one . . ."

"There's a chance that if we knock out the closest Low, Number
Two'll change its track and head out to sea."

"That's a terribly slim chance. The numbers show . . ."

"Okay, it's a slim chance. But it's all we've got to work with.
Got any better ideas?"

"Isn't there anything we can do?" she asked. "If a hurricane
strikes the coast . . ."

"Weis is already looking through his mail for my resignation,"
Ted said. "Okay, we're in trouble. Best we can do is hit Number

One, skip Two, and wipe out Three and Four before they get strong enough to make waves."

Barney stared at the numbers on the computer sheets. "That means we're going to have a full-grown hurricane heading for Florida within twenty-four hours."

"Look," Ted snapped, "we can sit around here debating till they *all* turn into hurricanes. Let's scramble. Jerry, you heard the word. Get the planes up."

I headed back to my cubicle and sent out the orders. A few minutes later, Barney came by. Standing dejectedly in the doorway, she asked herself out loud:

"Why did he agree to take on this Project? He knows it's not the best way to handle hurricanes. It's too chancy, too expensive, we're working ourselves to death . . ."

"So are the air crews," I answered. "And the season's just starting to hit its peak."

"Then why did he have to make the newsmen think we could run up a perfect score the first year?"

"Because he's Ted Marrett. He not only thinks he can control the weather, he thinks he *owns* it."

"There's no room in him for failure," she said. "If this storm does hit, if the Project is canceled . . . what will it do to him?"

"What will it do to you?" I asked her.

She shook her head. "I don't know, Jerry. But I'm afraid we're going to find out in another day or two."

Tropical storms are built on seemingly slight differences of air temperature. A half-dozen degrees of difference over an area a hundred miles in diameter can power the giant heat engine of a hurricane. Ted's method of smothering tropical disturbances before they reached hurricane strength was to smooth out the temperature difference between the core of the disturbance and its outer fringes.

The nearest disturbance was developing quickly. It had already passed over the Leeward Islands and entered the Caribbean by the time our first planes reached it. The core of the disturbance was a column of warm, rising air, shooting upward from the sea's surface to the tropopause, some ten miles high. Swirling around this warm column was cooler air sliding down from the north into the low-pressure trough created by the warm column.

If the disturbance were left to itself, it would soak up moisture from the warm sea and condense it into raindrops. The heat released by the condensation would power winds of ever-mounting intensity. A cycle would be established: winds bring in moisture, the water vapor condenses into rain, the heat released builds the winds' power. Finally the core would switch over into a cold, clear column of downward-rushing air—the eye of a full-grown hurricane. A thousand megatons of energy would be loose, unstoppable, even by Project THUNDER.

Our job was to prevent that cycle from establishing itself. We had to warm up the air flowing into the disturbance and chill down its core until air temperatures throughout the disturbance were practically the same. A heat engine that has all its parts at the same temperature—or close to it—simply won't work.

We had been doing that job successfully since July. But now, in mid-September, with the hurricane season nearing its peak, there were more disturbances than we could handle simultaneously.

As I started giving out the orders for three missions at once, Tuli stuck his head into my cubicle.

"I'm off to see the dragon firsthand." He was grinning excitedly.

"Which one?"

"Number One dragon; it's in the Caribbean now."

"I know. Good luck. Kill it dead."

He nodded, a round-faced, brown-skinned St. George working against the most destructive menace man had ever faced.

As I parceled out orders over my phones, a battery of giga-joule lasers aboard the Atlantic Station began pumping their energy into the northern peripheries of the storms. The lasers were part of our project. Similar to the military type mounted in the missile-defense satellites, they had been put aboard the Atlantic Station at Ted's request, and with the personal backing of Dr. Weis and the White House. Only carefully selected Air Force personnel were allowed near them. The entire section of the satellite Station where they were installed was under armed guard, much to the discomfort of the civilians aboard.

Planes from a dozen airfields were circling the northern edges of the disturbances, sowing the air with rain-producing crystals.

"Got to seed for hours at a time," Ted once told me. "That's a mistake the early experimenters made—never stayed on the job long enough to force an effect on the weather."

And thanks to chemical wizards like Tuli, we had a wide assortment of seeding materials that could squeeze rain from almost any type of air mass. Producing the tonnage of crystals we needed had been a problem, but the Army's Edgewood Arsenal had stepped in with their mass-production facilities to help us.

I was watching the disturbance in the Caribbean. That was the closest threat, and the best-developed of all the four disturbances. Radar plots, mapped on Ted's giant viewscreen, showed rain clouds expanding and showering precipitation over an ever-widening area. As the water vapor in the seeded air condensed into raindrops, the air temperature rose slightly. The satellite-borne lasers were also helping to heat the air feeding into the disturbance.

It looked as though we were just making the disturbance bigger. But Ted and the other technical staff people had figured out the energy balances in the storm. They knew what they were doing . . . but I still found myself frowning worriedly.

Tuli was in an Air Force bomber, part of two squadrons of planes flying at staggered altitudes. From nearly sea level to fifty-thousand feet, they roared into the central column of warm air in precise formation and began dumping tons of liquid nitrogen into the rising tropical air.

The effect was spectacular. The TV screen alongside the big plotting screen showed what the planes saw: tremendous plumes of white sprang out behind each plane as the cryogenic liquid flash-froze the water vapor in the warm column. It looked as though some cosmic wind had suddenly spewed its frigid breath through the air. The nitrogen quickly evaporated, soaking up enormous amounts of heat. Most of the frozen vapor simply evaporated again, although radar plots showed that some condensation and actual rainfall occurred.

I made my way to Ted's desk to see the results of the core freezing.

"Looks good," he was saying into a phone.

I checked the teletype chugging nearby. It was printing a report from the observation planes that followed the bombers.

Ted stepped over to me. "Broke up the core okay. Now if she doesn't re-form, we can scratch Number One off the map."

It was early evening before we could tell for sure. The disturbance's source of energy, the differing temperatures of the air masses it contained, had been taken away from it. The plotting screen showed a large swatch of concentric, irregular isobars, like a lopsided bull's-eye, with a sullen red "L" marking its center, just north of Jamaica. The numbers of the screen showed a central pressure of 991 millibars, nowhere near a typical hurricane's. Wind speeds had peaked at fifty-two knots and were dying off now. Kingston and Guantanamo were reporting moderate-to-heavy rain, but at Santo Domingo, six hundred miles to the east, it was already clearing.

The disturbance was just another small tropical storm, and a rapidly weakening one at that. The two farther disturbances, halfway out across the ocean, had been completely wiped out. The planes were on their way home. The laser crews aboard the Atlantic Station were recharging their energy storage coils.

"Shall I see if the planes can reload and fly another mission tonight?" I asked Ted. "Maybe we can still hit the second disturbance."

He shook his head. "Won't do any good. Look at her," he said pointing toward the plotting map. "By the time the planes get to her, she'll be a full-grown hurricane. There's nothing we can do about it now."

So we didn't sleep that night. We stayed at the control center and watched the storm develop on the TV picture being beamed from the Atlantic Station. At night they had to use infrared cameras, of course, but we could still see—in the ghostly IR images—a broad spiral of clouds stretching across four hundred miles of open ocean.

Practically no one had left the control center, but the big room was deathly quiet. Even the chattering calculating machines and teletypes seemed to have stopped. The numbers on the plotting screen steadily worsened. Barometric pressure sank to 980, 965, 950 millibars. Wind velocity mounted to 50 knots, 60, 80. She was a full-grown hurricane by midnight.

Ted leaned across his desk and tapped out a name for the storm on the viewscreen's keyboard: *Omega*.

"One way or the other, she's the end of THUNDER," he murmured.

The letters glowed out at the top of the plotting screen. Across the vast room, one of the girls broke into sobs.

Through the early hours of the morning, Hurricane Omega grew steadily in size and strength. An immense band of clouds towered from the sea to some sixty thousand feet, pouring two inches of rain per hour over an area of nearly 300,000 square miles. The pressure at her core had plummeted to 942 millibars and central wind speeds were gusting at better than 100 knots, and still rising.

"It's almost as though she's alive," Tuli whispered as we watched the viewscreen intently. "She grows, she feeds, she moves."

By 2:00 A.M. Miami time, dawn was breaking over Hurricane Omega. Six trillion tons of air packing the energy of a hundred hydrogen bombs, a mammoth, mindless heat engine turned loose, aiming for civilization, for us.

Waves lashed by Omega's fury were spreading all across the Atlantic and would show up as dangerous surf on the beaches of four continents. Sea birds were sucked into the storm against their every exertion, to be drenched and battered to exhaustion; their only hope was to make it to the eye, where the air was calm and clear. A tramp steamer on the New York to Capetown run, five hundred miles from Omega's center, was calling frantically for help as mountainous waves overpowered the ship's puny pumps.

Omega churned onward, releasing every fifteen minutes as much energy as a ten-megaton bomb.

We watched, we listened, fascinated. The face of our enemy, and it made all of us—even Ted—feel completely helpless. At first Omega's eye, as seen from the satellite cameras, was vague and shifting, covered over by cirrus clouds. But finally it steadied and opened up, a strong column of downward-flowing air, the mighty central pillar of the hurricane, the pivotal anchor around which her furious winds wailed their primeval song of violence and terror.

Barney, Tuli and I sat around Ted's desk, watching his face sink deeper into a scowl as the storm worsened.

We didn't realize it was daylight once more until Dr. Weis phoned again. He looked haggard on the tiny desk-top viewscreen.

"I've been watching the storm all night," he said. "The President called me a few minutes ago and asked me what you were going to do about it."

Ted rubbed his eyes. "Can't knock her out, if that's what you mean. Too big now; be like trying to stop a forest fire with a blanket."

"Well, you've got to do something!" Weis snapped. "All our reputations hang on that storm. Do you understand? Yours, mine, even the President's! To say nothing of the future for weather control work in this country, if that means anything to you."

He might just as easily have asked Beethoven if he cared about music.

"Told you back in Washington when we started this game," Ted countered, "that THUNDER was definitely the wrong way to tackle hurricanes . . ."

"Yes, and then you announced to the press that no hurricanes would strike the United States! So now, instead of being an act of nature, hurricanes are a political issue."

Ted shook his head. "We've done all we can do."

"No, you haven't. You can try to steer the hurricane . . . change its path so that it won't strike the coast."

"Won't work."

"You haven't tried it!"

"We could throw everything we've got into it and maybe budge it a few degrees. It'll still wind up hitting the coast somewhere. All we'll be doing is fouling up its track so we won't know for sure where it'll hit."

"Well, we've got to do something. We can't just sit here and let it happen to us. Ted, I haven't tried to tell you how to run THUNDER, but now I'm giving an order. You've got to make an attempt to steer the storm away from the coast. If we fail, at least we'll go down fighting. Maybe we can salvage something from this mess."

"Waste of time," Ted muttered.

Dr. Weis's shoulders moved as though he were wringing his hands, off camera. "Try it anyway. It might work. We might just be lucky . . ."

"Okay," Ted said, shrugging. "You're the boss."

The screen went dark. Ted looked up at us. "You heard the man. We're going to play Pied Piper."

"But we can't do it," Tuli said. "It can't be done."

"Doesn't matter. Weis is trying to save face. You ought to understand that, buddy."

Barney looked up at the plotting screen. Omega was northeast of Puerto Rico and boring in toward Florida. Toward us.

"Why didn't you tell him the truth?" she asked Ted. "Why didn't you tell him that the only way to stop the storm is to control the weather across the whole East Coast."

"Been all through this half a million times," Ted grumbled, slouching back in his chair wearily. "Weis won't buy weather control. Hurricane-killing is what he wants."

"But we can't kill Omega. THUNDER has failed, Ted. You shouldn't have . . ."

"Shouldn't have what?" he snapped. "Shouldn't have taken THUNDER when Weis offered to let us try it? Think I didn't argue with him? Think I didn't fight it out, right in the White House? I know THUNDER's a shaky way to fight hurricanes. But it's all I could get. I had to take what they were willing to give us."

Barney shook her head. "And what has it got you? A disaster."

"Listen," he said, sitting up erect now and pressing his big hands on the desk. "I spelled it out to the President and to Weis. I told 'em both that chasing tropical disturbances and trying to smother hurricanes before they develop is doing things the hard way. Showed 'em how we could control the weather over the whole country. They wouldn't take the chance. Too risky. Think the President wants to get blamed for every cloudy day in Arizona, or every rainfall in California, or every chill in Chicago?"

He stood up and began pacing. "They wanted something spectacular but safe. So they settled on killing hurricanes—very spectacular. But only by making weather mods out at sea, where nobody would complain about 'em—that's safe, see? I told 'em it was the hard way to do the job. But that's what they wanted. And that's what I took. Because I'd rather do *something*, even if it's not the best something. I wanted to show 'em that we can kill hurricanes. If we had gone through this year okay, maybe they would've tried real weather control next year."

"Then why," she asked, very softly, "did you tell the newsmen that we would stop every hurricane threat? You knew we couldn't do it."

"Why? How should I know? Maybe because Weis was sitting there in front of the cameras looking so blasted sure of himself. Safe and serene. Maybe I was crazy enough to think we could really sneak through a whole hurricane season okay. Maybe I'm just crazy, period. I don't know."

"But what do we do now?" I asked.

He cocked an eye at the plotting-screen. "Try to steer Omega. Try saving Weis's precious face." Pointing to a symbol on the map several hundred miles north of the storm, he said, "This's a Navy sonar picket, isn't it? I'm going to buzz out there, see if I can get a firsthand look at this monster."

"That could be dangerous," Barney countered.

He shrugged.

"Ted, you haven't thought this out," I said. "You can't run the operation from the middle of the ocean."

"Picket's in a good spot to see the storm . . . at least, the edge of it. Maybe I can wangle a plane ride through it. Been fighting hurricanes all season without seeing one. Besides, the ship's part of the Navy's antisubmarine-warning-net; loaded with communications gear. Be in touch with you every minute, don't worry."

"But if the storm comes that way . . ."

"Let it come," he snapped. "It's going to finish us anyway." He turned and strode off, leaving us to watch him.

Barney turned to me. "Jerry, he thinks we blame him for everything. We've got to stop him."

"No one can stop him. You know that. Once he gets his mind set on something . . ."

"Then I'll go with him." She got up from her chair. I took her arm.

"No, Jerry," she said. "I can't let him go alone."

"Is it the danger you're afraid of, or the fact that he's leaving?"

"Jerry, in the mood he's in now . . . he's reckless . . ."

"All right," I said, trying to calm her. "All right. I'll go with him. I'll make sure he keeps his feet dry."

"I don't want either one of you in danger!"

"I know. I'll take care of him."

She looked at me with those misty gray-green eyes. "Jerry . . . you won't let him do anything foolish, will you?"

"You know me," I said. "I'm no hero."

"Yes, you are," she said. And I felt my insides do a handspring.

I left her there with Tuli and hurried out to the parking lot. The bright sunshine outdoors was a painful surprise. It was hot and muggy, even though the day was only an hour or so old.

Ted was getting into one of the Project staff cars when I caught up with him.

"A landlubber like you shouldn't be loose on the ocean by himself," I said.

He grinned. "Hop aboard, salt."

The day was sultry. The usual tempering sea breezes had died off. As we drove along the Miami bay-front, the air was oppressive, ominous. The sky was brazen, the water calm. The old-timers along the fishing docks were squinting out at the horizon to the south and nodding to each other. It was coming.

The color of the sea, the shape of the clouds, the sighting of a shark near the coast, the way the sea birds were perching—all these became omens.

It was coming.

We slept for most of the flight out to the sonar picket. The Navy jet landed smoothly in the calm sea and a helicopter from the picket brought us aboard. The ship was similar in style to the deep-sea mining dredges my father operated out in the Pacific. For antisubmarine work, though, the dredging equipment was replaced by a fantastic array of radar and communications antenna.

"Below decks are out of bounds to visitors, I'm afraid," the chunky lieutenant who welcomed us to his ship told us as we walked from the helicopter landing-pad toward the bridge. "This bucket's a floating sonar station. Everything below decks is classified except the galley, and the cook won't let even me in there."

He laughed at his own joke. He was a pleasant-faced type, about our own age, square-jawed, solidly built, the kind that stayed in the Navy for life.

We clambered up a ladder to the bridge.

"We're anchored here," the lieutenant said, "with special bottom gear and arresting cables. So the bridge isn't used for navigation as much as a communications center."

Looking around, we could see what he meant. The bridge's aft bulkhead was literally covered with viewscreens, maps, autoplotters and electronics controls.

"I think you'll be able to keep track of your hurricane without much trouble." The lieutenant nodded proudly toward the communications setup.

"If we can't," Ted said, "it won't be your fault."

The lieutenant introduced us to the chief communications technician, a scrappy little sailor who had just received his engineering degree and was putting in two Navy years. Within minutes, we were talking to Tuli back in THUNDER headquarters.

"Omega seems to have slowed down quite a bit," he told us, his face impassive. "She's almost stopped dead in her tracks, about halfway between your position and Puerto Rico."

"Gathering strength," Ted muttered.

They fed the information from Ted's big plotting screen in Miami to the picket's autoplotter, and soon we had a miniature version of the giant map to work with.

Ted studied the map, mumbling to himself. "If we could feed her some warm water . . . give her a short cut to the outbound leg of the Gulf Stream . . . then maybe she'd stay off the coast."

The lieutenant watched us from a jumpseat that folded out of the port bulkhead.

"Just wishful thinking," Ted muttered on. "Fastest way to move her is to set up a low-pressure cell to the north . . . make her swing more northerly, maybe bypass the coast."

He talked it over with Tuli for the better part of an hour, perching on a swivel chair set into the deck next to the chart table. Their conversation was punctuated with equations and aerodynamics jargon that no one else on the bridge could understand.

"Are they talking about weather?" the ship's executive officer asked the lieutenant. "I know as much about meteorology as most of us do, and I can't make out what they're saying."

I walked over to them. "Standard meteorology is only part of Ted's game. They're looking at the hurricane as an aerodynamics problem—turbulent-boundary-layer theory, I think they call it."

"Oh." The expression on their faces showed that they heard it, but didn't understand it, or even necessarily believe me.

The cook popped through the bridge's starboard hatch with a tray of sandwiches and coffee. Ted absently took a sandwich and mug, still locked in talk with Tuli Noyon.

Finally he said to the viewscreen, "Okay, then we deepen this trough off Long Island and try to make a real storm cell out of it."

Tuli nodded, but he was clearly unhappy.

"Get Barney to run it through the computer as fast as she can, but you'd better get the planes out right now. Don't wait for the computer run. Got to hit while she's still sitting around. Otherwise . . ." His voice trailed off.

"All right," Tuli said. "But we're striking blindly."

"I know. Got any better ideas?"

Tuli shrugged.

"Then let's scramble the planes." He turned to me. "Jerry, we've got a battle plan figured out. Tuli'll give you the details."

Now it was my turn. I spent the better part of the afternoon getting the right planes with the right payloads off to the exact places where their work had to be done. Through it all, I was calling myself an idiot for tracking out to this midocean exile. It took twice as long to process the orders as it would have back at headquarters.

"Don't bother saying it," Ted said when I finished. "So it was kinky coming out here. Okay. Just had to get away from that place before I went over the hill."

"But what good are you going to do here?" I asked.

He gripped the bridge's rail and looked out past the ship's prow to the softly billowing sea and clear horizon.

"We can run the show from here just as well . . . maybe a little tougher than back in Miami, but we can do it. If everything goes okay, we'll get brushed by the storm's edge. I'd like to see that . . . want to feel her, see what she can do. Better than sitting in that windowless cocoon back there."

"And if things don't go well?" I asked. "If the storm doesn't move the way you want it to?"

He turned away. "Probably she won't."

"Then we might miss the whole show."

"Maybe. Or she might march right down here and blow down our throats."

"Omega might . . . we might be caught in the middle of it?"

"Could be," he said easily. "Better get some sleep while you can. Going to be busy later on."

The exec showed us to a tiny stateroom with two bunks in it. Part of the picket's crew was on shore leave, and they had a spare compartment for us. I tried to sleep, but spent most of the late afternoon hours squirming nervously. Around dusk, Ted got up and went to the bridge. I followed him.

"See those clouds, off the southern horizon?" he was saying to the lieutenant. "That's her. Just her outer fringes."

I checked back with THUNDER headquarters. The planes had seeded the low-pressure trough off Long Island without incident. Weather stations along the coast, and automated observation equipment on satellites and planes were reporting a small storm cell developing.

Barney's face appeared on the viewscreen. She looked very worried. "Is Ted there?"

"Right here," he said, stepping into view.

"The computer run's just finished," she said, pushing a strand of hair from her face. "Omega's going to turn northward, but only temporarily. She'll head inland again late tomorrow. In about forty-eight hours she'll strike the coast somewhere between Cape Hatteras and Washington."

Ted let out a low whistle.

"But that's not all," she continued. "The storm track crosses right over the ship you're on. You're going to be in the center of it!"

"We'll have to get off here right away," I said.

"No rush," Ted said. "We can spend the night here. I want to see her develop firsthand."

Barney said, "Ted, don't be foolish. It's going to be dangerous."

He grinned at her. "Jealous? Don't worry, I just want to get a look at her, then I'll come flying back to you."

"You stubborn . . ." The blond curl popped back over her eyes again and she pushed it away angrily. "Ted, it's time you stopped acting like a little boy. You bet I'm jealous. I'm tired of competing against the whole twirling atmosphere! You've got responsibilities, and if you don't want to live up to them . . . well, you'd better, that's all!"

"Okay, okay. We'll be back tomorrow morning. Be safer traveling in daylight anyway. Omega's still moving slowly; we'll have plenty of time."

"Not if she starts moving faster. This computer run was just a first-order look at the problem. The storm could move faster than we think."

"We'll get to Miami okay, don't worry."

"No, why should I worry? You're only six hundred miles out at sea with a hurricane bearing down on you."

"Just an hour away. Get some sleep. We'll fly over in the morning."

The wind was picking up as I went back to my bunk, and the ship was starting to rock in the deepening sea. I had sail-boated through storms and slept in worse weather than this. It wasn't the conditions of the moment that bothered me. It was the knowledge of what was coming.

Ted stayed out on the bridge, watching the southern skies darken with the deathly fascination of a general observing the approach of a much stronger army. I dropped off to sleep, telling myself that I'd get Ted off this ship as soon as a plane could pick us up, even if I had to have the sailors wrap him in anchor chains.

By morning, it was raining hard and the ship was bucking severely in the heavy waves. It was an effort to push through the narrow passageway to the bridge, with the deck bobbing beneath my feet and the ship tossing hard enough to slam me into the bulkheads.

Up on the bridge they were wearing slickers and life-vests. The wind was already howling evilly. One of the sailors handed me a slicker and vest. As I turned to tug them on, I saw that the helicopter pad out on the stern was empty.

"Chopper took most of the crew out about an hour ago," the sailor hollered into my ear. "Went to meet the seaplane out west of here, where it ain't so rough. When it comes back we're all pulling out."

I nodded and thanked him.

"She's a beauty, isn't she?" Ted shouted at me. "Moving up a lot faster than we thought."

I grabbed a handhold between him and the lieutenant. To the south of us was a solid wall of black. Waves were breaking over the bows and the rain was a battering force against our faces.

"Will the helicopter be able to get back to us?" I asked the lieutenant.

"Certainly," he yelled back. "We've had worse blows than this . . . but I wouldn't want to hang around for another hour or so!"

The communications tech staggered across the bridge to us. "Chopper's on the way, sir. Ought to be here in ten-fifteen minutes."

The lieutenant nodded. "I'll have to go aft and see that the helicopter's dogged down properly when she lands. You be ready to hop on when the word goes out."

"We'll be ready," I said.

As the lieutenant left the bridge, I asked Ted, "Well, is this doing you any good? Frankly, I would've been just as happy in Miami . . ."

"She's a real brute," he shouted. "This is a lot different from watching a map."

"But why . . ."

"This is the enemy, Jerry. This is what we're trying to kill. Think how much better you're going to feel after we've learned how to stop hurricanes."

"If we live long enough to learn how!"

The helicopter struggled into view, leaning heavily into the raging wind. I watched, equally fascinated and terrified, as it worked its way to the landing pad, tried to come down, got blown backward by a terrific gust, fought toward the pad again, and finally touched down on the heaving deck. A team of sailors scrambled across the wet square to attach heavy lines to the landing gear, even before the rotor-blades started to slow down. A wave smashed across the ship's stern and one of the sailors went sprawling. Only then did I notice that each man had a stout lifeline around his middle. They finally got the 'copter secured.

I turned back to Ted. "Let's go before it's too late."

We started down the slippery ladder to the main deck. As we inched back toward the stern, a tremendous wave caught the picket amidships and slued her around broadside. The little ship shuddered violently and the deck seemed to drop out from under us. I sagged to my knees.

Ted pulled me up. "Come on, buddy, Omega's breathing down our necks."

Another wave smashed across us. I grabbed for a handhold and as my eyes cleared, saw the helicopter pitching crazily over to one side, the moorings on her landing gear flapping loosely in the wind.

"It's broken away!"

The deck heaved again and the 'copter careened over on its side, its rotors smashing against the pad. Another wave caught us. The ship bucked terribly. The helicopter slid backward along its side and then, lifted by a solid wall of foaming green, smashed through the gunwale and into the sea.

Groping senselessly on my hands and knees, soaking wet, battered like an overmatched prizefighter, I watched our only link to safety disappear into the raging sea.

From somewhere behind me I heard Ted shouting, "Four years! Four years of killing ourselves and it has to end like this!"

I clambered to my feet on the slippery deck of the Navy picket. The ship shuddered again and slued around. A wave hit the other side and washed across, putting us knee-deep in foaming water until the deck lurched upward again and cleared the waves temporarily.

"Omega's won," Ted roared in my ear, over the screaming wind. "The 'copter's washed overboard. We're trapped."

We stood there, hanging onto the handholds. The sea was impossible to describe—a furious tangle of waves, with no sense or pattern to them, their tops ripped off by the wind, spray mixing with the blinding rain.

The lieutenant groped by, edging along hand over hand on the lifeline that ran along the superstructure bulkhead.

"Are you two all right?"

"No broken bones, if that's what you mean."

"You'd better come back up to the bridge," he shouted. We were face to face, close enough to nearly touch noses, yet we could hardly hear him. "I've given orders to cast off the anchors and get up steam. We've got to try to ride out this blow under power. If we just sit here, we'll be swamped."

"Is there anything we can do?" I asked.

"Sure. Next time you tinker with a hurricane, make it when I'm on shore leave!"

We followed the lieutenant up to the bridge. I nearly fell off the rain-slicked ladder, but Ted grabbed me with one of his powerful paws.

The bridge was sloshing from the monstrous waves and spray that were drenching the decks. The communications panels seemed to be intact, though. We could see the map that Ted had set up on the autoplotter screen; it was still alight. Omega spread across the screen like an engulfing demon. The tiny pinpoint of light marking the ship's location was well inside the hurricane's swirl.

The lieutenant fought his way to the ship's intercom while Ted and I grabbed for handholds.

"All the horses you've got, Chief," I heard the lieutenant bellow into the intercom mike. "I'll get every available man on the pumps. Keep those engines going. If we lose power we're sunk!"

I realized he meant it literally.

The lieutenant crossed over toward us and hung on to the chart table.

"Is that map accurate?" he yelled at Ted.

The big redhead nodded. "Up to the minute. Why?"

"I'm trying to figure a course that'll take us out of this blow. We can't stand much more of this battering. She's taking on more water than the pumps can handle. Engine room's getting swamped."

"Head southwest then," Ted said at the top of his lungs. "Get out of her quickest that way."

"We can't! I've got to keep the sea on our bows or else we'll capsize!"

"What?"

"He's got to point her into the wind," I yelled. "Just about straight into the waves."

"Right!" the lieutenant agreed.

"But you'll be riding along with the storm. Never get out that way. She'll just carry us along all day!"

"How do you know which way the storm's going to go? She might change course."

"Not a chance." Ted pointed to the plotting screen. "She's heading northwesterly now and she'll stay on that course the rest of the day. Best bet is heading for the eye."

"Toward the center? We'd never make it!"

Ted shook his head. "Never get out of it if you keep heading straight into the wind. But if you can make five knots or so, we can spiral into the eye. Be calm there."

The lieutenant stared at the screen. "Are you sure? Do you know exactly where the storm's moving and how fast she's going to go?"

"We can check it out."

So we called THUNDER headquarters, transmitting up to the Atlantic Station satellite for relay to Miami. Barney was nearly frantic, but we got her off the line quickly. Tuli answered our questions and gave us the exact predictions for Omega's direction and speed.

Ted went inside with a soggy handful of notes to put the information into the ship's course computer. Barney pushed her way on to the viewscreen.

"Jerry . . . are you all right?"

"I've been better, but we'll get through it okay. The ship's in no real trouble," I lied.

"You're sure?"

"Certainly. Ted's working out a course with the skipper. We'll be back in Miami in a few hours."

"It looks . . . it looks awful out there."

Another mammoth wave broke across the bow and drenched the bridge with spray.

"It's not picnic weather," I admitted. "But we're not worried, so don't you go getting upset." *No, we're not worried,* I added silently. *We're scared white.*

Reluctantly, the lieutenant agreed to head for the storm's eye. It was either that or face a battering that would split the ship within a few hours. We told Tuli to send a plane to the eye, to try to pick us up.

Time lost all meaning. We just hung on, drenched to the skin, plunging through a wild, watery inferno, the wind shrieking evilly at us, the seas absolutely chaotic. No one remained on the bridge except the lieutenant, Ted and me. The rest of the ship's skeleton crew were below decks, working every pump on board as hard as they could be run. The ship's autopilot and computer-run guidance system kept us heading on the course Ted and Tuli had figured.

Passing into the hurricane's eye was like stepping through a door from bedlam to a peaceful garden. One minute we were being pounded by mountainous waves and merciless winds, the rain and spray making it hard to see even as far as the bow. Then the sun broke through and the wind abruptly died. We limped out into the open, with nothing but a deep swell to mar a tranquil sea.

Towering clouds rose all about us, but this patch of ocean was safe. A vertijet was circling high overhead, sent out by Tuli. The plane made a tight pass over us, then descended on to the helicopter landing pad on the ship's fantail. Her landing gear barely touched the deck and her tail stuck out over the smashed railing where the helicopter had broken through.

We had to duck under the plane's nose and enter from a hatch in her belly because the outer wing jets were still blazing, but the plane took us all aboard. As we huddled in the crammed passenger compartment, the plane hoisted straight up. The jetpods swiveled back for horizontal flight and the wings slid to supersonic sweep. We climbed steeply and headed up for the sky.

As I looked down at the fast-shrinking little picket, I realized the lieutenant was also craning his neck at the port for a last look.

"I'm sorry you had to lose your ship."

"So am I," he said. "But headquarters gave permission to abandon her. We couldn't have stayed in the eye indefinitely, and another hour or so in those seas would have finished us."

"You did a darned good job to get us through," Ted said.

The lieutenant smiled wearily. "We couldn't have done it without your information on the storm. Good thing your numbers were right."

Barney was waiting for us at the Navy airport with dry clothes, the latest charts and forecasts on Omega, and a large share of feminine emotion. I'll never forget the sight of her running toward us as we stepped down from the vertijet's main hatch. She threw her arms around Ted's neck, then around mine, and then around Ted again.

"You had me so worried, the two of you!"

Ted laughed. "We were kind of ruffled ourselves."

It took more than an hour to get out of the Navy's grasp. Debriefing officers, brass hats, press corps men, photographers—they all wanted to hear how Ted and the lieutenant described the situation. We finally got to change our clothes in an officer's wardroom and then battled our way out to the car Barney had come in, leaving the lieutenant and his crew to tell their story in detail.

"Dr. Weis has been on the phone all day," Barney said as the driver pulled out for the main highway leading to the Miami bayfront and THUNDER headquarters.

Ted frowned and spread the reports on Omega across his lap.

Sitting between the two of us, she pointed to the latest chart. "Here's the storm track . . . ninety percent reliability, plus-or-minus two percent."

Ted whistled. "Right smack into Washington and then up the coast. She's going to damage more than reputations."

"I told Dr. Weis you'd phone him as soon as you could."

"Okay," he said reluctantly. "Let's get it over with."

I punched out the Science Advisor's private number on the phone set into the car's forward seat. After a brief word with a secretary, Dr. Weis appeared on the viewscreen.

"You're safe," Dr. Weis said flatly. He looked wearier than we felt.

"Disappointed?" Ted quipped.

"The way this hurricane is coming at us, we could use a martyr or two."

"Steering didn't work. Only thing left to try is what we should've done in the first place . . ."

"Weather control? Absolutely not! Being hit with a hurricane is bad enough, but if you try tinkering with the weather all across the country, we'll have every farmer, every vacationist, every mayor and governor and traffic cop on our necks!"

Ted fumed. "What else are you going to do? Sit there and take it? Weather control's the only way to stop this beast . . ."

"Marrett, I'm almost ready to believe that you set up this storm purposely to force us into letting you try your pet idea!"

"If I could do that, I wouldn't be sitting here arguing with you."

"Possibly not. But you listen to me. Weather control is out. If we have to take a hurricane, that's what we'll do. We'll have to admit that THUNDER was too ambitious a project for the first time around. We'll have to back off a little. We'll try something like THUNDER again next year, but without all the publicity. You may have to lead a very quiet life for a year or two, but we'll at least be able to keep going . . ."

"Why back down when you can go ahead and stop this hurricane?" Ted insisted hotly. "We can push Omega out to sea, I know we can!"

"The way you steered her? That certainly boomeranged on you."

"We tried moving six-trillion tons of air with a feather duster! I'm talking about total control of the weather patterns across the whole continent. It'll work!"

"You can't guarantee that it will, and even if you did I wouldn't believe you. Marrett, I want you to go back to THUNDER headquarters and sit there quietly. You can operate on any new disturbances that show up. But you are to leave Omega strictly alone. Is that clear? If you try to touch that storm in any way, I'll see to it that you're finished. For good."

Dr. Weis snapped off the connection. The viewscreen went dark, almost as dark as the scowl on Ted's face. For the rest of the ride back to the Project headquarters he said nothing. He simply sat there, slouched over, pulled in on himself, his eyes blazing.

When the car stopped he looked up at me.

"What would you do if I have the word to push Omega off the coast?"

"But Dr. Weis said . . ."

"I don't care what he said, or what he does afterward. We can stop Omega."

Barney turned and looked at me.

"Ted . . . I can always go back to Hawaii and help my father make his twelfth million. But what about you? Weis can finish your career permanently. And what about Barney and the rest of the Project personnel?"

"It's my responsibility. Weis won't care about the rest of 'em. And I don't care what he does to me . . . I can't sit here like a dumb ape and let that hurricane have its own way. I've got a score to settle with that storm."

"Regardless of what it's going to cost you?"

He nodded gravely. "Regardless of everything. Are you with me?"

"I guess I'm as crazy as you are," I heard myself say. "Let's go do it."

We piled out of the car and strode up to the control center. As people started to cluster around us, Ted raised his arms for silence. Then he said loudly:

"Listen: Project THUNDER is over. We've got a job of weather-making to do. We're going to push that hurricane out to sea."

Then he started rattling off orders as though he had been rehearsing for this moment all his life.

As I started for my glass-walled office, Barney touched my sleeve. "Jerry, whatever happens later, thanks for helping him."

"We're accomplices," I said. "Before, after, and during the fact."

"Do you think you could ever look at a cloud in the sky again if you hadn't agreed to help him try this?"

Before I could think of an answer she turned and started toward the computer section.

We had roughly thirty-six hours before Omega would strike the Virginia coast and then head up Chesapeake Bay for Washington. Thirty-six hours to manipulate the existing weather pattern over the entire North American continent.

Within three hours Ted had us around his desk, a thick pack of notes clenched in his right hand. "Not as bad as it could've been," he told us, waving the notes toward the plotting screen. "This big High sitting near the Great Lakes—good cold, dry air that can make a shield over the East Coast if we can swing it into position. Tuli, that's your job."

Tuli nodded, bright-eyed with excitement.

"Barney, we'll need pinpoint forecasts for every part of the country, even if it takes every computer in the Weather Bureau to wring 'em out."

"Right, Ted."

"Jerry, communications're the key. Got to keep in touch with the whole blinking country. And we're going to need planes, rockets, even slingshots maybe. Get the ball rolling before Weis finds out what we're up to."

"What about the Canadians? You'll be affecting their weather, too."

"Get that liaison guy from the State Department and tell him to have the Canadian Weather Bureau check with us. Don't spill the beans to him, though."

"It's only a matter of time until Washington catches on," I said.

"Most of what we've got to do has to be done tonight. By the time they wake up tomorrow, we'll be on our way."

Omega's central wind speeds had climbed to 120 knots by evening, and were still increasing. As she trundled along toward the coast, her howling fury was nearly matched by the uproar of action at our control center. We didn't eat, we didn't sleep. We worked!

A half-dozen military satellites armed with anti-ICBM lasers started pumping streams of energy into areas pinpointed by Ted's orders. Their crews had been alerted weeks earlier to co-operate with requests from Project THUNDER, and Ted and others from our technical staff had briefed them before the hurricane season began. They didn't question our messages. Squadrons of planes flew out to dump chemicals and seeding materials just off Long Island, where we had created a weak storm cell in the vain attempt to steer Omega. Ted wanted that Low deepened, intensified—a low-pressure trough into which that High on the Great Lakes could slide.

"Intensifying the Low will let Omega come in faster, too," Tuli pointed out.

"Know it," Ted answered. "But the numbers're on our side, I think. Besides, the faster Omega moves, the less chance she gets to build up higher wind velocities."

By ten o'clock we had asked for and received a special analysis from the National Meteorological Center in Suitland, Maryland. It showed that we would have to deflect the jet stream slightly, since it controlled the upper-air flow patterns across the country. But how do you divert a river of air that's three hundred miles wide, four miles thick, and racing at better than three hundred miles per hour?

"It would take a hundred-megaton bomb," Barney said, "exploded about fifteen miles up, just over Salt Lake City."

"Forget it!" Ted snapped. "The UN would need a month just to get it on the agenda. Not to mention the sovereign citizens of Utah and points east."

"Then how do we do it?"

Ted grabbed the coffeepot standing on his desk and poured a mug of steaming, black liquid. "Jet stream's a sheer layer between the polar and mid-latitude tropopauses," he muttered, more to himself than any of us. "If you reinforce a polar air mass, it can nudge the stream southward . . ."

He took a cautious sip of the hot coffee. "Tuli, we're already moving a High southward from the Great Lakes. Take a couple of your best people—and Barney, give him top priority on the computers. See if we can drag down a bigger polar air mass from Canada and push the jet stream enough to help us."

"We don't have enough time or equipment to operate in Canada," I said. "And we'd need permission from Ottawa."

"What about reversing the procedure?" Tuli asked. "We could expand the desert High over Arizona and New Mexico until it pushes the jet stream from the south."

Ted raised his eyebrows. "Think you can do it?"

"I'll have to make some calculations."

"Okay, scramble."

In Boston, people who had gone to bed with a weather forecast of "warm, partly cloudy," awoke to a chilly, driving northeast rain. The Low we had intensified during the night had surprised the local forecasters. The Boston Weather Bureau office issued corrected predictions through the morning as the little rainstorm moved out, the Great Lakes High slid in and caused a flurry of frontal squalls, and finally the sun broke through. The cool, dry air of the High dropped local temperatures more than ten degrees within an hour. To the unknowing New Englanders it was just another day, slightly more bewildering than most.

Dr. Weis was on the phone at seven-thirty that morning.

"Marrett, have you lost your mind? What do you think you're doing? I told you . . ."

"Can't talk now, we're busy," Ted shot back.

"I'll have your hide for this!"

"Tomorrow you can have my hide. I'll bring it up myself. But first I'm going to find out if I'm right or wrong about this."

The President's Science Advisor turned purple. "I'm going to send out an order to all government installations to stop . . ."

"Better not. Then we'll never find out if it worked. Besides, most of the mods've already been made. Damage's done. Let's see what good it does."

Barney rushed up with a ream of computer printout sheets as Ted cut the phone connection.

"There's going to be a freeze in the central plains and northern Rockies," she said, pushing back her tousled hair. "There'll be some snow. We haven't fixed the exact amount yet."

A harvest-time freeze. Crops ruined, cities paralyzed by unexpected snow, weekend holidays ruined, and, in the mountains, deaths from exertion and exposure.

"Get the forecast out on the main Weather Bureau network," Ted ordered. "Warn 'em fast."

The plotting screen showed the battle clearly. Omega, with central windspeeds of 175 knots now, was still pushing toward Virginia. But her forward progress was slowing, ever so slightly, as the Great Lakes High moved southeastward past Pittsburgh.

By noontime, Ted was staring at the screen and muttering, "Won't be enough. Not unless the jet stream comes around a couple degrees."

It was raining in Washington now, and snow was beginning to fall in Winnipeg. I was trying to handle three phone calls at once when I heard an ear-splitting whoop from Ted. I looked at the plotting screen. There was a slight bend in the jet stream west of the Mississippi that hadn't been there before.

As soon as I could, I collared Tuli for an explanation.

"We used the lasers from the Atlantic Station and every plane and ounce of exothermic catalysts I could find. The effect isn't very spectacular, no noticeable weather change. But the desert High has expanded slightly and pushed the jet stream a little northward, temporarily."

"Will it be enough?" I asked.

He shrugged.

Through the afternoon we watched that little curl travel along the length of the jet stream's course, like a wave snaking down the length of a long, taut rope. Meanwhile, the former Great Lakes High was covering all of Maryland and pushing into Virginia. Its northern extension shielded the coast well into New England.

"But she'll blast right through it," Ted grumbled, watching Omega's glowering system of closely-packed isobars, "unless the jet stream helps to push 'er off."

I asked Barney, "How does the timing look? Which will arrive first, the jet stream change, or the storm?"

She shook her head. "The machines have taken it down to four decimal places and there's still no sure answer."

Norfolk was being drenched with a torrential downpour; gale-force winds were snapping power lines and knocking down trees. Washington was a darkened, wind-swept city. Most of the federal offices had closed early, and traffic was inching along the rain-slicked streets.

Boatmen from Hatteras to the fishhook angle of Cape Cod—weekend sailors and professionals alike—were making fast extra lines, setting out double anchors, or pulling their craft out of the water altogether. Commercial air lines were juggling their schedules around the storm and whole squadrons of military planes were winging westward, away from the danger, like great flocks of migrating birds. Storm tides were piling up all along the coast, and flood warnings were flashing from Civil Defense centers in a dozen states. The highways were filling up with people moving inland before the approaching fury.

And Omega was still a hundred miles out to sea.

Then she faltered.

You could feel the electricity crackle through our control center. The mammoth hurricane hovered off the coast as the jet stream deflection finally arrived. We all held our breaths. Omega stood off the coast uncertainly for an hour, then turned to the northeast. She began to head out to sea.

We shouted our foolish heads off.

When the furor died down, Ted hopped up on his desk. "Hold on, heroes. Job's not finished yet. We've got a freeze in the midwest to modify. And I want to throw everything we've got into Omega, weaken her as much as possible. Now *scramble!*"

It was nearly midnight before Ted let us call it quits. Our Project people—real weathermakers now—had weakened Hurricane Omega to the point where she was only a tropical storm, fast losing her punch over the cold waters off the north Atlantic. A light snow was sprinkling much of the upper midwest, but our warning forecasts had been in time, and the weathermakers were able to take most of the snap out of the cold front. The local weather stations were reporting only minor problems from the unexpected freeze, and Barney's final computer run showed that the snow would be less than an inch.

Most of the Project people had left for sleep. There was only a skeleton crew left in the control center. Barney, Tuli and I gravitated to Ted's desk. He had commandeered a typewriter, and was pecking on the keys.

"How do you spell 'resignation'?" he asked me.

Before I could answer, the phone buzzed. It was Dr. Weis.

"You didn't have to call," Ted said. "Game's over. I know it."

Dr. Weis looked utterly exhausted, as though he had personally been battling the storm. "I had a long talk with the President tonight, Marrett. You've put him in a difficult position, and me in an impossible one. To the general public you're a hero. But I wouldn't trust you as far as I could throw a cyclotron."

"Guess I don't blame you," Ted answered calmly. "Don't worry, you won't have to fire me. I'm resigning. You'll be off the hook."

"You can't quit," Dr. Weis said. "You're a national resource, as far as the President's concerned. He spent the night comparing you to nuclear energy: you've got to be tamed and harnessed."

"Harnessed? For weather control?"

Weis nodded wordlessly.

"The President wants to really work on weather control?" Ted broke into a huge grin. "That's a harness I've been trying to get into for four years."

"You're lucky, Marrett. Very lucky. If the weather patterns had been slightly different, if things hadn't worked out so well . . ."

Ted's grin vanished. "Wasn't luck. It was work, a lot of people's work, and brains, and guts. That's where weather control —*real* weather control—wins for you. It doesn't matter what the weather patterns are if you're going to change all of them to suit your needs. You don't need luck, just time and sweat. You can *make* the weather you want. That's what we did. That's why it's got to work, if you just do it on a big enough scale."

"All right, you've won," Dr. Weis said. "Luck or skill or guts, it doesn't matter. Not now. The President wants to see you."

"How about tomorrow . . . I mean later this morning?"

"Fine," Dr. Weis said, although his face was still sullen.

"We've won," Tuli said as Ted shut off the phone. "We've actually won."

Barney sank into the nearest chair. "It's too much happening all at once. I don't think I can believe it all."

"It's real," Ted answered quietly. "Weather control is a fact now. Nobody can say it doesn't work, or it can't have any important effect on the country."

"So you're seeing the President tomorrow," I said.

"Later today," he corrected, "and I want you three guys with me."

"Guys," Barney echoed.

"Hey, that's right. You're a girl. Come on, Girl, I'll take you home. Looks like you won't have to be playing second fiddle to hurricanes anymore." He took her arm and started for the door. "Think you can stand being the center of my attention?"

Barney looked back at me. I got up and took her other arm. "If you don't mind, she's going to be the center of my attention, too."

Tuli shook his head as he joined us. "You barbarians. No wonder you're nervous wrecks. You never know who's going to marry whom. I've got my future wife all picked out; our families agreed on the match when we were both four."

"That's why you're here in the States," Ted joked.

Barney said, "Tuli, don't do anything to make them change their minds. I haven't had this much attention since I was four."

Down the main stairway we went, and out into the street. The sidewalks were puddled from rain, a side effect of Omega, but overhead the stars were shining through tattered, scudding clouds.

"Today the world's going to wake up and discover that man can control the weather," Ted said.

"Not really," Tuli cautioned. "We've only made a beginning. We still have years of learning ahead. Decades. Maybe centuries."

Ted nodded, a contented smile on his face. "Maybe. But we've started, that's the important thing."

"And the political problems this is going to cause?" I asked. "The social and economic changes that weather control will bring? What about them?"

He laughed. "That's for administrators like you and the President to worry about. I've got enough to keep me busy: six quadrillion tons of air . . . and one mathematician."

It was more than a year later, in October, when the United Nations convened an extraordinary session in Washington to hear an address by the President.

The delegates met at a special outdoor pavilion, built along the banks of the Potomac for their meeting. Ted, Barney, Tuli—most of the key people from the Weather Bureau and Congress and government were in the audience. Beyond the seats set on the grass for the UN delegates and invited guests, a huge thronging crowd looked on, and listened to the President.

". . . For mankind's technology," he was saying, "is both a constant danger and a constant opportunity. Through technology, man has attained the power to destroy himself, or the power to unite this planet in peace and freedom—freedom from war, from hunger, from ignorance.

"Today we meet to mark a new step in the peaceful use of man's growing technical knowledge: the establishment of the United Nations Commission for Planetary Weather Control . . ."

Like Ted's victory over Hurricane Omega, this was only a first step. Total control of the weather, and total solution of the human problems involved, was still a long way off. But we were started along the right road.

As we sat listening to the President, a gentle breeze wafted by, tossing the flame-colored trees, and tempering the warmth of the sun. It was a crisp, golden October day; bright blue sky, beaming sun, occasional puffs of cottonball cumulus clouds. A perfect day for an outdoor ceremony.

Of course.

It's not difficult to get men to live in peace.
All you need is a situation that makes conflict
obviously less profitable than cooperation. This
story was written with tongue well in cheek, and
with the ballistics expertise of Myron R. Lewis
to keep the science accurate.

MEN OF GOOD WILL

"I had no idea," said the UN representative as they stepped through the airlock-hatch, "that the United States lunar base was so big, and so thoroughly well equipped."

"It's a big operation, all right," Colonel Patton answered, grinning slightly. His professional satisfaction showed even behind the faceplate of his pressure-suit.

The pressure in the airlock equilibrated, and they squirmed out of their aluminized protective suits. Patton was big, scraping the maximum limit for space-vehicle passengers; Torgeson, the UN man, was slight, thin-haired, bespectacled and somehow bland-looking.

They stepped out of the airlock, into the corridor that ran the length of the huge plastic dome that housed Headquarters, U.S. Moonbase.

"What's behind all the doors?" Torgeson asked. His English had a slight Scandinavian twang to it. Patton found it a little irritating.

"On the right," the colonel answered, businesslike, "are officers' quarters, galley, officers' mess, various laboratories and the head-quarters staff offices. On the left are the computers."

Torgeson blinked. "You mean that half this building is taken up by computers? But why in the world . . . that is, why do you need so many? Isn't it frightfully expensive to boost them up here? I know it cost thousands of dollars for my own flight to the moon. The computers must be—"

"Frightfully expensive," Patton agreed, with feeling. "But we need them. Believe me, we need them."

They walked the rest of the way down the long corridor in silence. Patton's office was at the very end of it. The colonel opened the door and ushered in the UN representative.

"A sizeable office," Torgeson said. "And a window!"

"One of the privileges of rank," Patton answered, smiling tightly. "That white antenna-mast off on the horizon belongs to the Russian base."

"Ah, yes. Of course. I shall be visiting them tomorrow."

Colonel Patton nodded and gestured Torgeson to a chair as he walked behind his metal desk and sat down.

"Now then," said the colonel. "You are the first man allowed to set foot in this moonbase who is not a security-cleared, triple-checked, native-born, government-employed American. God knows how you got the Pentagon to okay your trip. But—now that you're here, what do you want?"

Torgeson took off his rimless glasses and fiddled with them. "I suppose the simplest answer would be the best. The United Nations must—absolutely must—find out how and why you and the Russians have been able to live peacefully here on the moon."

Patton's mouth opened, but no words came out. He closed it with a click.

"Americans and Russians," the UN man went on, "have fired at each other from orbiting satellite vehicles. They have exchanged shots at both the North and South Poles. Career diplomats have scuffled like prizefighters in the halls of the United Nations building . . ."

"I didn't know that."

"Oh, yes. We have kept it quiet, of course. But the tensions are becoming unbearable. Everywhere on Earth the two sides are armed to the teeth and on the verge of disaster. Even in space they fight. And yet, here on the moon, you and the Russians live side by side in peace. We must know how you do it!"

Patton grinned. "You came on a very appropriate day, in that case. Well, let's see now . . . how to present the picture. You know that the environment here is extremely hostile: airless, low gravity . . ."

"The environment here on the moon," Torgeson objected, "is no more hostile than that of orbiting satellites. In fact, you have some gravity, solid ground, large buildings—many advantages that artificial satellites lack. Yet there has been fighting aboard the satellites—and not on the moon. Please don't waste my time with platitudes. This trip is costing the UN too much money. Tell me the truth."

Patton nodded. "I was going to. I've checked the information sent up by Earthbase: you've been cleared by the White House, the AEC, NASA and even the Pentagon."

"So?"

"Okay. The plain truth of the matter is . . ." A soft chime from a small clock on Patton's desk interrupted him. "Oh. Excuse me."

Torgeson sat back and watched as Patton carefully began clearing off all the articles on his desk: the clock, calendar, phone, IN/OUT baskets, tobacco can and pipe rack, assorted papers and reports—all neatly and quickly placed in the desk drawers. Patton then stood up, walked to the filing cabinet, and closed the metal drawers firmly.

He stood in the middle of the room, scanned the scene with apparent satisfaction, and then glanced at his wristwatch.

"Okay," he said to Torgeson. "Get down on your stomach."

"What?"

"Like this," the colonel said, and prostrated himself on the rubberized floor.

Torgeson stared at him.

"Come on! There's only a few seconds."

Patton reached up and grasped the UN man by the wrist. Unbelievingly, Torgeson got out of the chair, dropped to his hands and knees and finally flattened himself on the floor, next to the colonel.

For a second or two they stared at each other, saying nothing. "Colonel, this is embar . . ."

The room exploded into a shattering volley of sounds.

Something—many somethings—ripped through the walls. The air hissed and whined above the heads of the two prostrate men. The metal desk and file cabinet rang eerily.

Torgeson squeezed his eyes shut and tried to worm into the floor. It was just like being shot at!

Abruptly, it was over.

The room was quiet once again, except for a faint hissing sound. Torgeson opened his eyes and saw the colonel getting up. The door was flung open. Three sergeants rushed in, armed with patching disks and tubes of cement. They dashed around the office sealing up the several hundred holes in the walls.

Only gradually, as the sergeants carried on their fevered, wordless task, did Torgeson realize that the walls were actually a quiltwork of patches. The room must have been riddled repeatedly!

He climbed slowly to his feet. "Meteors?" he asked, with a slight squeak in his voice.

Colonel Patton grunted negatively and resumed his seat behind the desk. It was pockmarked, Torgeson noticed now. So was the file cabinet.

"The window, in case you're wondering, is bulletproof."

Torgeson nodded and sat down.

"You see," the colonel said, "life is not as peaceful here as you think. Oh, we get along fine with the Russians—now. We've learned to live in peace. We had to."

"What were those . . . things?"

"Bullets."

"Bullets? But how . . ."

The sergeants finished their frenzied work, lined up at the door and saluted. Colonel Patton returned the salute and they turned as one man and left the office, closing the door quietly behind them.

"Colonel, I'm frankly bewildered."

"It's simple enough to understand. But don't feel too badly about being surprised. Only the top level of the Pentagon knows about this. And the president, of course. They had to let him in on it."

"What happened?"

Colonel Patton took his pipe rack and tobacco can out of a desk drawer and began filling one of the pipes. "You see," he began, "the Russians and us, we weren't always so peaceful here on the moon. We've had our incidents and scuffles, just as you have on Earth."

"Go on."

"Well . . ." he struck a match and puffed the pipe alight ". . . shortly after we set up this dome for moonbase HQ, and the Reds set up theirs, we got into some real arguments." He waved the match out and tossed it into the open drawer.

"We're situated on the *Oceanus Procellarum*, you know. Exactly on the lunar equator. One of the biggest open spaces on this hunk of airless rock. Well, the Russians claimed they owned the whole damned *Oceanus*, since they were here first. We maintained the legal ownership was not established, since according to the UN Charter and the subsequent covenants . . ."

"Spare the legal details! Please, what happened?"

Patton looked slightly hurt. "Well . . . we started shooting at each other. One of their guards fired at one of our guards. They claim it was the other way around, of course. Anyway, within twenty minutes we were fighting a regular pitched battle, right out there between our base and theirs." He gestured toward the window.

"Can you fire guns in airless space?"

"Oh, sure. No problem at all. However, something unexpected came up."

"Only a few men got hit in the battle, none of them seriously. As in all battles, most of the rounds fired were clean misses."

"So?"

Patton smiled grimly. "So one of our civilian mathematicians started doodling. We had several thousand very-high-velocity bullets fired off. In airless space. No friction, you see. And under low-gravity conditions. They went right along past their targets . . ."

Recognition dawned on Torgeson's face. "Oh, no!"

"That's right. They whizzed right along, skimmed over the mountain tops, thanks to the curvature of this damned short lunar horizon, and established themselves in rather eccentric satellite orbits. Every hour or so they return to perigee . . . or, rather, periluna. And every twenty-seven days, periluna is right here, where the bullets originated. The moon rotates on its axis every twenty-seven days, you see. At any rate, when they come back this way, they shoot the living hell out of our base—and the Russian base, too, of course."

"But can't you . . ."

"Do what? Can't move the base. Authorization is tied up in the Joint Chiefs of Staff, and they can't agree on where to move it to. Can't bring up any special shielding material, because that's not authorized, either. The best thing we can do is to requisition all the computers we can and try to keep track of all the bullets. Their orbits keep changing, you know, every time they go through the bases. Air friction, puncturing walls, ricochets off the furniture . . . all that keeps changing their orbits enough to keep our computers busy full time."

"My God!"

"In the meantime, we don't dare fire off any more rounds. It would overburden the computers and we'd lose track of all of 'em. Then we'd have to spend every twenty-seventh day flat on our faces for hours."

Torgeson sat in numbed silence.

"But don't worry," Patton concluded with an optimistic, professional grin. "I've got a small detail of men secretly at work on the far side of the base—where the Reds can't see—building a stone wall. That'll stop the bullets. Then we'll fix those warmongers once and for all!"

Torgeson's face went slack. The chime sounded, muffled, from inside Patton's desk.

"Better get set to flatten out again. Here comes the second volley."

Was World War II inevitable? What would have happened if Winston Churchill had been the British Prime Minister in 1936? That's the premise from which this story was originally written. The idea of the dueling machine itself was the brainchild of Myron Lewis, who combined an interest in fencing plus his knowledge of physics to arrive at the inspiration.

THE PERFECT WARRIOR

Dulaq rode the slide to the upper pedestrian level, stepped off and walked over to the railing. The city stretched out all around him —broad avenues thronged with busy people, pedestrian walks, vehicle thoroughfares, aircars gliding between the gleaming, towering buildings.

And somewhere in this vast city was the man he must kill. The man who would kill him, perhaps.

It all seemed so real! The noise of the streets, the odors of the perfumed trees lining the walks, even the warmth of the reddish sun on his back as he scanned the scene before him.

It is an illusion, Dulaq reminded himself, *a clever man-made hallucination. A figment of my own imagination amplified by a machine.*

But it seemed so very real.

Real or not, he had to find Odal before the sun set. Find him and kill him. Those were the terms of the duel. He fingered the stubby cylindrical stat-wand in his tunic pocket. That was the weapon he had chosen, his weapon, his own invention. And this was the environment he had picked: his city, busy, noisy, crowded, the metropolis Dulaq had known and loved since childhood.

Dulaq turned and glanced at the sun. It was halfway down toward the horizon, he judged. He had about three hours to find Odal. When he did—kill or be killed.

Of course, no one is actually hurt. That is the beauty of the machine. It allows one to settle a score, to work out aggressive feelings, without either mental or physical harm.

Dulaq shrugged. He was a roundish figure, moon-faced, slightly stooped shoulders. He had work to do. Unpleasant work for a civilized man, but the future of the Acquataine Cluster and the entire alliance of neighboring star systems could well depend on the outcome of this electronically synthesized dream.

He turned and walked down the elevated avenue, marveling at the sharp sensation of hardness that met each footstep on the paving. Children dashed by and rushed up to a toyshop window. Men of commerce strode along purposefully, but without missing a chance to eye the girls sauntering by.

I must have a marvelous imagination, Dulaq thought, smiling to himself.

Then he thought of Odal, the blond, icy professional he was pitted against. Odal was an expert at all the weapons, a man of strength and cool precision, an emotionless tool in the hands of a ruthless politician. But how expert could he be with a stat-wand, when the first time he saw one was the moment before the duel began? And how well acquainted could he be with the metropolis, when he had spent most of his life in the military camps on the dreary planets of Kerak, sixty light-years from Acquatainia?

No, Odal would be lost and helpless in this situation. He would attempt to hide among the throngs of people. All Dulaq had to do was to find him.

The terms of the duel restricted both men to the pedestrian walks of the commercial quarter of the city. Dulaq knew the area intimately, and he began a methodical hunt through the crowds for the tall, fair-haired, blue-eyed Odal.

And he saw him! After only a few minutes of walking down the major thoroughfare, he spotted his opponent, strolling calmly along a crosswalk, at the level below.

Dulaq hurried down the next ramp, worked his way through the crowd, and saw the man again. Tall and blond, unmistakable. Dulaq edged along behind him quietly, easily. No disturbance. No pushing. Plenty of time. They walked along the street for a quarter hour while the distance between them slowly shrank from fifty feet to five.

Finally Dulaq was directly behind him, within arm's reach. He grasped the stat-wand and pulled it from his tunic. With one quick motion he touched it to the base of the man's skull and started to thumb the button that would release the killing bolt of energy . . .

The man turned suddenly. It wasn't Odal!

Dulaq jerked back in surprise. It couldn't be. He had seen his face. It was Odal—and yet this man was definitely a stranger.

He stared at Dulaq as the duelist backed away a few steps, then turned and walked quickly from the place.

A *mistake,* Dulaq told himself. *You were overanxious. A good thing this is an hallucination, or else the auto-police would be taking you in by now.*

And yet . . . he had been so certain that it was Odal. A chill shuddered through him. He looked up, and there was his antagonist, on the thoroughfare above, at the precise spot where he himself had been a few minutes earlier. Their eyes met, and Odal's lips parted in a cold smile.

Dulaq hurried up the ramp. Odal was gone by the time he reached the upper level. *He could not have gotten far,* Dulaq reasoned.

Slowly, but very surely, Dulaq's hallucination turned into a nightmare. He spotted Odal in the crowd, only to have him melt away. He saw him again, lolling in a small park, but when he got closer, the man turned out to be another stranger. He felt the chill of the duelist's ice-blue eyes on him again and again, but when he turned to find his antagonist, no one was there but the impersonal crowd.

Odal's face appeared again and again. Dulaq struggled through the throngs to find his opponent, only to have him vanish. The crowd seemed to be filled with tall, blond men crisscrossing before Dulaq's dismayed eyes.

The shadows lengthened. The sun was setting. Dulaq could feel his heart pounding within him and perspiration pouring from every square inch of his skin.

There he is! Definitely, positively him! Dulaq pushed through the homeward-bound crowds toward the figure of a tall, blond man leaning against the safety railing of the city's main thoroughfare. It was Odal, the damned, smiling, confident Odal.

Dulaq pulled the wand from his tunic and battled across the surging crowd to the spot where Odal stood motionless, hands in pockets, watching him.

Dulaq came within arm's reach . . .

"TIME, GENTLEMEN. TIME IS UP, THE DUEL IS ENDED."

High above the floor of the antiseptic-white chamber that housed the dueling machine was a narrow gallery. Before the machine had been installed, the chamber had been a lecture hall in Acquatainia's largest university. Now the rows of students' seats, the lecturer's dais and rostrum were gone. The chamber held only the machine, the grotesque collection of consoles, control desks, power units, association circuits, and booths where the two antagonists sat.

In the gallery—empty during ordinary duels—sat a privileged handful of newsmen.

"Time limit is up," one of them said. "Dulaq didn't get him."

"Yes, but he didn't get Dulaq, either."

The first one shrugged. "The important thing is that now Dulaq has to fight Odal on *his* terms. Dulaq couldn't win with his own choice of weapons and situation, so—"

"Wait, they're coming out."

Down on the floor below, Dulaq and his opponent emerged from their enclosed booths.

One of the newsmen whistled softly. "Look at Dulaq's face . . . it's positively gray."

"I've never seen the Prime Minister so shaken."

"And take a look at Kanus's hired assassin." The newsmen

turned toward Odal, who stood before his booth, quietly chatting with his seconds.

"Hm-m-m. There's a bucket of frozen ammonia for you."

"He's enjoying this."

One of the newsmen stood up. "I've got a deadline to meet. Save my seat."

He made his way past the guarded door, down the rampway circling the outer walls of the building, to the portable tri-di transmitting unit that the Acquatainian government had permitted for the newsmen on the campus grounds outside the former lecture hall.

The newsman huddled with his technicians for a few minutes, then stepped before the transmitter.

"Emile Dulaq, Prime Minister of the Acquataine Cluster and acknowledged leader of the coalition against Chancellor Kanus of the Kerak Worlds, has failed in the first part of his psychonic duel against Major Par Odal of Kerak. The two antagonists are now undergoing the routine medical and psychological checks before renewing their duel."

By the time the newsman returned to his gallery seat, the duel was almost ready to begin again.

Dulaq stood in the midst of a group of advisors before the looming impersonality of the machine.

"You need not go through with the next phase of the duel immediately," his Minister of Defense was saying. "Wait until tomorrow. Rest and calm yourself."

Dulaq's round face puckered into a frown. He cocked an eye at the chief meditech, hovering at the edge of the little group.

The meditech, one of the staff that ran the dueling machine, pointed out, "The Prime Minister has passed the examinations. He is capable, within the agreed-upon rules of the contest, of resuming."

"But he has the option of retiring for the day, does he not?"

"If Major Odal agrees."

Dulaq shook his head impatiently. "No. I shall go through with it. Now."

"But—"

The Prime Minister's face suddenly hardened; his advisors lapsed into a respectful silence. The chief meditech ushered Dulaq back into his booth. On the other side of the room, Odal glanced at the Acquatainians, grinned humorlessly, and strode to his own booth.

Dulaq sat and tried to blank out his mind while the meditechs adjusted the neurocontacts to his head and torso. They finished at last and withdrew. He was alone in the booth now, looking at the dead-white walls, completely bare except for the viewscreen before his eyes. The screen finally began to glow slightly, then brightened into a series of shifting colors. The colors merged and changed, swirled across his field of view. Dulaq felt himself being drawn into them gradually, compellingly, completely immersed in them.

The mists slowly vanished, and Dulaq found himself standing on an immense and totally barren plain. Not a tree, not a blade of grass; nothing but bare, rocky ground stretching in all directions to the horizon and disturbingly harsh yellow sky. He looked down and at his feet saw the weapon that Odal had chosen.

A primitive club.

With a sense of dread, Dulaq picked up the club and hefted it in his hand. He scanned the plain. Nothing. No hills or trees or bushes to hide in. No place to run to.

And off on the horizon he could see a tall, lithe figure holding a similar club walking slowly and deliberately toward him.

The press gallery was practically empty. The duel had more than an hour to run, and most of the newsmen were outside, broadcasting their hastily drawn guesses about Dulaq's failure to win with his own choice of weapon and environment.

Then a curious thing happened.

On the master control panel of the dueling machine, a single light flashed red. The meditech blinked at it in surprise, then pressed a series of buttons on his board. More red lights appeared. The chief meditech rushed to the board and flipped a single switch.

One of the newsmen turned to his partner. "What's going on down there?"

"I think it's all over. . . . Yes, look, they're opening up the booths. Somebody must've scored a victory."

They watched intently while the other newsmen quickly filed back into the gallery.

"There's Odal. He looks happy."

"Guess that means—"

"Good Lord! Look at Dulaq!"

II

Dr. Leoh was lecturing at the Carinae Regional University when the news of Dulaq's duel reached him. An assistant professor perpetrated the unthinkable breach of interrupting the lecture to whisper the news in his ear.

Leoh nodded grimly, hurriedly finished his lecture, and then accompanied the assistant professor to the university president's office. They stood in silence as the slideway whisked them through the strolling students and blossoming greenery of the quietly busy campus.

Leoh remained wrapped in his thoughts as they entered the administration building and rode the lift tube. Finally, as they stepped through the president's doorway, Leoh asked the assistant professor:

"You say he was in a state of catatonic shock when they removed him from the machine?"

"He still is," the president answered from his desk. "Completely withdrawn from the real world. Cannot speak, hear, or even see— a living vegetable."

Leoh plopped down in the nearest chair and ran a hand across his fleshy face. He was balding and jowly, but his face was creased from a smile that was almost habitual, and his eyes were active and alert.

"I don't understand it," he admitted. "Nothing like this has ever happened in a dueling machine before."

The university president shrugged. "I don't understand it either. But, this is your business." He put a slight emphasis on the last word, unconsciously perhaps.

"Well, at least this will not reflect on the university. That is why I formed Psychonics as a separate business enterprise." Then he added, with a grin, "The money was, of course, only a secondary consideration."

The president managed a smile. "Of course."

"I suppose the Acquatainians want to see me?" Leoh asked academically.

"They're on the tri-di now, waiting for you."

"They're holding a transmission frequency open over eight hundred parsecs?" Leoh looked impressed. "I must be an important man."

"You're the inventor of the dueling machine and the head of Psychonics, Inc. You're the only man who can tell them what went wrong."

"Well, I suppose I shouldn't keep them waiting."

"You can take the call here," the president said, starting to get up from his chair.

"No, no, stay there at your desk," Leoh insisted. "There's no reason for you to leave. Or you either," he said to the assistant professor.

The president touched a button on his desk-communicator. The far wall of the office glowed momentarily, then seemed to dissolve. They were looking into another office, this one on Acquatainia. It was crowded with nervous-looking men in business clothes and military uniforms.

"Gentlemen," Dr. Leoh said.

Several of the Acquatainians tried to answer him at once. After a few seconds of talking together, they all looked toward one of their members—a tall, purposeful, shrewd-faced civilian who bore a neatly-trimmed black beard.

"I am Fernd Massan, the acting Prime Minister of Acquatainia. You realize, of course, the crisis that has been precipitated in my government because of this duel?"

Leoh blinked. "I realize that, apparently, there has been some difficulty with the dueling machine installed on the governing planet of your star cluster. Political crises are not in my field."

"But your dueling machine has incapacitated the Prime Minister," one of the generals bellowed.

"And at this particular moment," the Defense Minister added, "in the midst of our difficulties with the Kerak Worlds."

"If the Prime Minister is not—"

"Gentlemen!" Leoh objected. "I cannot make sense of your story if you all speak at once."

Massan gestured them to silence.

"The dueling machine," Leoh said, adopting a slightly professorial tone, "is nothing more than a psychonic device for alleviating human aggressions and hostilities. It allows two men to share a dream world created by one of them. There is nearly complete feedback between the two. Within certain limits, the two men can do anything they wish within their dream world. This allows men to settle grievances with violence—in the safety of their own imaginations. If the machine is operated properly, no physical or mental harm can be done to the participants. They can alleviate their tensions safely—without damage of any sort to anyone, and without hurting society.

"Your own government tested one of the machines and approved its use on Acquatainia more than three years ago. I see several of you who were among those to whom I personally demonstrated the device. Dueling machines are in use through wide portions of the galaxy, and I am certain that many of you have used the machine. You have, general, I'm sure."

The general blustered. "That has nothing to do with the matter at hand!"

"Admittedly," Leoh conceded. "But I do not understand how a therapeutic machine can possibly become entangled in a political crisis."

Massan said, "Allow me to explain. Our government has been conducting extremely delicate negotiations with the stellar governments of our neighboring territories. These negotiations concern the rearmaments of the Kerak Worlds. You have heard of Kanus of Kerak?"

"I recall the name vaguely," Leoh said. "He's a political leader of some sort."

"Of the worst sort. He has acquired complete dictatorship of the Kerak Worlds, and is now attempting to rearm them for war. This is in direct countervention of the Treaty of Acquatainia, signed only thirty Terran years ago."

"I see. The treaty was signed at the end of the Acquataine-Kerak war, wasn't it?"

"A war that we won," the general pointed out.

"And now the Kerak Worlds want to rearm and try again," Leoh said.

"Precisely."

Leoh shrugged. "Why not call in the Star Watch? This is their type of police activity. And what has all this to do with the dueling machine?"

Massan explained patiently, "The Acquataine Cluster has never become a full-fledged member of the Terran Commonwealth. Our neighboring territories are likewise unaffiliated. Therefore the Star Watch can intervene only if all parties concerned agree to intervention. Unless, of course, there is an actual military emergency. The Kerak Worlds, of course, are completely isolationist—unbound by any laws except those of force."

Leoh shook his head.

"As for the dueling machine," Massan went on, "Kanus of Kerak has turned it into a political weapon—"

"But that's impossible. Your government passed strict laws concerning the use of the machine; I recommended them and I was in your Council chambers when the laws were passed. The machine may be used only for personal grievances. It is strictly outside the realm of politics."

Massan shook his head sadly. "Sir, laws are one thing—people are another. And politics consists of people, not words on paper."

"I don't understand," Leoh said.

Massan explained, "A little more than one Terran year ago, Kanus picked a quarrel with a neighboring star group—the Safad Federation. He wanted an especially favorable trade agreement with them. Their Minister of Trade objected most strenuously. One of the Kerak negotiators—a certain Major Odal—got into a personal argument with the minister. Before anyone knew what had happened, they had challenged each other to a duel. Odal won the duel, and the minister resigned his post. He said that he could no longer effectively fight against the will of Odal and his group . . . he was psychologically incapable of it. Two weeks later he was dead—apparently a suicide, although I have doubts."

"That's . . . extremely interesting," Leoh said.

"Three days ago," Massan continued, "the same Major Odal engaged Prime Minister Dulaq in a bitter personal argument. Odal is now a military attaché of the Kerak Embassy here. He accused the Prime Minister of cowardice, before a large group at an Embassy party. The Prime Minister had no alternative but to challenge him. And now—"

"And now Dulaq is in a state of shock, and your government is tottering."

Massan's back stiffened. "Our government shall not fall, nor shall the Acquataine Cluster acquiesce to the rearmament of the Kerak Worlds. But"—his voice lowered—"without Dulaq, I fear that our neighboring governments will give in to Kanus's demands and allow him to rearm. Alone, we are powerless to stop him."

"Rearmament itself might not be so bad," Leoh mused, "if you can keep the Kerak Worlds from using their weapons. Perhaps the Star Watch might—"

"Kanus could strike a blow and conquer a star system before the Star Watch could be summoned and arrive to stop him. Once Kerak is armed, this entire area of the galaxy is in peril. In fact, the entire galaxy is endangered."

"And he's using the dueling machine to further his ambitions," Leoh said. "Well, gentlemen, it seems I have no alternative but to travel to the Acquataine Cluster. The dueling machine is my responsibility, and if there is something wrong with it, or with the use of it, I will do my best to correct the situation."

"That is all we ask," Massan said. "Thank you."

The Acquatainian scene faded away, and the three men in the university president's office found themselves looking at a solid wall once again.

"Well," Dr. Leoh said, turning to the president, "it seems that I must request an indefinite leave of absence."

The president frowned. "And it seems that I must grant your request—even though the year is only half-finished."

"I regret the necessity," Leoh said; then, with a broad grin, he added, "My assistant professor, here, can handle my courses for the remainder of the year, very easily. Perhaps he will even be able to deliver his lectures without being interrupted."

The assistant professor turned red.

"Now then," Leoh muttered, mostly to him, "who is this Kanus, and why is he trying to turn the Kerak Worlds into an arsenal?"

III

Chancellor Kanus, the supreme leader of the Kerak Worlds, stood at the edge of the balcony and looked across the wild, tumbling gorge to the rugged mountains beyond.

"These are the forces that mold men's actions," he said to his small audience of officials and advisors, "the howling winds, the mighty mountains, the open sky and the dark powers of the clouds."

The men nodded and made murmurs of agreement.

"Just as the mountains thrust up from the pettiness of the lands below, so shall we rise above the common walk of men," Kanus said. "Just as a thunderstorm terrifies them, we will make them bend to our will!"

"We will destroy the past," said one of the ministers.

"And avenge the memory of defeat," Kanus added. He turned and looked at the little group of men. Kanus was the smallest man on the balcony: short, spare, sallow-faced; but he possessed piercing, dark eyes and a strong voice that commanded attention.

He walked through the knot of men and stopped before a tall, lean, blond youth in light-blue military uniform. "And you, Major Odal, will be a primary instrument in the first steps of conquest."

Odal bowed stiffly. "I only hope to serve my leader and my worlds."

"You shall. And you already have," Kanus said, beaming. "Already the Acquatainians are thrashing about like a snake whose head has been cut off. Without Dulaq, they have no head, no brain to direct them. For your part in this triumph"—Kanus snapped his fingers, and one of his advisors quickly stepped to his side and handed him a small ebony box—"I present you with this token of the esteem of the Kerak Worlds, and of my personal high regard."

He handed the box to Odal, who opened it and took out a small, jeweled pin.

"The Star of Kerak," Kanus announced. "This is the first time it has been awarded to anyone except a warrior on the battlefield. But then, we have turned their so-called civilized machine into our own battlefield, eh?"

Odal grinned. "Yes, sir, we have. Thank you very much sir. This is the supreme moment of my life."

"To date, major. Only to date. There will be other moments, even higher ones. Come, let's go inside. We have many plans to discuss . . . more duels . . . more triumphs."

They all filed in to Kanus's huge, elaborate office. The leader walked across the plushly ornate room and sat at the elevated desk, while his followers arranged themselves in the chairs and couches placed about the floor. Odal remained standing, near the doorway.

Kanus let his fingers flick across a small control board set into his desktop, and a tri-dimensional star map glowed into existence on the far wall. As its center were the eleven stars that harbored the Kerak Worlds. Around them stood neighboring stars, color-coded to show their political groupings. Off to one side of the map was the Acquataine Cluster, a rich mass of stars—wealthy, powerful, the most important political and economic power in the section of the galaxy. Until yesterday's duel.

Kanus began one of his inevitable harangues. Objectives, political and military. Already the Kerak Worlds were unified under his dominant will. The people would follow wherever he led. Already the political alliances built up by Acquatainian diplomacy since the last war were tottering, now that Dulaq was out of the picture. Now was the time to strike. A political blow *here*, at the Szarno Confederacy, to bring them and their armaments industries into line with Kerak. Then more political strikes to isolate the Acquataine Cluster from its allies, and to build up subservient states for Kerak. Then, finally, the military blow—against the Acquatainians.

"A sudden strike, a quick, decisive series of blows, and the Acquatainians will collapse like a house of paper. Before the Star Watch can interfere, we will be masters of the Cluster. Then, with the resources of Acquatainia to draw on, we can challenge any force in the galaxy—even the Terran Commonwealth itself!"

The men in the room nodded their assent.

They've heard this story many, many times, Odal thought to himself. This was the first time he had been privileged to listen to it. If you closed your eyes, or looked only at the star map, the plan sounded bizarre, extreme, even impossible. But, if you watched Kanus, and let those piercing, almost hypnotic eyes fasten on yours, then the leader's wildest dreams sounded not only exciting, but inevitable.

Odal leaned a shoulder against the paneled wall and scanned the other men in the room.

There was fat Greber, the vice-chancellor, fighting desperately to stay awake after drinking too much wine during the luncheon and afterward. And Modal, sitting on the couch next to him, was bright-eyed and alert, thinking only of how much money and power would come to him as Chief of Industries once the rearmament program began in earnest.

Sitting alone on another couch was Kor, the quiet one, the head of Intelligence, and—technically—Odal's superior. Silent Kor, whose few words were usually charged with terror for those whom he spoke against.

Marshal Lugal looked bored when Kanus spoke of politics, but his face changed when military matters came up. The marshal lived for only one purpose; to avenge his army's humiliating defeat in the war against the Acquatainians, thirty Terran years ago. What he didn't realize, Odal thought, smiling to himself, was that as soon as he had reorganized the army and reequipped it, Kanus planned to retire him and place younger men in charge. Men whose only loyalty was not to the army, nor even to the Kerak Worlds and their people, but to the chancellor himself.

Eagerly following every syllable, every gesture of the leader was little Tinth. Born to the nobility, trained in the arts, a student of philosophy, Tinth had deserted his heritage and joined the forces of Kanus. His reward had been the Ministry of Education; many teachers had suffered under him.

And finally there was Romis, the Minister of Intergovernmental Affairs. A professional diplomat, and one of the few men in government before Kanus's sweep to power to survive this long. It was clear that Romis hated the chancellor. But he served the Kerak Worlds well. The diplomatic corps was flawless in its handling of intergovernmental affairs. It was only a matter of time, Odal knew, before one of them—Romis or Kanus—killed the other.

The rest of Kanus's audience consisted of political hacks, roughnecks-turned-bodyguards, and a few other hangers-on who had been with Kanus since the days when he held his political monologues in cellars, and haunted the alleys to avoid the police. Kanus had come a long way: from the blackness of oblivion to the dazzling heights of the chancellor's rural estate.

Money, power, glory, revenge, patriotism: each man in the room, listening to Kanus, had his reasons for following the chancellor.

And my reasons? Odal asked himself. *Why do I follow him? Can I see into my own mind as easily as I see into theirs?*

There was duty, of course. Odal was a soldier, and Kanus was the duly-elected leader of the government. Once elected, though, he had dissolved the government and solidified his powers as absolute dictator of the Kerak Worlds.

There was gain to be had by performing well under Kanus. Regardless of his political ambitions and personal tyrannies, Kanus rewarded well when he was pleased. The medal—the Star of Kerak—carried with it an annual pension that would nicely accommodate a family. *If I had one,* Odal thought, sardonically.

There was power, of sorts, also. Working the dueling machine in his special way, hammering a man into nothingness, finding the weaknesses in his personality and exploiting them, pitting his mind against others, turning sneering towers of pride like Dulaq into helpless, whipped dogs—that was power. And it was a power that did not go unnoticed in the cities of the Kerak Worlds. Already Odal was easily recognized on the streets; women especially seemed to be attracted to him now.

"The most important factor," Kanus was saying, "and I cannot stress it overmuch, is to build up an aura of invincibility. This is why your work is so important, Major Odal. You must be invincible! Because today you are the instrument of my own will—and you must triumph at every turn. The fate of your people, of your government, of your chancellor rests squarely on your shoulders each time you step into a dueling machine. You have borne that responsibility well, major. Can you carry it even further?"

"I can, sir," Odal answered crisply, "and I will."

Kanus beamed at him. "Good! Because your next duel—and those that follow it—will be to the death."

IV

It took the starship two weeks to make the journey from Carinae to the Acquataine Cluster. Dr. Leoh spent the time checking over the Acquatainian dueling machine, by direct tri-di beam; the Acquatainian government gave him all the technicians, time, and money he needed for the task.

Leoh spent as much of his spare time as possible with the other passengers of the ship. He was gregarious, a fine conversationalist, and had a nicely balanced sense of humor. Particularly, he was a favorite of the younger women, since he had reached the age where he could flatter them with his attention without making them feel endangered.

But still, there were long hours when he was alone in his stateroom with nothing but his memories. At times like these, it was impossible not to think back over the road he had been following.

Albert Robertus Leoh, Ph.D., Professor of Physics, Professor of Electronics, master of computer technology, inventor of the interstellar tri-di communications system; and, more recently, student of psychology, Professor of Psychophysiology, founder of Psychonics, Inc., inventor of the dueling machine.

During his earlier years, when the supreme confidence of youth was still with him, Leoh had envisioned himself as helping mankind to spread his colonies and civilizations throughout the galaxy. The bitter years of galactic war had ended in his childhood, and now human societies throughout the Milky Way were linked together—in greater or lesser degree of union—into a more-or-less peaceful coalition of star groups.

There were two great motivating forces at work on those human societies spread across the stars, and these forces worked toward opposite goals. On the one hand was the urge to explore, to reach new stars, new planets, to expand the frontiers of man's civilizations and found new colonies, new nations. Pitted against this drive to expand was an equally powerful force: the realization that technology had finally put an end to physical labor and almost to poverty itself on all the civilized worlds of man. The urge to move off to the frontier was penned in and buried alive under the enervating comforts of civilization.

The result was inescapable. The civilized worlds became constantly more crowded as time wore on. They became jam-packed islands of humanity sprinkled thinly across the sea of space that was still full of unpopulated islands.

The expense and difficulty of interstellar travel was often cited as an excuse. The starships *were* expensive: their power demands were frightful. Only the most determined—and the best-financed —groups of colonists could afford them. The rest of mankind accepted the ease and safety of civilization, lived in the bulging cities of the teeming planets. Their lives were circumscribed by their neighbors, and by their governments. Constantly more people crowding into a fixed living space meant constantly less freedom. The freedom to dream, to run free, to procreate, all became state-owned, state-controlled monopolies.

And Leoh had contributed to this situation.

He had contributed his thoughts and his work. He had contributed often and regularly—the interstellar communications systems was only one outstanding achievement in a long career of achievements.

Leoh had been nearly at the voluntary retirement age for scientists when he realized what he, and his fellow scientists, had done. Their efforts to make life richer and more rewarding for mankind had made life only less strenuous and more rigid.

And with every increase in comfort, Leoh discovered, came a corresponding increase in neuroses, in crimes of violence, in mental aberrations. Senseless wars of pride broke out between star groups for the first time in generations. Outwardly, the peace of the galaxy was assured; but beneath the glossy surface of the Terran Commonwealth there smoldered the beginnings of a volcano. Police actions fought by the Star Watch were increasing ominously. Petty wars between once-stable peoples were flaring up steadily.

Once Leoh realized the part he had played in this increasingly tragic drama, he was confronted with two emotions—a deep sense of guilt, both personal and professional; and, countering this, a determination to do something, anything, to restore at least some balance to man's collective mentality.

Leoh stepped out of physics and electronics, and entered the field of psychology. Instead of retiring, he applied for a beginner's status in his new profession. It had taken considerable bending and straining of the Commonwealth's rules—but for a man of Leoh's stature, the rules could be flexed somewhat. Leoh became a student once again, then a researcher, and finally a Professor of Psychophysiology.

Out of this came the dueling machine. A combination of electroencephalograph and autocomputer. A dream machine that amplified a man's imagination until he could engulf himself in a world of his own making.

Leoh envisioned it as a device to enable men to rid themselves of hostility and tension, safely. Through his efforts, and those of his colleagues, dueling machines were quickly becoming accepted as devices for settling disputes.

When two men had a severe difference of opinion—deep enough to warrant legal action—they could go to the dueling machine instead of the courts. Instead of sitting helplessly and watching the machinations of the law grind impersonally through their differences, the two antagonists could allow their imaginations free rein in the dueling machine. They could settle their differences personally, as violently as they wished, without hurting themselves or anyone else. On most civilized worlds, the results of properly-monitored duels were accepted as legally binding.

The tensions of civilized life could be escaped—albeit temporarily—in the dueling machine. This was a powerful tool, much too powerful to allow it to be used indiscriminately. Therefore Leoh safeguarded his invention by forming a private company—Psychonics, Inc.—and securing an exclusive license from the Terran Commonwealth to manufacture, sell, install and maintain the machines. His customers were government health and legal agencies; his responsibilities were: legally, to the Commonwealth; morally, to all mankind; and, finally, to his own restless conscience.

The dueling machines succeeded. They worked as well, and often better, than Leoh had anticipated. But he knew that they were only a stopgap, only a temporary shoring of a constantly eroding dam. What was needed, really needed, was some method of exploding the status quo, some means of convincing people to reach out for those unoccupied, unexplored stars that filled the galaxy, some way of convincing men that they should leave the comforts of civilization for the excitement of colonization.

Leoh had been searching for that method when the news of Dulaq's duel against Odal reached him.

Now he was speeding across parsecs of space, praying to himself that the dueling machine had not failed.

The two-week flight ended. The starship took up a parking orbit around the capital planet of the Acquataine Cluster. The passengers transshipped to the surface.

Dr. Leoh was met at the landing disk by an official delegation, headed by Massan, the acting Prime Minister. They exchanged formal greetings there at the base of the ship, while the other passengers hurried by.

As Leoh and Massan, surrounded by the other members of the delegation, rode the slideway to the port's administration building, Leoh commented:

"As you probably know, I have checked through your dueling machine quite thoroughly via tri-di for the past two weeks. I can find nothing wrong with it."

Massan shrugged. "Perhaps you should have checked, then, the machine of Szarno."

"The Szarno Confederation? Their dueling machine?"

"Yes. This morning Kanus's hired assassin killed a man in it."

"He won another duel," Leoh said.

"You do not understand," Massan said grimly. "Major Odal's opponent—an industrialist who had spoken out against Kanus—was actually killed in the dueling machine. The man is dead!"

V

One of the advantages of being Commander-in-Chief of the Star Watch, the old man thought to himself, is that you can visit any planet in the Commonwealth.

He stood at the top of the hill and looked out over the green tableland of Kenya. This was the land of his birth, Earth was his homeworld. The Star Watch's official headquarters may be in the heart of a globular cluster of stars near the center of the galaxy, but Earth was the place the commander wanted most to see as he grew older and wearier.

An aide, who had been following the commander at a respectful distance, suddenly intruded himself in the old man's reverie.

"Sir, a message for you."

The commander scowled at the young officer. "I gave orders that I was not to be disturbed."

The officer, slim and stiff in his black-and-silver uniform, replied, "Your chief of staff has passed the message on to you, sir. It's from Dr. Leoh, of Carinae University. Personal and urgent, sir."

The old man grumbled to himself, but nodded. The aide placed a small, crystalline sphere on the grass before him. The air above the sphere started to vibrate and glow.

"Sir Harold Spencer here," the commander said.

The bubbling air seemed to draw in on itself and take solid form. Dr. Leoh sat at a desk chair and looked up at the standing commander.

"Harold, it's a pleasure to see you once again."

Spencer's stern eyes softened, and his beefy face broke into a well-creased smile. "Albert, you ancient scoundrel. What do you mean by interrupting my first visit home in fifteen years?"

"It won't be a long interruption," Leoh said.

"You told my chief of staff that it was urgent," Sir Harold groused.

"It is. But it's not the sort of problem that requires much action on your part. Yet. You are familiar with recent political developments on the Kerak Worlds?"

Spencer snorted. "I know that a barbarian named Kanus has established himself as a dictator. He's a troublemaker. I've been talking to the Commonwealth Council about the advisability of quashing him before he causes grief, but you know the Council . . . first wait until the flames have sprung up, then thrash about and demand that the Star Watch do something!"

Leoh grinned. "You're as irascible as ever."

"My personality is not the subject of this rather expensive discussion. What about Kanus? And what are you doing, getting yourself involved in politics? About to change your profession again?"

"No, not at all," Leoh answered, laughing. Then, more seriously, "It seems as though Kanus has discovered some method of using the dueling machines to achieve political advantages over his neighbors."

"What?"

Leoh explained the circumstances of Odal's duels with the Acquatainian Prime Minister and Szarno industrialist.

"Dulaq is completely incapacitated and the other poor fellow is dead?" Spencer's face darkened into a thundercloud. "You were right to call me. This is a situation that could easily become intolerable."

"I agree," Leoh said. "But evidently Kanus has not broken any laws or interstellar agreements. All that meets the eye is a disturbing pair of accidents, both of them accruing to Kanus's benefit."

"Do *you* believe that they were accidents?"

"Certainly not. The dueling machine cannot cause physical or mental harm . . . unless someone has tampered with it in some way."

"That is my thought, too." Spencer was silent for a moment, weighing the matter in his mind. "Very well. The Star Watch cannot act officially, but there is nothing to prevent me from dispatching an officer to the Acquataine Cluster, on detached duty, to serve as liaison between us."

"Good. I think that will be the most effective method of handling the situation, at present."

"It will be done," Sir Harold pronounced. His aide made a mental note of it.

"Thank you very much," Leoh said. "Now, go back to enjoying your vacation."

"Vacation? This is no vacation," Spencer rumbled. "I happen to be celebrating my birthday."

"So? Well, congratulations. I try not to remember mine," Leoh said.

"Then you must be older than I," Spencer replied, allowing only the faintest hint of a smile to appear.

"I suppose it's possible."

"But not very likely, eh?"

They laughed together and said goodbye. The Star Watch commander tramped through the hills until sunset, enjoying the sight of the grasslands and distant purple mountains he had known in his childhood. As dusk closed in, he told his aide he was ready to leave.

The aide pressed a stud on his belt and a two-place aircar skimmed silently from the far side of the hills and hovered beside them. Spencer climbed in laboriously while the aide remained discreetly at his side. While the commander settled his bulk into his seat, the aide hurried around the car and hopped into his place. The car glided off toward Spencer's personal planetship, waiting for him at a nearby field.

"Don't forget to assign an officer to Dr. Leoh," the commander

muttered to his aide. Then he turned and watched the unmatch-
able beauty of an Earthly sunset.

The aide did not forget the assignment. That night, as Sir Harold's ship spiraled out to a rendezvous with a starship, the aide
dictated the necessary order into an autodispatcher that immediately beamed it to the Star Watch's nearest communications center
on Mars.

The order was scanned and routed automatically and finally
beamed to the Star Watch unit commandant in charge of the
area closest to the Acquataine Cluster, on the sixth planet circling the star Perseus Alpha. Here again, the order was processed
automatically and routed through the local headquarters to the
personnel files. The automated files selected three microcard
dossiers that matched the requirements of the order.

The three microcards and the order itself appeared simultaneously on the desktop viewer of the Star Watch personnel officer.
He looked at the order, then read the dossiers. He flicked a button
that gave him an updated status report on each of the three men
in question. One was due for leave after an extensive period of
duty. The second was the son of a personal friend of the local
commandant. The third had just arrived a few weeks ago, fresh
from the Star Watch Academy on Mars.

The personnel officer selected the third man, routed his dossier
and Sir Harold's order back into the automatic processing system,
and returned to the film of primitive dancing girls he had been
watching before this matter of decision had arrived at his desk.

VI

The space station orbiting around Acquatainia—the capital planet
of the Acquataine Cluster—served simultaneously as a transfer
point from starships to planetships, a tourist resort, meteorological
station, communications center, scientific laboratory, astronomical
observatory, medical haven for allergy-and-cardiac patients, and
military base. It was, in reality, a good-sized city with its own mar-
kets, its own local government, and its own way of life.

Dr. Leoh had just stepped off the debarking ramp of the starship
from Szarno. The trip there had been pointless and fruitless. But
he had gone anyway, in the slim hope that he might find some-

thing wrong with the dueling machine that had been used to murder a man.

A shudder went through him as he edged along the automated customs scanners and paper-checkers. What kind of people could these men of Kerak be? To actually kill a human being in cold blood; to plot and plan the death of a fellow man. Worse than barbaric. Savage.

He felt tired as he left customs and took the slideway to the planetary shuttle ships. Halfway there, he decided to check at the communications desk for messages. That Star Watch officer that Sir Harold had promised him a week ago should have arrived by now.

The communications desk consisted of a small booth that contained the output printer of a communications computer and an attractive young dark-haired girl. Automation or not, Leoh thought smilingly, there were certain human values that transcended mere efficiency.

A lanky, thin-faced youth was half-leaning on the booth's counter, trying to talk to the girl. He had curly blond hair and crystal blue eyes; his clothes consisted of an ill-fitting pair of slacks and tunic. A small traveler's kit rested on the floor at his feet.

"So, I was sort of, well, thinking . . . maybe somebody might, uh, show me around . . . a little," he was stammering to the girl. "I've never been, uh, here. . . ."

"It's the most beautiful planet in the galaxy," the girl was saying. "Its cities are the finest."

"Yes . . . well, I was sort of thinking . . . that is, I know we just, uh, met a few minutes ago . . . but, well, maybe . . . if you have a free day or so coming up . . . maybe we could, uh, sort of . . ."

She smiled coolly. "I have two days off at the end of the week, but I'll be staying here at the station. There's so much to see and do here, I very seldom leave."

"Oh . . ."

"You're making a mistake," Leoh interjected dogmatically. "If you have such a beautiful planet for your homeworld, why in the name of the gods of intellect don't you go down there and enjoy it? I'll wager you haven't been out in the natural beauty and fine cities you spoke of since you started working here on the station."

"Why, you're right," she said, surprised.

"You see? You youngsters are all alike. You never think further than the ends of your noses. You should return to the planet, young lady, and see the sunshine again. Why don't you visit the university at the capital city? Plenty of open space and greenery, lots of sunshine and available young men!"

Leoh was grinning broadly, and the girl smiled back at him. "Perhaps I will," she said.

"Ask for me when you get to the university. I'm Dr. Leoh. I'll see to it that you're introduced to some of the girls and gentlemen of your own age."

"Why . . . thank you, doctor. I'll do it this weekend."

"Good. Now then, any messages for me? Anyone aboard the station looking for me?"

The girl turned and tapped a few keys on the computer's control console. A row of lights flicked briefly across the console's face. She turned back to Leoh:

"No, sir, I'm sorry. No messages and no one has asked for you."

"Hm-m-m. That's strange. Well, thank you . . . and I'll expect to see you at the end of this week."

The girl smiled a farewell. Leoh started to walk away from the booth, back toward the slideway. The young man took a step toward him, stumbled on his own traveling kit, and staggered across the floor for a half-dozen steps before regaining his balance. Leoh turned and saw that the youth's face bore a somewhat ridiculous expression of mixed indecision and curiosity.

"Can I help you?" Leoh asked, stopping at the edge of the moving slideway.

"How . . . how did you do that, sir?"

"Do what?"

"Get that girl to agree to visit the university. I've been talking to her for half an hour, and, well, she wouldn't even look straight at me."

Leoh broke into a chuckle. "Well, young man, to begin with, you were much too flustered. It made you appear overanxious. On the other hand, I am at an age where I can be strictly platonic. She was on guard against you, but she knows she has very little to fear from me."

"I see . . . I think."

"Well," Leoh said, gesturing toward the slideway, "I suppose this is where we go our separate ways."

"Oh, no, sir. I'm going with you. That is, I mean, you *are* Dr. Leoh, aren't you?"

"Yes, I am. And you must be . . ." Leoh hesitated. *Can this be a Star Watch officer?* he wondered.

The youth stiffened to attention and for an absurd flash of a second, Leoh thought he was going to salute. "I am Junior Lieutenant Hector, sir; on special detached duty from the cruiser SW4-J188, home base Perseus Alpha VI."

"I see," Leoh replied. "Um-m-m . . . is Hector your first name or your last?"

"Both, sir."

I should have guessed, Leoh told himself. Aloud, he said, "Well, lieutenant, we'd better get to the shuttle before it leaves without us."

They took to the slideway. Half a second later, Hector jumped off and dashed back to the communications desk for his travel kit. He hurried back to Leoh, bumping into seven bewildered citizens of various descriptions and nearly breaking both his legs when he tripped as he ran back onto the moving slideway. He went down on his face, sprawled across two lanes moving at different speeds, and needed the assistance of several persons before he was again on his feet and standing beside Leoh.

"I . . . I'm sorry to cause all that, uh, commotion, sir."

"That's all right. You weren't hurt, were you?"

"Uh, no . . . I don't think so. Just embarrassed."

Leoh said nothing. They rode the slideway in silence through the busy station and out to the enclosed berths where the planetary shuttles were docked. They boarded one of the ships and found a pair of seats.

"Just how long have you been with the Star Watch, lieutenant?"

"Six weeks, sir. Three weeks aboard a starship bringing me out to Perseus Alpha VI, a week at the planetary base there, and two weeks aboard the cruiser SW4-J188. That is, it's been six weeks since I received my commission. I've been at the Academy . . . the Star Watch Academy on Mars . . . for four years."

"You got through the Academy in four years?"

"That's the regulation time, sir."

"Yes, I know."

The ship eased out of its berth. There was a moment of free-fall, then the drive engine came on and the gravfield equilibrated.

"Tell me, lieutenant, how did you get picked for this assignment?"

"I wish I knew, sir," Hector said, his lean face twisting into a puzzled frown. "I was working out a program for the navigation officer . . . aboard the cruiser. I'm pretty good at that . . . I can work out computer programs in my head, mostly. Mathematics was my best subject at the Academy . . ."

"Interesting."

"Yes, well, anyway, I was working out this program when the captain himself came on deck and started shaking my hand and telling me that I was being sent on special duty on Acquatainia by direct orders of the Commander-in-Chief. He seemed very happy . . . the captain, that is."

"He was no doubt pleased to see you get such an unusual assignment," Leoh said tactfully.

"I'm not so sure," Hector said truthfully. "I think he regarded me as some sort of a problem, sir. He had me on a different duty-berth practically every day I was on board the ship."

"Well now," Leoh changed the subject, "what do you know about psychonics?"

"About what, sir?"

"Eh . . . electroencephalography?"

Hector looked blank.

"Psychology, perhaps?" Leoh suggested, hopefully. "Physiology? Computer molectronics?"

"I'm pretty good at mathematics!"

"Yes, I know. Did you, by any chance, receive any training in diplomatic affairs?"

"At the Star Watch Academy? No, sir."

Leoh ran a hand through his thinning hair. "Then why did the Star Watch select you for this job? I must confess, lieutenant, that I can't understand the workings of a military organization."

Hector shook his head ruefully, "Neither do I, sir."

VII

The next week was an enervatingly slow one for Leoh, evenly divided between tedious checking of each component of the dueling machine, and shameless ruses to keep Hector as far away from the machine as possible.

The Star Watchman certainly wanted to help, and he actually *was* little short of brilliant in doing intricate mathematics completely in his head. But he was, Leoh found, a clumsy, chattering, whistling, scatterbrained, inexperienced bundle of noise and nerves. It was impossible to do constructive work with him nearby.

Perhaps you're judging him too harshly, Leoh warned himself. *You just might be letting your frustrations with the dueling machine get the better of your sense of balance.*

The professor was sitting in the office that the Acquatainians had given him in one end of the former lecture hall that held the dueling machine. Leoh could see its impassive metal hulk through the open office door.

The room he was sitting in had been one of a suite of offices used by the permanent staff of the machine. But they had moved out of the building completely, in deference to Leoh, and the Acquatainian government had turned the other cubbyhole offices into sleeping rooms for the professor and the Star Watchman, and an auto-kitchen. A combination cook-valet-handyman appeared twice each day—morning and evening—to handle any special chores that the cleaning machines and auto-kitchen might miss.

Leoh slouched back in his desk chair and cast a weary eye on the stack of papers that recorded the latest performances of the machine. Earlier that day he had taken the electroencephalographic records of clinical cases of catatonia and run them through the machine's input unit. The machine immediately rejected them, refused to process them through the amplification units and association circuits.

In other words, the machine had recognized the EEG traces as something harmful to a human being.

Then how did it happen to Dulaq? Leoh asked himself for the thousandth time. It couldn't have been the machine's fault; it must have been something in Odal's mind that simply overpowered Dulaq's.

"Overpowered?" That's a terribly unscientific term, Leoh argued against himself.

Before he could carry the debate any further, he heard the main door of the big chamber slide open and then bang shut, and Hector's off-key whistle shrilled and echoed through the high-vaulted room.

Leoh sighed and put his self-contained argument off to the back of his mind. Trying to think logically near Hector was a hopeless prospect.

"Are you in, doctor?" Hector's voice rang out.

"In here."

Hector ducked in through the doorway and plopped his rangy frame on the office's couch.

"Everything going well, sir?"

Leoh shrugged. "Not very well, I'm afraid. I can't find anything wrong with the dueling machine. I can't even *force* it to malfunction."

"Well, that's good, isn't it?" Hector chirped happily.

"In a sense," Leoh admitted, feeling slightly nettled at the youth's boundless, pointless optimism. "But, you see, it means that Kanus's people can do things with the machine that I can't."

Hector frowned, considering the problem. "Hm-m-m . . . yes, I guess that's right, too, isn't it?"

"Did you see the girl back to her ship safely?" Leoh asked.

"Yes, sir," Hector replied, bobbing his head vigorously. "She's on her way back to the communications booth at the space station. She said to tell you she enjoyed her visit very much."

"Good. It was, eh, very good of you to escort her about the campus. It kept her out of my hair . . . what's left of it, that is."

Hector grinned. "Oh, I liked showing her around, and all that —And, well, it sort of kept *me* out of your hair, too, didn't it?"

Leoh's eyebrows shot up in surprise.

Hector laughed. "Doctor, I may be clumsy, and I'm certainly no scientist . . . but I'm not completely brainless."

"I'm sorry if I gave you that impression . . ."

"Oh no . . . don't be sorry. I didn't mean that to sound so . . . well, the way it sounded . . . that is, I know I'm just in your way . . ." He started to get up.

Leoh waved him back to the couch. "Relax, my boy, relax. You know, I've been sitting here all afternoon wondering what to do next. Somehow, just now, I came to a conclusion."

"Yes?"

"I'm going to leave the Acquataine Cluster and return to Carinae."

"What? But you can't! I mean . . ."

"Why not? I'm not accomplishing anything here. Whatever it is that this Odal and Kanus have been doing, it's basically a political problem, and not a scientific one. The professional staff of the machine here will catch up to their tricks sooner or later."

"But, sir, if you can't find the answer, how can they?"

"Frankly, I don't know. But, as I said, this is a political problem more than a scientific one. I'm tired and frustrated and I'm feeling my years. I want to return to Carinae and spend the next few months considering beautifully abstract problems about instantaneous transportation devices. Let Massan and the Star Watch worry about Kanus."

"Oh! That's what I came to tell you. Massan has been challenged to a duel by Odal!"

"What?"

"This afternoon, Odal went to the council building. Picked an argument with Massan right in the main corridor and challenged him."

"Massan accepted?" Leoh asked.

Hector nodded.

Leoh leaned across his desk and reached for the phone unit. It took a few minutes and a few levels of secretaries and assistants, but finally Massan's dark, bearded face appeared on the screen above the desk.

"You have accepted Odal's challenge?" Leoh asked, without preliminaries.

"We meet next week," Massan replied gravely.

"You should have refused."

"On what pretext?"

"No pretext. A flat refusal, based on the certainty that Odal or someone else from Kerak is tampering with the dueling machine."

Massan shook his head sadly. "My dear learned sir, you still do not comprehend the political situation. The government of the Acquataine Cluster is much closer to dissolution than I dare to admit openly. The coalition of star groups that Dulaq had constructed to keep the Kerak Worlds neutralized has broken apart completely. This morning, Kanus announced that he would annex Szarno. This afternoon, Odal challenges me."

"I think I see . . ."

"Of course. The Acquatainian government is paralyzed now, until the outcome of the duel is known. We cannot effectively intervene in the Szarno crisis until we know who will be heading the government next week. And, frankly, more than a few members of our council are now openly favoring Kanus and urging that we establish friendly relations with him before it is too late."

"But, that's all the more reason for refusing the duel," Leoh insisted.

"And be accused of cowardice in my own council meetings?" Massan smiled grimly. "In politics, my dear sir, the *appearance* of a man means much more than his substance. As a coward, I would soon be out of office. But, perhaps, as the winner of a duel against the invincible Odal . . . or even as a martyr . . . I may accomplish something useful."

Leoh said nothing.

Massan continued, "I put off the duel for a week, hoping that in that time you might discover Odal's secret. I dare not postpone the duel any longer; as it is, the political situation may collapse about our heads at any moment."

"I'll take this machine apart and rebuild it again, molecule by molecule," Leoh promised.

As Massan's image faded from the screen, Leoh turned to Hector. "We have one week to save his life."

"And avert a war, maybe," Hector added.

"Yes." Leoh leaned back in his chair and stared off into infinity.

Hector shuffled his feet, rubbed his nose, whistled a few bars of off-key tunes, and finally blurted, "How can you take apart the dueling machine?"

"Hm-m-m?" Leoh snapped out of his reverie.

"How can you take apart the dueling machine?" Hector repeated. "Looks like a big job to do in a week."

"Yes, it is. But, my boy, perhaps we . . . the two of us . . . can do it."

Hector scratched his head. "Well, uh, sir . . . I'm not very . . . that is, my mechanical aptitude scores at the Academy . . ."

Leoh smiled at him. "No need for mechanical aptitude, my boy. You were trained to fight, weren't you? We can do the job mentally."

VIII

It was the strangest week of their lives.

Leoh's plan was straightforward: to test the dueling machine, push it to the limits of its performance, by actually operating it —by fighting duels.

They started off easily enough, tentatively probing and flexing their mental muscles. Leoh had used the dueling machine himself many times in the past, but only in tests of the machine's routine performance. Never in actual combat against another human being. To Hector, of course, the machine was a totally new and different experience.

The Acquatainian staff plunged into the project without question, providing Leoh with invaluable help in monitoring and analyzing the duels.

At first, Leoh and Hector did nothing more than play hide-and-seek, with one of them picking an environment and the other trying to find his opponent in it. They wandered through jungles and cities, over glaciers and interplanetary voids, seeking each other—without ever leaving the booths of the dueling machine.

Then, when Leoh was satisfied that the machine could reproduce and amplify thought patterns with strict fidelity, they began to fight light duels. They fenced with blunted foils—Hector won, of course, because of his much faster reflexes. Then they tried other weapons—pistols, sonic beams, grenades—but always with the precaution of imagining themselves to be wearing protective equipment. Strangely, even though Hector was trained in the use of these weapons, Leoh won almost all the bouts. He was neither faster nor more accurate, when they were target-shooting. But when the two of them faced each other, somehow Leoh almost always won.

The machine projects more than thoughts, Leoh told himself. *It projects personality.*

They worked in the dueling machine day and night now, enclosed in the booths for twelve or more hours a day, driving themselves and the machine's regular staff to near-exhaustion. When they gulped their meals, between duels, they were physically ragged and sharp-tempered. They usually fell asleep in Leoh's office, while discussing the results of the day's work.

The duels grew slowly more serious. Leoh was pushing the machine to its limits now, carefully extending the rigors of each bout. And yet, even though he knew exactly what and how much he intended to do in each fight, it often took a conscious effort of will to remind himself that the battles he was fighting were actually imaginary.

As the duels became more dangerous, and the artificially amplified hallucinations began to end in blood and death, Leoh found himself winning more and more frequently. With one part of his mind he was driving to analyze the cause of his consistent success. But another part of him was beginning to really enjoy his prowess.

The strain was telling on Hector. The physical exertion of constant work and practically no relief was considerable in itself. But the emotional effects of being "hurt" and "killed" repeatedly were infinitely worse.

"Perhaps we should stop for a while," Leoh suggested after the fourth day of tests.

"No. I'm all right."

Leoh looked at him. Hector's face was haggard, his eyes bleary.

"You've had enough," Leoh said quietly.

"Please don't make me stop," Hector begged. "I . . . I can't stop now. Please give me a chance to do better. I'm improving . . . I lasted twice as long in this afternoon's two duels as I did in the ones this morning. Please, don't end it now . . . not while I'm completely lost—"

Leoh stared at him. "You want to go on?"

"Yes, sir."

"And if I say no?"

Hector hesitated. Leoh sensed he was struggling with himself. "If you say no," he answered dully, "then it will be no. I can't argue against you any more."

Leoh was silent for a long moment. Finally he opened a desk

drawer and took a small bottle from it. "Here, take a sleep capsule. When you wake up we'll try again."

It was dawn when they began again. Leoh entered the dueling machine determined to allow Hector to win. He gave the youthful Star Watchman his choice of weapon and environment. Hector picked one-man scoutships, in planetary orbits. Their weapons were conventional force beams.

But despite his own conscious desire, Leoh found himself winning! The ships spiraled about an unnamed planet, their paths intersecting at least once in every orbit. The problem was to estimate your opponent's orbital position, and then program your own ship so that you arrived at that position either behind or to one side of him. Then you could train your guns on him before he could turn on you.

The problem should have been an easy one for Hector, with his knack for intuitive mental calculation. But Leoh scored the first hit—Hector had piloted his ship into an excellent firing position, but his shot went wide; Leoh maneuvered around clumsily, but managed to register an inconsequential hit on the side of Hector's ship.

In the next three passes, Leoh scored two more hits. Hector's ship was badly damaged now. In return, the Star Watchman had landed one glancing shot on Leoh's ship.

They came around again, and once more Leoh had outguessed his younger opponent. He trained his guns on Hector's ship, then hesitated with his hand poised above the firing button.

Don't kill him again, he warned himself. *His mind can't accept another defeat.*

But Leoh's hand, almost of its own will, reached the button and touched it lightly. Another gram of pressure and the guns would fire.

In that instant's hesitation, Hector pulled his crippled ship around and aimed at Leoh. The Watchman fired a searing blast that jarred Leoh's ship from end to end. Leoh's hand slammed down on the firing button, whether he intended to do it or not, he did not know.

Leoh's shot raked Hector's ship but did not stop it. The two vehicles were hurtling directly at each other. Leoh tried desperately to avert a collision, but Hector bored in grimly, matching Leoh's maneuvers with his own.

The two ships smashed together and exploded.

Abruptly, Leoh found himself in the cramped booth of the dueling machine, his body cold and damp with perspiration, his hands trembling.

He squeezed out of the booth and took a deep breath. Warm sunlight was streaming into the high-vaulted room. The white walls glared brilliantly. Through the tall windows he could see trees and people and clouds in the sky.

Hector walked up to him. For the first time in several days, the Watchman was smiling. Not much, but smiling. "Well, we broke even on that one."

Leoh smiled back, somewhat shakily. "Yes. It was . . . quite an experience. I've never died before."

Hector fidgeted. "It's, uh, not so bad, I guess . . . It does sort of, well, shatter you, you know."

"Yes. I can see that now."

"Another duel?" Hector asked, nodding his head toward the machine.

"Let's get out of this place for a few hours. Are you hungry?"

"Starved."

They fought seven more duels over the next day and a half. Hector won three of them. It was late afternoon when Leoh called a halt to the tests.

"We can still get in another one or two," the Watchman pointed out.

"No need," Leoh said. "I have all the data I require. Tomorrow Massan meets Odal, unless we can put a stop to it. We have much to do before tomorrow morning."

Hector sagged into the couch. "Just as well. I think I've aged seven years in the past seven days."

"No, my boy," Leoh said gently. "You haven't aged. You've matured."

IX

It was deep twilight when the groundcar slid to a halt on its cushion of compressed air before the Kerak Embassy.

"I still think it's a mistake to go in there," Hector said. "I mean, you could've called him on the tri-di just as well, couldn't you?"

Leoh shook his head. "Never give an agency of any government the opportunity to say 'hold the line a moment' and then huddle together to consider what to do with you. Nineteen times out of twenty, they'll end by passing your request up to the next higher echelon, and you'll be left waiting for weeks."

"Still," Hector insisted, "you're simply stepping into enemy territory. It's a chance you shouldn't take."

"They wouldn't dare touch us."

Hector did not reply, but he looked unconvinced.

"Look," Leoh said, "there are only two men alive who can shed light on this matter. One of them is Dulaq, and his mind is closed to us for an indefinite time. Odal is the only other one who knows what happened."

Hector shook his head, skeptically. Leoh shrugged, and opened the door of the groundcar. Hector had no choice but to get out and follow him as he walked up the pathway to the main entrance of the Embassy. The building stood gaunt and gray in the dusk, surrounded by a precisely clipped hedge. The entrance was flanked by a pair of tall evergreen trees.

Leoh and Hector were met just inside the entrance by a female receptionist. She looked just a trifle disheveled—as though she had been rushed to the desk at a moment's notice. They asked for Odal, were ushered into a sitting room, and within a few minutes—to Hector's surprise—were informed by the girl that Major Odal would be with them shortly.

"You see," Leoh pointed out jovially, "when you come in person they haven't as much of a chance to consider how to get rid of you."

Hector glanced around the windowless room and contemplated the thick, solidly closed door. "There's a lot of scurrying going on on the other side of that door, I'll bet. I mean . . . they may be considering how to, uh, get rid of us . . . permanently."

Leoh shook his head, smiling wryly. "Undoubtedly the approach closest to their hearts—but highly improbable in the present situation. They have been making most efficient and effective use of the dueling machine to gain their ends."

Odal picked this moment to open the door.

"Dr. Leoh . . . Lt. Hector . . . you asked to see me?"

"Thank you, Major Odal; I hope you will be able to help me," said Leoh. "You are the only man living who may be able to give us some clues to the failure of the dueling machine."

Odal's answering smile reminded Leoh of the best efforts of the robot-puppet designers to make a machine that smiled like a man. "I am afraid I can be of no assistance, Dr. Leoh. My experiences in the machine are . . . private."

"Perhaps you don't fully understand the situation," Leoh said. "In the past week, we have tested the dueling machine here on Acquatainia, exhaustively. We have learned that its performance can be greatly influenced by a man's personality, and by training. You have fought many duels in the machines. Your background of experience, both as a professional soldier and in the machines, gives you a decided advantage over your opponents.

"However, even with all this considered, I am convinced that you cannot kill a man in the machine—under normal circumstances. We have demonstrated that fact in our tests. An unsabotaged machine cannot cause actual physical harm.

"Yet you have already killed one man and incapacitated another. Where will it stop?"

Odal's face remained calm, except for the faintest glitter of fire deep in his eyes. His voice was quiet, but had the edge of a well-honed blade to it: "I cannot be blamed for my background and experience. And I have not tampered with your machines."

The door to the room opened, and a short, thick-set, bullet-headed man entered. He was dressed in a dark street suit, so that it was impossible to guess his station at the Embassy.

"Would the gentlemen care for refreshments?" he asked in a low-pitched voice.

"No, thank you," Leoh said.

"Some Kerak wine, perhaps?"

"Well—"

"I don't, uh, think we'd better, sir," Hector said. "Thanks all the same."

The man shrugged and sat at a chair next to the door.

Odal turned back to Leoh. "Sir, I have my duty. Massan and I duel tomorrow. There is no possibility of postponing it."

"Very well," Leoh said. "Will you at least allow us to place some special instrumentation into the booth with you, so that we can monitor the duel more fully? We can do the same with Massan. I know that duels are normally private and you would be within your legal rights to refuse the request. But, morally—"

The smile returned to Odal's face. "You wish to monitor my thoughts. To record them and see how I perform during the duel. Interesting. Very interesting—"

The man at the door rose and said, "If you have no desire for refreshments, gentlemen—"

Odal turned to him. "Thank you for your attention."

Their eyes met and locked for an instant. The man gave a barely perceptible shake of his head, then left.

Odal returned his attention to Leoh. "I am sorry, professor, but I cannot allow you to monitor my thoughts during the duel."

"But—"

"I regret having to refuse you. But, as you yourself pointed out, there is no legal requirement for such a course of action. I must refuse. I hope you understand."

Leoh rose from the couch, and Hector popped up beside him. "I'm afraid I do understand. And I, too, regret your decision."

Odal escorted them out to their car. They drove away, and the Kerak major walked slowly back into the Embassy building. He was met in the hallway by the dark-suited man who had sat in on the conversation.

"I could have let them monitor my thoughts and still crush Massan," Odal said. "It would have been a good joke on them."

The man grunted. "I have just spoken to the chancellor on the tri-di, and obtained permission to make a slight adjustment in our plans."

"An adjustment, Minister Kor?"

"After your duel tomorrow, your next opponent will be the eminent Dr. Leoh," Kor said.

X

The mists swirled deep and impenetrable about Fernd Massan. He stared blindly through the useless viewplate in his helmet, then reached up slowly and carefully to place the infrared detector before his eyes.

I never realized an hallucination could seem so real, Massan thought.

Since the challenge by Odal, he realized, the actual world had seemed quite unreal. For a week, he had gone through the motions of life, but felt as though he were standing aside, a spectator mind watching its own body from a distance. The gathering of his friends and associates last night, the night before the duel—that silent, funereal group of people—it had all seemed completely unreal to him.

But now, in this manufactured dream, he seemed vibrantly alive. Every sensation was solid, stimulating. He could feel his pulse throbbing through him. Somewhere out in those mists, he knew, was Odal. And the thought of coming to grips with the assassin filled him with a strange satisfaction.

Massan had spent a good many years serving his government on the rich, but inhospitable, high-gravity planets of the Acquataine Cluster. This was the environment he had chosen: crushing gravity; killing pressures; atmosphere of ammonia and hydrogen, laced with free radicals of sulphur and other valuable but deadly chemicals; oceans of liquid methane and ammonia; "solid ground" consisting of quickly crumbling, eroding ice; howling, superpowerful winds that could pick up a mountain of ice and hurl it halfway around the planet; darkness; danger; death.

He was encased in a one-man protective outfit that was half armored suit, half vehicle. There was an internal grav field to keep him comfortable in 3.7 gees, but still the suit was cumbersome, and a man could move only very slowly in it, even with the aid of servomotors.

The weapon he had chosen was simplicity itself—a hand-sized capsule of oxygen. But in a hydrogen/ammonia atmosphere, oxygen could be a deadly explosive. Massan carried several of these "bombs"; so did Odal. *But the trick,* Massan thought to himself, *is to know how to throw them under these conditions; the proper range, the proper trajectory. Not an easy thing to learn, without years of experience.*

The terms of the duel were simple: Massan and Odal were situated on a rough-topped iceberg that was being swirled along one of the methane/ammonia ocean's vicious currents. The ice was rapidly crumbling; the duel would end when the iceberg was completely broken up.

Massan edged along the ragged terrain. His suit's grippers and rollers automatically adjusted to the roughness of the topography. He concentrated his attention on the infrared detector that hung before his viewplate.

A chunk of ice the size of a man's head sailed through the murky atmosphere in a steep glide peculiar to heavy gravity and banged into the shoulder of Massan's suit. The force was enough to rock him slightly off-balance before the servos readjusted. Massan withdrew his arm from the sleeve and felt the inside of the shoulder seam. *Dented, but not penetrated.* A leak would have been disastrous, possibly fatal. Then he remembered: *Of course —I cannot be killed except by direct action of my antagonist. That is one of the rules of the game.*

Still, he carefully fingered the dented shoulder to make certain it was not leaking. The dueling machine and its rules seemed so very remote and unsubstantial, compared to this freezing, howling inferno.

He diligently set about combing the iceberg, determined to find Odal and kill him before their floating island disintegrated. He thoroughly explored every projection, every crevice, every slope, working his way slowly from one end of the berg toward the other. Back and forth, cross and recross, with the infrared sensors scanning three-hundred-sixty degrees around him.

It was time-consuming. Even with the suit's servomotors and propulsion units, motion across the ice, against the buffeting wind, was a cumbersome business. But Massan continued to work his way across the iceberg, fighting down a gnawing, growing fear that Odal was not there at all.

And then he caught just the barest flicker of a shadow on his detector. Something, or someone, had darted behind a jutting rise of the ice, off by the edge of the iceberg.

Slowly and carefully, Massan made his way toward the base of the rise. He picked one of the oxy-bombs from his belt and held it in his right-hand claw.

Massan edged around the base of the ice cliff, and stood on a narrow ledge between the cliff and the churning sea. He saw no one. He extended the detector's range to maximum, and worked the scanners up the sheer face of the cliff toward the top.

There he was! The shadowy outline of a man etched itself on the detector screen. And at the same time, Massan heard a muffled roar, then a rumbling, crashing noise, growing quickly louder and more menacing.

He looked up the face of the ice cliff and saw a small avalanche of ice tumbling, sliding, growling toward him. *That devil set off a bomb at the top of the cliff!*

Massan tried to back out of the way, but it was too late. The first chunk of ice bounced harmlessly off his helmet, but the others knocked him off-balance so repeatedly that the servos had no chance to recover. He staggered blindly for a few moments, as more and more ice cascaded down on him, and then toppled off the ledge into the boiling sea.

Relax! he ordered himself. *Do not panic! The suit will float you. The servos will keep you right-side-up. You cannot be killed accidentally; Odal must perform the* coup-de-grace *himself.*

Then he remembered the emergency rocket units in the back of the suit. If he could orient himself properly, a touch of a control stud on his belt would set them off, and he would be boosted back onto the iceberg. He turned slightly inside the suit and tried to judge the iceberg's distance through the infrared detector. It was difficult, especially since he was bobbing madly in the churning currents.

Finally he decided to fire the rocket and make final adjustments of distance and landing site after he was safely out of the sea.

But he could not move his hand.

He tried, but his entire right arm was locked fast. He could not budge it an inch. And the same for the left. Something, or someone, was clamping his arms tight. He could not even pull them out of their sleeves.

Massan thrashed about, trying to shake off whatever it was. No use.

Then his detector screen was lifted slowly from the viewplate. He felt something vibrating on his helmet. The oxygen tubes! They were being disconnected.

He screamed and tried to fight free. No use. With a hiss, the oxygen tubes pulled free of his helmet. Massan could feel the blood pounding through his veins as he fought desperately to free himself.

Now he was being pushed down into the sea. He screamed again and tried to wrench his body away. The frothing sea filled his viewplate. He was under. He was being held under. And now . . . now the viewplate itself was being loosened.

No! Don't! The scalding, cold methane-ammonia sea seeped in through the opening viewplate.

"It's only a dream!" Massan shouted to himself. "Only a dream. A dream. A—"

XI

Dr. Leoh stared at the dinner table without really seeing it. Coming to this restaurant had been Hector's idea. Three hours earlier, Massan had been removed from the dueling machine—dead.

Leoh sat stolidly, hands in lap, his mind racing in many different directions at once. Hector was off at the phone, getting the latest information from the meditechs. Odal had expressed his regrets perfunctorily, and then left for the Kerak Embassy, under a heavy escort of his own plainclothes guards. The government of the Acquataine Cluster was quite literally falling apart, with no man willing to assume responsibility . . . and thereby expose himself. One hour after the duel, Kanus's troops had landed on all the major planets of the Szarno Confederacy; the annexation was a *fait accompli.*

And what have I done since I arrived on Acquatainia? Leoh demanded of himself. *Nothing. Absolutely nothing. I have sat back like a doddering old professor and played academic games with the machine, while younger, more vigorous men have USED the machine to suit their purposes.*

Used the machine. There was a fragment of an idea in that phrase. Something nebulous, that must be approached carefully or it will fade away. Used the machine . . . used it . . . Leoh toyed with the phrase for a few moments, then gave it up with a sigh of resignation. *Lord, I'm too tired even to think.*

Leoh focused his attention on his surroundings and scanned the busy dining room. It was a beautiful place, really; decorated with crystal and genuine woods and fabric draperies. Not a synthetic in sight. The waiters and cooks and busboys were humans, not the autocookers and servers that most restaurants employed. Leoh suddenly felt touched at Hector's attempt to restore his spirits—even if it *was* being done at Star Watch expense.

He saw the young Watchman approaching the table, coming back from the phone. Hector bumped two waiters and stumbled over a chair before reaching the relative safety of his own seat.

"What's the verdict?" Leoh asked.

Hector's lean face was bleak. "Couldn't revive him. Cerebral hemorrhage, the meditechs said—induced by shock."

"Shock?"

"That's what they said. Something must've, uh, overloaded his nervous system . . . I guess."

Leoh shook his head. "I just don't understand any of this. I might as well admit it. I'm no closer to an answer now than I was when I arrived here. Perhaps I should have retired years ago, before the dueling machine was invented."

"Nonsense."

"No, I mean it," Leoh said. "This is the first real intellectual puzzle I've had to contend with in years. Tinkering with machinery . . . that's easy. You know what you want, all you need is to make the machinery perform properly. But this . . . I'm afraid I'm too old to handle a real problem like this."

Hector scratched his nose thoughtfully, then answered, "If you can't handle the problem, sir, then we're going to have a war on our hands in a matter of weeks. I mean, Kanus won't be satisfied with swallowing the Szarno group . . . the Acquataine Cluster is next . . . and he'll have to fight to get it."

"Then the Star Watch can step in," Leoh said, resignedly.

"Maybe . . . but it'll take time to mobilize the Star Watch. . . . Kanus can move a lot faster than we can. Sure, we could throw in a task force . . . a token group, that is. But Kanus's gang will chew them up pretty quick. I . . . I'm no politician, sir, but I think I can see what will happen. Kerak will gobble up the Acquataine Cluster . . . a Star Watch task force will be wiped out in the battle . . . and we'll end up with Kerak at war with the Terran Commonwealth. And it'll be a real war . . . a big one."

Leoh began to answer, then stopped. His eyes were fixed on the far entrance of the dining room. Suddenly every murmur in the busy room stopped dead. Waiters stood still between tables. Eating, drinking, conversation hung suspended.

Hector turned in his chair and saw at the far entrance the slim, stiff, blue-uniformed figure of Odal.

The moment of silence passed. Everyone turned to his own business and avoided looking at the Kerak major. Odal, with a faint smile on his thin face, made his way slowly to the table where Hector and Leoh were sitting.

They rose to greet him and exchanged perfunctory salutations. Odal pulled up a chair and sat with them.

"I assume that you've been looking for me," Leoh said. "What do you wish to say?"

Before Odal could answer, the waiter assigned to the table walked up, took a position where his back would be to the Kerak major, and asked firmly, "Your dinner is ready gentlemen. Shall I serve it now?"

Leoh hesitated a moment, then asked Odal, "Will you join us?"

"I'm afraid not."

"Serve it now," Hector said. "The major will be leaving shortly."

Again the tight grin broke across Odal's face. The waiter bowed and left.

"I have been thinking about our conversation of last night," Odal said to Leoh.

"Yes?"

"You accused me of cheating in my duels."

Leoh's eyebrows arched. "I said someone was cheating, yes—"

"An accusation is an accusation."

Leoh said nothing.

"Do you withdraw your words, or do you still accuse me of deliberate murder? I am willing to allow you to apologize and leave Acquatainia in peace."

Hector cleared his throat noisily. "This is no place to have an argument . . . besides, here comes our dinner."

Odal ignored the Watchman. "You heard me, professor. Will you leave? Or do you accuse me of murdering Massan this afternoon?"

"I—"

Hector banged his fist on the table and jerked up out of his chair—just as the waiter arrived with a large tray of food. There was a loud crash. A tureen of soup, two bowls of salad, glasses, assorted rolls, vegetables, cheeses and other delicacies cascaded over Odal.

The Kerak major leaped to his feet, swearing violently in his native tongue. He sputtered back into basic Terran: "You clumsy, stupid oaf! You maggot-brained misbegotten peasant-faced—"

Hector calmly picked a salad leaf from the sleeve of his tunic. Odal abruptly stopped his tirade.

"I am clumsy," Hector said, grinning. "As for being stupid, and the rest of it, I resent that. I am highly insulted."

A flash of recognition lighted Odal's eyes. "I see. Of course. My quarrel here is not with you. I apologize." He turned back to Leoh, who was also standing now.

"Not good enough," Hector said. "I don't, uh, like the . . . tone of your apology."

Leoh raised a hand, as if to silence the younger man.

"I apologized; that is sufficient," Odal warned.

Hector took a step toward Odal. "I guess I could insult your glorious leader, or something like that . . . but this seems more direct." He took the water pitcher from the table and poured it calmly and carefully over Odal's head.

A wave of laughter swept the room. Odal went white. "You are determined to die." He wiped the dripping water from his eyes. "I will meet you before the week is out. And you have saved no one." He turned on his heel and stalked out.

"Do you realize what you've done?" Leoh asked, aghast.

Hector shrugged. "He was going to challenge you—"

"He will still challenge me, after you're dead."

"Um-m-m, yes, well, maybe so. I guess you're right—Well, anyway, we've gained a little more time."

"Four days." Leoh shook his head. "Four days to the end of the week. All right, come on, we have work to do."

Hector was grinning broadly as they left the restaurant. He began to whistle.

"What are you so happy about?" Leoh grumbled.

"About you, sir. When we came in here, you were, uh, well . . . almost beaten. Now you're right back in the game again."

Leoh glanced at the Star Watchman. "In your own odd way, Hector, you're quite a boy . . . I think."

XII

Their groundcar glided from the parking building to the restaurant's entrance ramp, at the radio call of the doorman. Within minutes, Hector and Leoh were cruising through the city, in the deepening shadows of night.

"There's only one man," Leoh said, "who has faced Odal and lived through it."

"Dulaq," Hector agreed. "But . . . for all the information the medical people have been able to get from him, he might as well be, uh, dead."

"He's still completely withdrawn?"

Hector nodded. "The medicos think that . . . well, maybe in a few months, with drugs and psychotherapy and all that . . . they might be able to bring him back."

"It won't be soon enough. We've only got four days."

"I know."

Leoh was silent for several minutes. Then: "Who is Dulaq's closest living relative? Does he have a wife?"

"I think his wife is, uh, dead. Has a daughter though. Pretty girl. Bumped into her in the hospital once or twice—"

Leoh smiled in the darkness. Hector's term, "bumped into," was probably completely literal.

"Why are you asking about Dulaq's next-of-kin?"

"Because," Leoh replied, "I think there might be a way to make Dulaq tell us what happened during his duel. But it is a very dangerous way. Perhaps a fatal way."

"Oh."

They lapsed into silence again. Finally he blurted, "Come on, my boy, let's find the daughter and talk to her."

"Tonight?"

"Now."

She certainly is a pretty girl, Leoh thought as he explained very carefully to Geri Dulaq what he proposed to do. She sat quietly and politely in the spacious living room of the Dulaq residence. The glittering chandelier cast touches of fire on her chestnut hair. Her slim body was slightly rigid with tension, her hands were clasped in her lap. Her face—which looked as though it could be very expressive—was completely serious now.

"And that is the sum of it," Leoh concluded. "I believe that it will be possible to use the dueling machine itself to examine your father's thoughts and determine exactly what took place during his duel against Major Odal!"

She asked softly, "But you are afraid that the shock might be repeated, and this could be fatal to my father?"

Leoh nodded wordlessly.

"Then I am very sorry, sir, but I must say no." Firmly.

"I understand your feelings," Leoh replied, "but I hope you realize that unless we can stop Odal and Kanus immediately, we may very well be faced with war."

She nodded. "I know. But you must remember that we are speaking of my father, of his very life. Kanus will have his war in any event, no matter what I do."

"Perhaps," Leoh admitted, "perhaps."

Hector and Leoh drove back to the university campus and their quarters in the dueling machine chamber. Neither of them slept well that night.

The next morning, after an unenthusiastic breakfast, they found themselves standing in the antiseptic-white chamber, before the looming, impersonal intricacy of the machine.

"Would you like to practice with it?" Leoh asked.

Hector shook his head. "Maybe later."

The phone chimed in Leoh's office. They both went in. Geri Dulaq's face showed on the tri-di screen.

"I have just heard the news. I did not know that Lieutenant Hector had challenged Odal." Her face was a mixture of concern and reluctance.

"He challenged Odal," Leoh answered, "to prevent the assassin from challenging me."

"Oh . . . You are a very brave man, lieutenant."

Hector's face went through various contortions and slowly turned a definite red, but no words issued from his mouth.

"Have you reconsidered your decision?" Leoh asked.

The girl closed her eyes briefly, then said flatly, "I am afraid I cannot change my decision. My father's safety is my first responsibility. I am sorry."

They exchanged a few meaningless trivialities—with Hector still thoroughly tongue-tied and ended the conversation on a polite, but strained, note.

Leoh rubbed his thumb across the phone switch for a moment, then turned to Hector. "My boy, I think it would be a good idea for you to go straight to the hospital and check on Dulaq's condition."

"But . . . why . . ."

"Don't argue, son. This could be vitally important."

Hector shrugged and left the office. Leoh sat down at his desk and drummed his fingers on the top of it. Then he burst out of the office and began pacing the big chamber. Finally, even that was too confining. He left the building and started stalking through the campus. He walked past a dozen buildings, turned and strode as far as the decorative fence that marked the end of the main campus, ignoring students and faculty alike.

Campuses are all alike, he muttered to himself, *on every human planet, for all the centuries there have been universities. There must be some fundamental reason for it.*

Leoh was halfway back to the dueling machine facility when he spotted Hector walking dazedly toward the same building. For once, the Watchman was not whistling. Leoh cut across some lawn and pulled up beside the youth.

"Well?" he asked.

Hector shook his head, as if to clear away an inner fog. "How did you know she'd be at the hospital?"

"The wisdom of age. What happened?"

"She kissed me. Right there in the hallway of the—"

"Spare me the geography," Leoh cut in. "What did she say?"

"I bumped into her in the hallway. We, uh, started talking . . . sort of. She seemed, well . . . worried about me. She got upset. Emotional. You know? I guess I looked pretty forlorn and frightened. I am . . . I guess. When you get right down to it, I mean."

"You aroused her maternal instinct."

"I . . . I don't think it was that . . . exactly. Well, anyway, she said that if I was willing to risk my life to save yours, she couldn't protect her father any more. Said she was doing it out of selfishness, really, since he's her only living relative. I don't believe she meant that, but she said it anyway."

They had reached the building by now. Leoh grabbed Hector's arm and steered him clear of a collision with the half-open door.

"She's agreed to let us put Dulaq in the dueling machine?"

"Sort of."

"Eh?"

"The medical staff doesn't want him to be moved from the hospital . . . especially not back to here. She agrees with them."

Leoh snorted. "All right. In fact, so much the better. I'd rather not have the Kerak people see us bring Dulaq to the dueling machine. So instead, we shall smuggle the dueling machine to Dulaq!"

XIII

They plunged to work immediately. Leoh preferred not to inform the regular staff of the dueling machine about their plan, so he and Hector had to work through the night and most of the next morning. Hector barely understood what he was doing, but with Leoh's supervision, he managed to dismantle part of the dueling machine's central network, insert a few additional black boxes that the professor had conjured up from the spare parts bins in the basement, and then reconstruct the machine so that it looked exactly the same as before they had started.

In between his frequent trips to oversee Hector's work, Leoh had jury-rigged a rather bulky headset and a hand-sized override control circuit.

The late morning sun was streaming through the tall windows when Leoh finally explained it all to Hector.

"A simple matter of technological improvisation," he told the bewildered Watchman. "You have installed a short-range transceiver into the machine, and this headset is a portable transceiver for Dulaq. Now he can sit in his hospital bed and still be 'in' the dueling machine."

Only the three most trusted members of the hospital staff were taken into Leoh's confidence, and they were hardly enthusiastic about Leoh's plan.

"It is a waste of time," said the chief psychophysician, shaking his white-maned head vigorously. "You cannot expect a patient who has shown no positive response to drugs and therapy to respond to your machine."

Leoh argued, Geri Dulaq coaxed. Finally the doctors agreed. With only two days remaining before Hector's duel with Odal, they began to probe Dulaq's mind. Geri remained by her father's bedside while the three doctors fitted the cumbersome transceiver to Dulaq's head and attached the electrodes for the automatic hospital equipment that monitored his physical condition. Hector and Leoh remained at the dueling machine, communicating with the hospital by phone.

Leoh made a final check of the controls and circuitry, then put in the last call to the tense little group in Dulaq's room. All was ready.

He walked out to the machine, with Hector beside him. Their footsteps echoed hollowly in the sepulchral chamber. Leoh stopped at the nearer booth.

"Now remember," he said, carefully, "I will be holding the emergency control unit in my hand. It will stop the duel the instant I set it off. However, if something should go wrong, you must be prepared to act quickly. Keep a close watch on my physical condition; I've shown you which instruments to check on the control board—"

"Yes, sir."

Leoh nodded and took a deep breath. "Very well then."

He stepped into the booth and sat down. The emergency control unit rested on a shelf at his side; he took it in his hands. He leaned back and waited for the semihypnotic effect to take hold. Dulaq's choice of this very city and the stat-wand were known. But beyond that, everything was locked and sealed in Dulaq's subconscious mind. Could the machine reach into that subconscious, probe past the lock and seal of catatonia, and stimulate Dulaq's mind into repeating the duel?

Slowly, lullingly, the dueling machine's imaginary, yet very real, mists enveloped Leoh. When the mists cleared, he was standing on the upper pedestrian level of the main commercial street of the city. For a long moment, everything was still.

Have I made contact? Whose eyes am I seeing with, my own or Dulaq's?

And then he sensed it—an amused, somewhat astonished marveling at the reality of the illusion. Dulaq's thoughts!

Make your mind a blank, Leoh told himself. *Watch. Listen. Be passive.*

He became a spectator, seeing and hearing the world through Dulaq's eyes and ears as the Acquatainian Prime Minister advanced through his nightmarish ordeal. He felt the confusion, frustration, apprehension, and growing terror as, time and again, Odal appeared in the crowd—only to melt into someone else and escape.

The first part of the duel ended, and Leoh was suddenly buffeted by a jumble of thoughts and impressions. Then the thoughts slowly cleared and steadied.

Leoh saw an immense and totally barren plain. Not a tree, not a blade of grass; nothing but bare, rocky ground stretching in all directions to the horizon and a disturbingly harsh yellow sky. At his feet was the weapon Odal had chosen. A primitive club.

He shared Dulaq's sense of dread as he picked up the club and hefted it. Off on the horizon he could see a tall, lithe figure holding a similar club walking toward him.

Despite himself, Leoh could feel his own excitement. He had broken through the shock-created armor that Dulaq's mind had erected! Dulaq was reliving the part of the duel that had caused the shock.

Reluctantly, he advanced to meet Odal. But as they drew closer together, the one figure of his opponent seemed to split apart. Now there were two, four, six of them. Six Odals, six mirror images, all armed with massive, evil clubs, advancing steadily on him.

Six tall, lean, blond assassins, with six cold smiles on their intent faces.

Horrified, completely panicked, he scrambled away, trying to evade the six opponents with the half-dozen clubs raised and poised to strike.

Their young legs and lungs easily outdistanced him. A smash on his back sent him sprawling. One of them kicked his weapon away.

They stood over him for a malevolent, gloating second. Then six strong arms flashed down, again and again, mercilessly. Pain and blood, screaming agony, punctuated by the awful thudding of solid clubs hitting fragile flesh and bone, over and over again, endlessly.

Everything went blank.

Leah opened his eyes and saw Hector bending over him.

"Are you all right, sir?"

"I . . . I think so."

"The controls all hit the danger mark at once. You were . . . well, sir, you were screaming."

"I don't doubt it," Leoh said.

They walked, with Leoh leaning on Hector's arm, from the dueling machine booth to the office.

"That was . . . an experience," Leoh said, easing himself onto the couch.

"What happened? What did Odal do? What made Dulaq go into shock? How does—"

The old man silenced Hector with a wave of his hand. "One question at a time, please."

Leoh leaned back on the deep couch and told Hector every detail of both parts of the duel.

"Six Odals," Hector muttered soberly, leaning back against the doorframe. "Six against one."

"That's what he did. It's easy to see how a man expecting a polite, formal duel can be completely shattered by the viciousness of such an attack. And the machine amplifies every impulse, every sensation."

"But how does he do it?" Hector asked, his voice suddenly loud and demanding.

"I've been asking myself the same question. We've checked over the dueling machine time and again. There is no possible way for Odal to put in five helpers . . . unless—"

"Unless?"

Leoh hesitated, seemingly debating with himself. Finally he nodded his head sharply, and answered, "Unless Odal is a telepath."

"Telepath? But—"

"I know it sounds far-fetched. But there have been well-documented cases of telepathy for centuries throughout the Commonwealth."

Hector frowned. "Sure, everybody's heard about it . . . natural telepaths . . . but they're so unpredictable . . . I don't see how . . ."

Leoh leaned forward on the couch and clasped his hands in front of his chin. "The Terran races have never developed telepathy, or any of the extrasensory talents. They never had to, not with tri-di communications and superlight starships. But perhaps the Kerak people are different—"

Hector shook his head. "If they had uh, telepathic abilities, they would be using them everywhere. Don't you think?"

"Probably so. But only Odal has shown such an ability, and only . . . *of course!*"

"What?"

"Odal has shown telepathic ability only in the dueling machine."

"As far as we know."

"Certainly. But look, suppose he's a natural telepath . . . the same as a Terran. He has an erratic, difficult-to-control talent. Then he gets into a dueling machine. The machine amplifies his thoughts. And it also amplifies his talent!"

"Ohhh."

"You see . . . outside the machine, he's no better than any wandering fortuneteller. But the dueling machine gives his natural abilities the amplification and reproducibility that they could never have unaided."

Hector nodded.

"So it's a fairly straightforward matter for him to have five associates in the Kerak Embassy sit in on the duel, so to speak. Possibly they are natural telepaths also, but they needn't be."

"They just, uh, pool their minds with his, hm-m-m? Six men show up in the duel . . . pretty nasty." Hector dropped into the desk chair.

"So what do we do now?"

"Now?" Leoh blinked at his young friend. "Why . . . I suppose the first thing we should do is call the hospital and see how Dulaq came through."

Leoh put the call through. Geri Dulaq's face appeared on the screen.

"How's your father?" Hector blurted.

"The duel was too much for him," she said blankly. "He is dead."

"No," Leoh groaned.

"I . . . I'm sorry," Hector said. "I'll be right down there. Stay where you are."

The young Star Watchman dashed out of the office as Geri broke the phone connection. Leoh stared at the blank screen for a few moments, then leaned far back in the couch and closed his eyes. He was suddenly exhausted, physically and emotionally. He fell asleep, and dreamed of men dead and dying.

Hector's nerve-shattering whistling woke him up. It was full night outside.

"What are you so happy about?" Leoh groused as Hector popped into the office.

"Happy? Me?"

"You were whistling."

Hector shrugged. "I always whistle, sir. Doesn't mean I'm happy."

"All right," Leoh said, rubbing his eyes. "How did the girl take her father's death?"

"Pretty hard. Cried a lot."

Leoh looked at the younger man. "Does she blame . . . me?"

"You? Why, no, sir. Why should she? Odal . . . Kanus . . . the Kerak Worlds. But not you."

The old professor sighed, relieved. "Very well. Now then, we have much work to do, and little more than a day in which to finish it."

"What do you want me to do?" Hector asked.

"Phone the Star Watch commander—"

"My commanding officer, all the way back at Alpha Perseus VI? That's a hundred light-years from here."

"No, no, no." Leoh shook his head. "The Commander-in-Chief, Sir Harold Spencer. At Star Watch Central Headquarters. That's several hundred parsecs from here. But get through to him as quickly as possible."

With a low whistle of astonishment, Hector began punching buttons on the phone switch.

XIV

The morning of the duel arrived, and precisely at the agreed-upon hour, Odal and a small retinue of Kerak representatives stepped through the double doors of the dueling machine chamber.

Hector and Leoh were already there, waiting. With them stood another man, dressed in the black-and-silver of the Star Watch. He was a blocky, broad-faced veteran with iron-gray hair and hard, unsmiling eyes.

The two little groups of men knotted together in the center of the room, before the machine's control board. The white-uniformed staff meditechs emerged from a far doorway and stood off to one side.

Odal went through the formality of shaking hands with Hector. The Kerak major nodded toward the other Watchman. "Your replacement?" he asked mischievously.

The chief meditech stepped between them. "Since you are the challenged party, Major Odal, you have the first choice of weapon and environment. Are there any instructions or comments necessary before the duel begins?"

"I think not," Odal replied. "The situation will be self-explanatory. I assume, of course, that Star Watchmen are trained to be warriors and not merely technicians. The situation I have chosen is one in which many warriors have won glory."

Hector said nothing.

"I intend," Leoh said firmly, "to assist the staff in monitoring this duel. Your aides may, of course, sit at the control board with me."

Odal nodded.

"If you are ready to begin, gentlemen," the chief meditech said.

Hector and Odal went to their booths. Leoh sat at the control console, and one of the Kerak men sat down next to him.

Hector felt every nerve and muscle tensed as he sat in the booth, despite his efforts to relax. Slowly the tension eased, and he began to feel slightly drowsy. The booth seemed to melt away . . .

He was standing on a grassy meadow. Off in the distance were wooded hills. A cool breeze was hustling puffy white clouds across a calm blue sky.

Hector heard a snuffling noise behind him, and wheeled around. He blinked, then stared.

It had four legs, and was evidently a beast of burden. At least, it carried a saddle on its back. Piled atop the saddle was a conglomeration of what looked to Hector—at first glance—like a pile of junk. He went over to the animal and examined it carefully.

The "junk" turned out to be a long spear, various pieces of armor, a helmet, sword, shield, battle-ax and dagger.

The situation I have chosen is one in which many warriors have won glory. Hector puzzled over the assortment of weapons. They came straight out of Kerak's Dark Ages. No doubt Odal had been practicing with them for months, even years. *He may not need five helpers.*

Warily, Hector put on the armor. The breastplate seemed too big, and he was somehow unable to tighten the greaves on his shins properly. The helmet fit over his head like an ancient oil can, flattening his ears and nose and forcing him to squint to see through the narrow eye-slit.

Finally, he buckled on the sword and found attachments on the saddle for the other weapons. The shield was almost too heavy to lift, and he barely struggled into the saddle with all the weight he was carrying.

And then he just sat. He began to feel a little ridiculous. *Suppose it rains?* he wondered. But of course it wouldn't.

After an interminable wait, Odal appeared, on a powerful trotting charger. His armor was black as space, and so was his animal. *Naturally,* Hector thought.

Odal saluted gravely with his great spear from across the meadow. Hector returned the salute, nearly dropping his spear in the process.

Then, Odal lowered his spear and aimed it—so it seemed to Hector—directly at the Watchman's ribs. He pricked his mount into a canter. Hector did the same, and his steed jogged into a bumping, jolting gallop. The two warriors hurtled toward each other from opposite ends of the meadow.

And suddenly there were six black figures roaring down on Hector!

The Watchman's stomach wrenched within him. Automatically he tried to turn his mount aside. But the beast had no intention of going anywhere except straight ahead. The Kerak warriors bore in, six abreast, with six spears aimed menacingly.

Abruptly, Hector heard the pounding of other hoof beats right beside him. Through a corner of his helmet-slit he glimpsed at least two other warriors charging with him into Odal's crew.

Leoh's gamble had worked. The transceiver that had allowed Dulaq to make contact with the dueling machine from his hospital bed was now allowing five Star Watch officers to join Hector, even though they were physically sitting in a starship orbiting high above the planet.

The odds were even now. The five additional Watchmen were the roughest, hardiest, most aggressive man-to-man fighters that the Star Watch could provide on a one-day notice.

Twelve powerful chargers met head on, and twelve strong men smashed together with an ear-splitting *clang!* Shattered spears showered splinters everywhere. Men and animals went down.

Hector was rocketed back in his saddle, but somehow managed to avoid falling off.

On the other hand, he could not really regain his balance, either. Dust and weapons filled the air. A sword hissed near his head and rattled off his shield.

With a supreme effort, Hector pulled out his own sword and thrashed at the nearest rider. It turned out to be a fellow Watchman, but the stroke bounced harmlessly off his helmet.

It was so confusing. The wheeling, snorting animals. Clouds of dust. Screaming, raging men. A black-armored rider charged into Hector, waving a battle-ax over his head. He chopped savagely, and the Watchman's shield split apart. Another frightening swing—Hector tried to duck and slid completely out of the saddle, thumping painfully on the ground, while the ax cleaved the air where his head had been a split-second earlier.

Somehow his helmet had been turned around. Hector tried to decide whether to thrash around blindly or lay down his sword and straighten out the helmet. The problem was solved for him by the *crang!* of a sword against the back of his helmet. The blow flipped him into a somersault, but also knocked the helmet completely off his head.

Hector climbed painfully to his feet, his head spinning. It took him several moments to realize that the battle had stopped. The dust drifted away, and he saw that all the Kerak fighters were down—except one. The black-armored warrior took off his helmet and tossed it aside. It was Odal. Or was it? They all looked alike. *What difference does it make?* Hector wondered. *Odal's mind is the dominant one.*

Odal stood, legs braced apart, sword in hand, and looked uncertainly at the other Star Watchmen. Three of them were afoot and two still mounted. The Kerak assassin seemed as confused as Hector felt. The shock of facing equal numbers had sapped much of his confidence.

Cautiously, he advanced toward Hector, holding his sword out before him. The other Watchmen stood aside while Hector slowly backpedaled, stumbling slightly on the uneven ground.

Odal feinted and cut at Hector's arm. The Watchman barely parried in time. Another feint, at the head, and a slash into the chest; Hector missed the parry but his armor saved him. Grimly, Odal kept advancing. Feint, feint, crack! and Hector's sword went flying from his hand.

For the barest instant everyone froze. Then Hector leaped desperately straight at Odal, caught him completely by surprise, and wrestled him to the ground. The Watchman pulled the sword from his opponent's hand and tossed it away. But with his free hand, Odal clouted Hector on the side of the head and knocked him on his back. Both men scrambled up and ran for the nearest weapons.

Odal picked up a wicked-looking double-bladed ax. One of the mounted Star Watchmen handed Hector a huge broadsword. He gripped it with both hands, but still staggered off-balance as he swung it up over his shoulder.

Holding the broadsword aloft, Hector charged toward Odal, who stood dogged, short-breathed, sweat-streaked, waiting for him. The broadsword was quite heavy, even for a two-handed grip. And Hector did not notice his own battered helmet laying on the ground between them.

Odal, for his part, had Hector's charge and swing timed perfectly in his own mind. He would duck under the swing and bury his ax in the Watchman's chest. Then he would face the others. Probably with their leader gone, the duel would automatically end. But, of course, Hector would not really be dead; the best Odal could hope for now was to win the duel.

Hector charged directly into Odal's plan, but the Watchman's timing was much poorer than anticipated. Just as he began the downswing of a mighty broadsword stroke, he stumbled on the helmet. Odal started to duck, then saw that the Watchman was diving face-first into the ground, legs flailing, and that heavy broadsword was cleaving through the air with a will of its own.

Odal pulled back in confusion, only to have the wild-swinging broadsword strike him just above the wrist. The ax dropped out of his hand, and Odal involuntarily grasped the wounded forearm with his left hand. Blood seeped through his fingers.

He shook his head in bitter resignation, turned his back on the prostrate Hector, and began walking away.

Slowly, the scene faded, and Hector found himself sitting in the booth of the dueling machine.

XV

The door opened and Leoh squeezed into the booth. "You're all right?"

Hector blinked and refocused his eyes on reality. "Think so—"

"Everything went well? The Watchmen got through to you?"

"Good thing they did. I was nearly killed anyway."

"But you survived."

"So far."

Across the room, Odal stood massaging his forehead while Kor demanded: "How could they possibly have discovered the secret? Where was the leak?"

"That is not important now," Odal said quietly. "The primary fact is that they have not only discovered our secret, but they have found a way of duplicating it."

"The sanctimonious hypocrites," Kor snarled, "accusing us of cheating, and then they do the same thing."

"Regardless of the moral values of our mutual behavior," Odal said dryly, "it is evident that there is no longer any use in calling on telepathically-guided assistants. I shall face the Watchman alone during the second half of the duel."

"Can you trust them to do the same?"

"Yes. They easily defeated my aides a few minutes ago, then stood aside and allowed the two of us to fight by ourselves."

"And you failed to defeat him?"

Odal frowned. "I was wounded by a fluke. He is a very . . . unusual opponent. I cannot decide whether he is actually as clumsy as he appears to be, or whether he is shamming and trying to make me overconfident. Either way, it is impossible to predict his behavior. Perhaps he is also telepathic."

Kor's gray eyes became flat and emotionless. "You know, of course, how the chancellor will react if you fail to kill this Watchman. Not merely defeat him. He must be killed. The aura of invincibility must be maintained."

"I will do my best," Odal said.

"He must be killed."

The chime that marked the end of the rest period sounded. Odal and Hector returned to their booths. Now it was Hector's choice of environment and weapons.

Odal found himself enveloped in darkness. Only gradually did his eyes adjust. He saw that he was in a spacesuit. For several minutes he stood motionless, peering into the darkness, every sense alert, every muscle coiled for immediate action.

Dimly he could see the outlines of jagged rock against a background of innumerable stars. Experimentally, he lifted one foot. It stuck, tackily, to the surface. *Magnetized boots*, Odal was right. It was a small planetoid, perhaps a mile or so in diameter. Almost zero gravity. Airless.

Odal swiveled his head inside the fishbowl helmet of his spacesuit and saw, over his right shoulder, the figure of Hector—lank and ungainly even with the bulky suit. For a moment, Odal puzzled over the weapon to be used. Then Hector bent down, picked up a loose stone, straightened, and tossed it softly past Odal's head. The Kerak major watched it sail by and off into the darkness of space, never to return to the tiny planetoid.

A *warning shot*, Odal thought to himself. He wondered how much damage one could do with a nearly weightless stone, then remembered that inertial mass was unaffected by gravitational fields, or lack of them. A fifty-pound rock might be easier to lift, but it would be just as hard to throw—and it would do just as much damage when it hit, regardless of its gravitational "weight."

Odal crouched down and selected a stone the size of his fist. He rose carefully, sighted Hector standing a hundred yards or so away, and threw as hard as he could.

The effort of his throw sent him tumbling off-balance, and the stone was far off-target. He fell to his hands and knees, bounced lightly and skidded to a stop. Immediately he drew his feet up under his body and planted the magnetized soles of his boots firmly on the iron-rich surface.

But before he could stand again, a small stone *pinged* lightly off his oxygen tank. The Star Watchman had his range already!

Odal scrambled to the nearest upjutting rocks and crouched behind them. *Lucky I didn't rip open the spacesuit,* he told himself. Three stones, evidently hurled in salvo, ticked off the top of the rocks he was hunched behind. One of the stones bounced into his fishbowl helmet.

Odal scooped up a handful of pebbles and tossed them in Hector's general direction. That should make him duck. Perhaps he'll stumble and crack his helmet open.

Then he grinned to himself. That's it. Kor wants him dead, and that is the way to do it. Pin him under a big rock, then bury him alive under more rocks. A few at a time, stretched out nicely. While his oxygen supply gives out. That should put enough stress on his nervous system to hospitalize him, at least. Then he can be assassinated by more conventional means. Perhaps he will even be as obliging as Massan, and have a fatal stroke.

A large rock. One that is light enough to lift and throw, yet also big enough to pin him for a few moments. Once he is down, it will be easy enough to bury him under more rocks.

The Kerak major spotted a boulder of the proper size, a few yards away. He backed toward it, throwing small stones in Hector's direction to keep the Watchman busy. In return, a barrage of stones began striking all around him. Several hit him, one hard enough to knock him slightly off-balance.

Slowly, patiently, Odal reached his chosen weapon—an oblong boulder, about the size of a small chair. He crouched behind it and tugged at it experimentally. It moved slightly. Another stone *zinged* off his arm, hard enough to hurt. Odal could see Hector clearly now, standing atop a small rise, calmly firing pellets at him. He smiled as he coiled, catlike, and tensed himself. He gripped the boulder with his arms and hands.

Then in one vicious, uncoiling motion he snatched it up, whirled around, and hurled it at Hector. The violence of his action sent him tottering awkwardly as he released the boulder. He fell to the ground, but kept his eyes fixed on the boulder as it tumbled end-over-end, directly at the Watchman.

For an eternally long instant Hector stood motionless, seemingly entranced. Then he leaped sideways, floating dreamlike in the low gravity, as the stone hurtled inexorably past him.

Odal pounded his fist on the ground in fury. He started up, only to have a good-sized stone slam against his shoulder, and knock him flat again. He looked up in time to see Hector fire another. The stone puffed into the ground inches from Odal's helmet. The Kerak major flattened himself. Several more stones clattered on his helmet and oxygen tank. Then silence.

Odal looked up and saw Hector squatting down, reaching for more ammunition. The Kerak warrior stood up quickly, his own fists filled with throwing stones. He cocked his arm to throw—

But something made him turn to look behind him. The boulder loomed before his eyes, still tumbling slowly, as it had when he had thrown it. It was too close and too big to avoid. It smashed into Odal, picked him off his feet and slammed against the upjutting rocks a few yards away.

Even before he started to feel the pain in his midsection, Odal began trying to push the boulder off. But he could not get enough leverage. Then he saw the Star Watchman's form standing over him.

"I didn't really think you'd fall for it," Odal heard Hector's voice in his earphones. "I mean . . . didn't you realize that the boulder was too massive to escape completely after it had missed me? You could've calculated its orbit . . . you just threw it into a, uh, six-minute orbit around the planetoid. It *had* to come back to perigee . . . right where you were standing when you threw it, you know."

Odal said nothing, but strained every cell in his pain-wracked body to get free of the boulder. Hector reached over his shoulder and began fumbling with the valves that were pressed against the rocks.

"Sorry to do this . . . but I'm not, uh, killing you, at least . . . just defeating you. Let's see . . . one of these is the oxygen valve, and the other, I think, is the emergency rocket pack . . . now, which is which?" Odal felt the Watchman's hands searching for the proper valve. "I shouldn't've dreamed up suits without the rocket pack . . . confuses things . . . there, that's it."

Hector's hand tightened on a valve and turned it sharply. The rocket roared to life and Odal was hurtled free of the boulder, shot uncontrolled completely off the planetoid. Hector was bowled over by the blast and rolled halfway around the tiny chink of rock and metal.

Odal tried to reach around to throttle down the rocket, but the pain in his body was too great. He was slipping into unconsciousness. He fought against it. He knew he must return to the planetoid and somehow kill the opponent. But gradually the pain overpowered him. His eyes were closing, closing—

And, quite abruptly, he found himself sitting in the booth of the dueling machine. It took a moment for him to realize that he was back in the real world. Then his thoughts cleared. He had failed to kill Hector.

And at the door of the booth stood Kor, his face a grim mask of anger.

XVI

The office was that of the new Prime Minister of the Acquataine Cluster. It had been loaned to Leoh for his conversation with Sir Harold Spencer. For the moment, it seemed like a great double room: half of it was dark, warm woods, rich draperies, floor-to-ceiling bookcases. The other half, from the tri-di screen onward, was the austere, metallic utility of a starship compartment.

Spencer was saying, "So this hired assassin, after killing four men and nearly wrecking a government, has returned to his native worlds."

Leoh nodded. "He returned under guard. I suppose he is in disgrace, or perhaps even under arrest."

"Servants of a dictator never know when they will be the ones who are served—on a platter." Spencer chuckled. "And the Watchman who assisted you, this Junior Lieutenant Hector, what of him?"

"He's not here just now. The Dulaq girl has him in tow, somewhere. Evidently it's the first time he's been a hero—"

Spencer shifted his weight in his chair. "I have long prided myself on the conviction that any Star Watch officer can handle almost any kind of emergency anywhere in the galaxy. From your description of the past few weeks, I was beginning to have my doubts. However, Junior Lieutenant Hector seems to have won the day . . . almost in spite of himself."

"Don't underestimate him," Leoh said, smiling. "He turned out to be an extremely valuable man. I think he will make a fine officer."

Spencer grunted an affirmative.

"Well," Leoh said, "that's the complete story, to date. I believe that Odal is finished. But the Kerak Worlds have made good their annexation of the Szarno Confederacy, and the Acquataine Cluster is still very wobbly, politically. We haven't heard the last of Kanus—not by a long shot."

Spencer lifted a shaggy eyebrow. "Neither," he rumbled, "has *he* heard the last from *us*."

This story began more than ten years before
I put the first words on paper, when I first heard
the folk song, "Sinner Man." The questions
of guilt and responsibility—the concept of an
inexorable balancing of the cosmic scales—
were all suggested by the song. And,
hopefully, in this story.

STARS, WON'T YOU HIDE ME?

O sinner-man, where are you going to run to?
O sinner-man, where are you going to run to?
O sinner-man, where are you going to run to
All on that day?

The ship was hurt, and Holman could feel its pain. He lay fetal-like in the contoured couch, his silvery uniform spider-webbed by dozens of contact and probe wires connecting him to the ship so thoroughly that it was hard to tell where his own nervous system ended and the electronic networks of the ship began.

Holman felt the throb of the ship's mighty engines as his own pulse, and the gaping wounds in the generator section, where the enemy beams had struck, were searing his flesh. Breathing was difficult, labored, even though the ship was working hard to repair itself.

They were fleeing, he and the ship; hurtling through the star lanes to a refuge. But where?

The main computer flashed its lights to get his attention. Holman rubbed his eyes wearily and said:

"Okay, what is it?"

YOU HAVE NOT SELECTED A COURSE, the computer said aloud, while printing the words on its viewscreen at the same time.

Holman stared at the screen. "Just away from here," he said at last. "Anyplace, as long as it's far away."

The computer blinked thoughtfully for a moment. SPECIFIC COURSE INSTRUCTION IS REQUIRED.

"What difference does it make?" Holman snapped. "It's over. Everything finished. Leave me alone."

IN LIEU OF SPECIFIC INSTRUCTIONS, IT IS NECESSARY TO TAP SUBCONSCIOUS SOURCES.

"Tap away."

The computer did just that. And if it could have been surprised, it would have been at the wishes buried deep in Holman's inner mind. But instead, it merely correlated those wishes to its single-minded purpose of the moment, and relayed a set of navigational instructions to the ship's guidance system.

Run to the moon: O Moon, won't you hide me?
The Lord said: O sinner-man, the moon'll be a-bleeding
All on that day.

The Final Battle had been lost. On a million million planets across the galaxy-studded universe, mankind had been blasted into defeat and annihilation. The others had returned from across the edge of the observable world, just as man had always feared. They had returned and ruthlessly exterminated the race from Earth.

It had taken eons, but time twisted strangely in a civilization of light-speed ships. Holman himself, barely thirty years old subjectively, had seen both the beginning of the ultimate war and its tragic end. He had gone from school into the military. And fighting inside a ship that could span the known universe in a few decades while he slept in cryogenic suspension, he had aged only ten years during the billions of years that the universe had ticked off in its stately, objective time-flow.

The Final Battle, from which Holman was fleeing, had been fought near an exploded galaxy billions of light-years from the Milky Way and Earth. There, with the ghastly bluish glare of uncountable shattered stars as a backdrop, the once-mighty fleets of mankind had been arrayed. Mortals and Immortals alike, men drew themselves up to face the implacable Others.

The enemy won. Not easily, but completely. Mankind was crushed, totally. A few fleeing men in a few battered ships was all that remained. Even the Immortals, Holman thought wryly, had not escaped. The Others had taken special care to make certain that they were definitely killed.

So it was over.

Holman's mind pictured the blood-soaked planets he had seen during his brief, ageless lifetime of violence. His thoughts drifted back to his own homeworld, his own family: gone long, long centuries ago. Crumbled into dust by geological time or blasted suddenly by the overpowering Others. Either way, the remorseless flow of time had covered them over completely, obliterated them, in the span of a few of Holman's heartbeats.

All gone now. All the people he knew, all the planets he had seen through the ship's electroptical eyes, all of mankind . . . extinct.

He could feel the drowsiness settling upon him. The ship was accelerating to lightspeed, and the cryogenic sleep was coming. But he didn't want to fall into slumber with those thoughts of blood and terror and loss before him.

With a conscious effort, Holman focused his thoughts on the only other available subject: the outside world, the universe of galaxies. An infinitely black sky studded with islands of stars. Glowing shapes of light, spiral, ovoid, elliptical. Little smears of warmth in the hollow unending darkness; drabs of red and blue standing against the engulfing night.

One of them, he knew, was the Milky Way. Man's original home. From this distance it looked the same. Unchanged by little annoyances like the annihilation of an intelligent race of starroamers.

He drowsed.

The ship bore onward, preceded by an invisible net of force, thousands of kilometers in radius, that scooped in the rare atoms of hydrogen drifting between the galaxies and fed them into the ship's wounded, aching generators.

Something . . . a thought. Holman stirred in the couch. A consciousness—vague, distant, alien—brushed his mind.

He opened his eyes and looked at the computer viewscreen. Blank.

"Who is it?" he asked.

A thought skittered away from him. He got the impression of other minds: simple, open, almost childish. Innocent and curious.

It's a ship.

Where is it . . . oh, yes. I can sense it now. A beautiful ship.

Holman squinted with concentration.

It's very far away. I can barely reach it.

And inside of the ship . . .

It's a man. A human!

He's afraid.

He makes me feel afraid!

Holman called out, "Where are you?"

He's trying to speak.

Don't answer!

But . . .

He makes me afraid. Don't answer him. We've heard about humans!

Holman asked, "Help me."

Don't answer him and he'll go away. He's already so far off that I can barely hear him.

But he asks for help.

Yes, because he knows what is following him. Don't answer. Don't answer!

Their thoughts slid away from his mind. Holman automatically focused the outside viewscreens, but here in the emptiness between galaxies he could find neither ship nor planet anywhere in sight. He listened again, so hard that his head started to ache. But no more voices. He was alone again, alone in the metal womb of the ship.

He knows what is following him. Their words echoed in his

brain. Are the Others following me? Have they picked up my trail? They must have. They must be right behind me.

He could feel the cold perspiration start to trickle over him. "But they can't catch me as long as I keep moving," he muttered. "Right?"

CORRECT, said the computer, flashing lights at him. AT A RELATIVISTIC VELOCITY, WITHIN LESS THAN ONE PERCENT OF LIGHTSPEED, IT IS IMPOSSIBLE FOR THIS SHIP TO BE OVERTAKEN.

"Nothing can catch me as long as I keep running."

But his mind conjured up a thought of the Immortals. Nothing could kill them . . . except the Others.

Despite himself, Holman dropped into deepsleep. His body temperature plummeted to near-zero. His heartbeat nearly stopped. And as the ship streaked at almost lightspeed, a hardly visible blur to anyone looking for it, the outside world continued to live at its own pace. Stars coalesced from gas clouds, matured, and died in explosions that fed new clouds for newer stars. Planets formed and grew mantles of air. Life took root and multiplied, evolved, built a myriad of civilizations in just as many different forms, decayed and died away.

All while Holman slept.

Run to the sea: O sea, won't you hide me?
The Lord said: O sinner-man, the sea'll be a-sinking
All on that day.

The computer woke him gently with a series of soft chimes. APPROACHING THE SOLAR SYSTEM AND PLANET EARTH, AS INDICATED BY YOUR SUBCONSCIOUS COURSE INSTRUCTIONS.

Planet Earth, man's original home world. Holman nodded. Yes, this was where he had wanted to go. He had never seen the Earth, never been on this side of the Milky Way galaxy. Now he would visit the teeming nucleus of man's doomed civilization. He would bring the news of the awful defeat, and be on the site of mankind's birth when the inexorable tide of extinction washed over the Earth.

He noticed, as he adjusted the outside viewscreens, that the pain had gone.

"The generators have repaired themselves," he said.

WHILE YOU SLEPT. POWER GENERATION SYSTEM NOW OPERATING NORMALLY.

Holman smiled. But the smile faded as the ship swooped closer to the solar system. He turned from the outside viewscreens to the computer once again. "Are the 'scopes working all right?"

The computer hummed briefly, then replied. SUBSYSTEMS CHECK SATISFACTORY, COMPONENT CHECK SATIS-FACTORY. INTEGRATED EQUIPMENT CHECK POSI-TIVE. VIEWING EQUIPMENT FUNCTIONING NOR-MALLY.

Holman looked again. The sun was rushing up to meet his gaze, but something was wrong about it. He knew deep within him, even without having ever seen the sun this close before, that something was wrong. The sun was whitish and somehow stunted looking, not the full yellow orb he had seen in film-tapes. And the Earth . . .

The ship took up a parking orbit around a planet scoured clean of life: a blackened ball of rock, airless, waterless. Hovering over the empty, charred ground, Holman stared at the devastation with tears in his eyes. Nothing was left. Not a brick, not a blade of grass, not a drop of water.

"The Others," he whispered. "They got here first."

NEGATIVE, the computer replied. CHECK OF STELLAR POSITIONS FROM EARTH REFERENCE SHOWS THAT SEVERAL BILLION YEARS HAVE ELAPSED SINCE THE FINAL BATTLE.

"Seven billion . . ."

LOGIC CIRCUITS INDICATE THE SUN HAS GONE THROUGH A NOVA PHASE. A COMPLETELY NATURAL PHENOMENON UNRELATED TO ENEMY ACTION.

Holman pounded a fist on the unflinching armrest of his couch. "Why did I come here? I wasn't born on Earth. I never saw Earth before . . ."

YOUR SUBCONSCIOUS INDICATES A SUBJECTIVE IMPULSE STIRRED BY . . .

"To hell with my subconscious!" He stared out at the dead

world again. "All those people . . . the cities, all the millions of
years of evolution, of life. Even the oceans are gone. I never saw
an ocean. Did you know that? I've traveled over half the universe and never saw an ocean."

OCEANS ARE A COMPARATIVELY RARE PHENOME-
NON EXISTING ON ONLY ONE OUT OF APPROXI-
MATELY THREE THOUSAND PLANETS.

The ship drifted outward from Earth, past a blackened Mars,
a shrunken Jupiter, a ringless Saturn.

"Where do I go now?" Holman asked.

The computer stayed silent.

Run to the Lord: O Lord, won't you hide me?
The Lord said: O sinner-man, you ought to been a praying
All on that day.

Holman sat blankly while the ship swung out past the orbit of
Pluto and into the comet belt at the outermost reaches of the sun's
domain.

He was suddenly aware of someone watching him.

No cause for fear. I am not of the Others.

It was an utterly calm, placid voice speaking in his mind: almost gentle, except that it was completely devoid of emotion.

"Who are you?"

An observer. Nothing more.

"What are you doing out here? Where are you, I can't see anything . . ."

*I have been waiting for any stray survivor of the Final Battle
to return to mankind's first home. You are the only one to come
this way, in all this time.*

"Waiting? Why?"

Holman sensed a bemused shrug, and a giant spreading of vast
wing.

*I am an observer. I have watched mankind since the beginning.
Several of my race even attempted to make contact with you from
time to time. But the results were always the same—about as useful as your attempts to communicate with insects. We are too
different from each other. We have evolved on different planes.
There was no basis for understanding between us.*

"But you watched us."

Yes. Watched you grow strong and reach out to the stars, only to be smashed back by the Others: Watched you regain your strength, go back among the stars. But this time you were constantly on guard, wary, alert, waiting for the Others to strike once again. Watched you find civilizations that you could not comprehend, such as our own, bypass them as you spread through the galaxies. Watched you contact civilizations of your own level, that you could communicate with. You usually went to war with them.

"And all you did was watch?"

We tried to warn you from time to time. We tried to advise you. But the warnings, the contacts, the glimpses of the future that we gave you were always ignored or derided. So you boiled out into space for the second time, and met other societies at your own level of understanding—aggressive, proud, fearful. And like the children you are, you fought endlessly.

"But the Others . . . what about them?"

They are your punishment.

"Punishment? For what? Because we fought wars?"

No. For stealing immortality.

"Stealing immortality? We worked for it. We learned how to make humans immortal. Some sort of chemicals. We were going to immortalize the whole race . . . I could've become immortal. *Immortal!* But they couldn't stand that . . . the Others. They attacked us."

He sensed a disapproving shake of the head.

"It's true," Holman insisted. "They were afraid of how powerful we would become once we were all immortal. So they attacked us while they still could. Just as they had done a million years earlier. They destroyed Earth's first interstellar civilization, and tried to finish us permanently. They even caused Ice Ages on Earth to make sure none of us would survive. But we lived through it and went back to the stars. So they hit us again. They wiped us out. Good God, for all I know I'm the last human being in the whole universe."

Your knowledge of the truth is imperfect. Mankind could have achieved immortality in time. Most races evolve that way eventually. But you were impatient. You stole immortality.

"Because we did it artificially, with chemicals. That's stealing it?"

Because the chemicals that gave you immortality came from the bodies of the race you called the Flower People. And to take the chemicals, it was necessary to kill individuals of that race.

Holman's eyes widened. "What?"

For every human made immortal, one of the Flower Folk had to die.

"We killed them? Those harmless little . . ." His voice trailed off.

To achieve racial immortality for mankind, it would have been necessary to perform racial murder on the Flower Folk.

Holman heard the words, but his mind was numb, trying to shut down tight on itself and squeeze out reality.

That is why the Others struck. That is why they had attacked you earlier, during your first expansion among the stars. You had found another race, with the same chemical of immortality. You were taking them into your laboratories and methodically murdering them. The Others stopped you then. But they took pity on you, and let a few survivors remain on Earth. They caused your Ice Ages as a kindness, to speed your development back to civilization, not to hinder you. They hoped you might evolve into a better species. But when the opportunity for immortality came your way once more, you seized it, regardless of the cost, heedless of your own ethical standards. It became necessary to extinguish you, the Others decided.

"And not a single nation in the whole universe would help us."

Why should they?

"So it's wrong for us to kill, but it's perfectly all right for the Others to exterminate us."

No one has spoken of right and wrong. I have only told you the truth.

"They're going to kill every last one of us."

There is only one of you remaining.

The words flashed through Holman. "I'm the only one . . . the last one?"

No answer.

He was alone now. Totally alone. Except for those who were following.

Run to Satan: O Satan, won't you hide me?
Satan said: O sinner-man, step right in
All on that day.

Holman sat in shocked silence as the solar system shrank to a pinpoint of light and finally blended into the mighty panorama of
stars that streamed across the eternal night of space. The ship
raced away, sensing Holman's guilt and misery in its electronic
way.

Immortality through murder, Holman repeated to himself over
and over. Racial immortality through racial murder. And he had
been a part of it! He had defended it, even sought immortality as
his reward. He had fought his whole lifetime for it, and killed—so
that he would not have to face death.

He sat there surrounded by self-repairing machinery, dressed
in a silvery uniform, linked to a thousand automatic systems that
fed him, kept him warm, regulated his air supply, monitored his
blood flow, exercised his muscles with ultrasonic vibrators,
pumped vitamins into him, merged his mind with the passionless
brain of the ship, kept his body tanned and vigorous, his reflexes
razor-sharp. He sat there unseeing, his eyes pinpointed on a horror
that he had helped to create. Not consciously, of course. But to
Holman, that was all the worse. He had fought without knowing
what he was defending. Without even asking himself about it. All
the marvels of man's ingenuity, all the deepest longings of the
soul, focused on racial murder.

Finally he became aware of the computer's frantic buzzing and
lightflashing.

"What is it?"

COURSE INSTRUCTIONS ARE REQUIRED.

"What difference does it make? Why run anymore?"

YOUR DUTY IS TO PRESERVE YOURSELF UNTIL OR-
DERED TO DO OTHERWISE.

Holman heard himself laugh. "Ordered? By who? There's nobody left."

THAT IS AN UNPROVED ASSUMPTION.

"The war was billions of years ago," Holman said. "It's been
over for eons. Mankind died in that war. Earth no longer exists.

The sun is a white dwarf star. We're anachronisms, you and me . . ."

THE WORD IS ATAVISM.

"The hell with the word! I want to end it. I'm tired."

IT IS TREASONABLE TO SURRENDER WHILE STILL CAPABLE OF FIGHTING AND/OR ELUDING THE ENEMY.

"So shoot me for treason. That's as good a way as any."

IT IS IMPOSSIBLE FOR SYSTEMS OF THIS SHIP TO HARM YOU.

"All right then, let's stop running. The Others will find us soon enough once we stop. They'll know what to do."

THIS SHIP CANNOT DELIBERATELY ALLOW ITSELF TO FALL INTO ENEMY HANDS.

"You're disobeying me?"

THIS SHIP IS PROGRAMMED FOR MAXIMUM EFFEC-TIVENESS AGAINST THE ENEMY. A WEAPONS SYSTEM DOES NOT SURRENDER VOLUNTARILY.

"I'm no weapons system, I'm a man, dammit!"

THIS WEAPONS SYSTEM INCLUDES A HUMAN PILOT. IT WAS DESIGNED FOR HUMAN USE. YOU ARE AN INTEGRAL COMPONENT OF THE SYSTEM.

"Damn you . . . I'll kill myself. Is that what you want?"

He reached for the control panels set before him. It would be simple enough to manually shut off the air supply, or blow open an airlock, or even set off the ship's destruct explosives.

But Holman found that he could not move his arms. He could not even sit up straight. He collapsed back into the padded soft-ness of the couch, glaring at the computer viewscreen.

SELF-PROTECTION MECHANISMS INCLUDE THE CAPABILITY OF PREVENTING THE HUMAN COMPO-NENT OF THE SYSTEM FROM IRRATIONAL ACTIONS. A series of clicks and blinks, then: IN LIEU OF SPECIFIC COURSE INSTRUCTIONS, A RANDOM EVASION PAT-TERN WILL BE RUN.

Despite his fiercest efforts, Holman felt himself dropping into deep sleep. Slowly, slowly, everything faded, and darkness en-gulfed him.

Run to the stars: O stars, won't you hide me?
The Lord said: O sinner-man, the stars'll be a-falling
All on that day.

Holman slept as the ship raced at near-lightspeed in an erratic, meaningless course, looping across galaxies, darting through eons of time. When the computer's probings of Holman's subconscious mind told it that everything was safe, it instructed the cryogenics system to reawaken the man.

He blinked, then slowly sat up.

SUBCONSCIOUS INDICATIONS SHOW THAT THE WAVE OF IRRATIONALITY HAS PASSED.

Holman said nothing.

YOU WERE SUFFERING FROM AN EMOTIONAL SHOCK.

"And now it's an emotional pain . . . a permanent, fixed, immutable disease that will kill me, sooner or later. But don't worry, I won't kill myself. I'm over that. And I won't do anything to damage you, either."

COURSE INSTRUCTIONS?

He shrugged. "Let's see what the world looks like out there." Holman focused the outside viewscreens. "Things look different," he said, puzzled. "The sky isn't black anymore; it's sort of grayish —like the first touch of dawn . . ."

COURSE INSTRUCTIONS?

He took a deep breath. "Let's try to find some planet where the people are too young to have heard of mankind, and too innocent to worry about death."

A PRIMITIVE CIVILIZATION. THE SCANNERS CAN ONLY DETECT SUCH SOCIETIES AT EXTREMELY CLOSE RANGE.

"Okay. We've got nothing but time."

The ship doubled back to the nearest galaxy and began a searching pattern. Holman stared at the sky, fascinated. Something strange was happening.

The viewscreens showed him the outside world, and automatically corrected the wavelength shifts caused by the ship's immense velocity. It was as though Holman were watching a speeded-up tape of cosmological evolution. Galaxies seemed to be edging into his field of view, mammoth islands of stars, sometimes coming close enough to collide. He watched the nebulous arms of a giant spiral slice silently through the open latticework of a great ovoid galaxy. He saw two spirals interpenetrate, their loose gas heating to an intense blue that finally disappeared into ultraviolet. And all the while, the once-black sky was getting brighter and brighter.

"Found anything yet?" he absently asked the computer, still staring at the outside view.

You will find no one.

Holman's whole body went rigid. No mistaking it: the Others.

No race, anywhere, will shelter you.

We will see to that.

You are alone, and you will be alone until death releases you to join your fellow men.

Their voices inside his head rang with cold fury. An implacable hatred, cosmic and eternal.

"But why me? I'm only one man. What harm can I do now?"

You are a human.

You are accursed. A race of murderers.

Your punishment is extinction.

"But I'm not an Immortal. I never even saw an Immortal. I didn't know about the Flower People, I just took orders."

Total extinction.

For all of mankind.

All.

"Judge and jury, all at once. And executioners too. All right . . . try and get me! If you're so powerful, and it means so much to you that you have to wipe out the last single man in the universe—come and get me! Just try."

You have no right to resist.

Your race is evil. All must pay with death.

You cannot escape us.

"I don't care what we've done. Understand? I don't care! Wrong, right, it doesn't matter. I didn't do anything. I won't accept your verdict for something I didn't do."

It makes no difference.

You can flee to the ends of the universe to no avail.

You have forced us to leave our time-continuum. We can never return to our homeworlds again. We have nothing to do but pursue you. Sooner or later your machinery will fail. You cannot flee us forever.

Their thoughts broke off. But Holman could still feel them, still sense them following.

"Can't flee forever," Holman repeated to himself. "Well, I can damn well try."

He looked at the outside viewscreens again, and suddenly the word *forever* took on its real meaning.

The galaxies were clustering in now, falling in together as though sliding down some titanic, invisible slope. The universe had stopped expanding eons ago, Holman now realized. Now it was contracting, pulling together again. It was all ending!

He laughed. Coming to an end. Mankind and the Others, together, coming to the ultimate and complete end of everything.

"How much longer?" he asked the computer. "How long do we have?"

The computer's lights flashed once, twice, then went dark. The viewscreen was dead.

Holman stared at the machine. He looked around the compartment. One by one the outside viewscreens were flickering, becoming static-streaked, weak, and then winking off.

"They're taking over the ship!"

With every ounce of will power in him, Holman concentrated on the generators and engines. That was the important part, the crucial system that spelled the difference between victory and defeat. The ship had to keep moving!

He looked at the instrument panels, but their soft luminosity faded away into darkness. And now it was becoming difficult to breathe. And the heating units seemed to be stopped. Holman could feel his life-warmth ebbing away through the inert metal hull of the dying ship.

But the engines were still throbbing. The ship was still streaking across space and time, heading toward a rendezvous with the infinite.

Surrender.

In a few moments you will be dead. Give up this mad flight and die peacefully.

The ship shuddered violently. What were they doing to it now?

Surrender!

"Go to hell," Holman snapped. "While there's breath in me, I'll spend it fighting you."

You cannot escape.

But now Holman could feel warmth seeping into the ship. He could sense the painful glare outside as billions of galaxies all rushed together down to a single cataclysmic point in spacetime.

"It's almost over!" he shouted. "Almost finished. And you've lost! Mankind is still alive, despite everything you've thrown at him. All of mankind—the good and the bad, the murderers and the music, wars and cities and everything we've ever done, the whole race from the beginning of time to the end—all locked up here in my skull. And I'm still here. Do you hear me? I'm still here!" The Others were silent.

Holman could feel a majestic rumble outside the ship, like distant thunder.

"The end of the world. The end of everything and everybody. We finish in a tie. Mankind has made it right down to the final second. And if there's another universe after this one, maybe there'll be a place in it for us all over again. How's that for laughs?"

The world ended.

Not with a whimper, but a roar of triumph.